Small Town Miracles

A CLEAN SMALL TOWN ROMANCE COLLECTION

MAPLEWOOD GROVE
BOOK THREE

DAISY LANDISH

BEACHES AND TRAILS
PUBLISHING

Sweet Mistletoe

CLEAN SMALL TOWN ROMANCE

Christmas Lights and Second Chances

DOT

Maplewood Grove comes alive in the winter, especially during the Christmas season. As soon as December arrives, the streets are adorned with twinkling lights, wreaths hang on every door, and a giant Christmas tree stands proudly in the town square, its ornaments sparkling like jewels against the frosty air. The town has a way of pulling everyone into the holiday spirit, whether they want it or not. The air is crisp, carrying the scent of pine, cinnamon, and the promise of snow, while the sound of carolers echoes softly from every corner.

Nestled among the snow-covered hills, Maplewood Grove is the kind of place where everyone knows each other's name and business, whether they want them to or not. It's a small town with a big heart, where time seems to slow down just enough for everyone to savor the little things—like the way the snow crunches underfoot or the warmth of a steaming cup of hot cocoa on a cold night.

This year, the excitement of Christmas hums a little louder, as if the town itself knows that something special is in the air. And if anyone can confirm that, it's Dorothy Simmons, the unofficial historian of Maplewood Grove. Dot is a woman who knows everyone's business and has a story for every occasion. She's in her mid-fifties, though she carries herself with the energy of someone half her age, her sharp eyes always twinkling with curiosity.

Today, Dot perches in her usual spot at the Maplewood Grove General Store, a mug of peppermint tea warming her hands as she observes the bustle around her. The store is a hub of activity, with townsfolk coming in to pick up last-minute decorations or ingredients for their Christmas feasts. Dot takes it all in, her keen eyes missing nothing.

She chuckles softly as she watches Mrs. Peterman, the librarian, argue with Mr. Grady over the last string of multicolored lights. She knows the outcome before it even happens—Mrs. Peterman always wins those little tiffs, and Mr. Grady relents with a good-natured grumble, just as he's doing now.

"How's the tea today, Dot?" asks Jenny, the store's young clerk, as she rings up a customer's purchase.

"Perfect, as always," Dot replies with a smile. "You know, Jenny, you remind me of your grandmother, God rest her soul. She had the same sparkle in her eye when she was your age. And she made the best gingerbread in all of Maplewood Grove. Did I ever tell you about the time she won the bake-off three years in a row?"

Jenny smiles politely, used to Dot's stories by now. "I think you might have mentioned it once or twice."

"Well, it's worth hearing again," Dot says, her voice filled with warmth. "Your grandmother was quite the woman. She'd be so proud of you."

Jenny's face goes wistful. "I can imagine. I only wish to be half the woman she was."

"You are on your way there, trust me. I would know." Dot chuckles into her mug.

"Do you ever wonder..." Jenny begins, faltering.

"What's that? Out with it, girl, it's not going to bite."

Jenny sighs, struggling with the right way to put her words. "Sometimes I just wonder maybe I'm missing out on life by staying in this town. What if there's some other thing I'm missing out on that's out there."

Dot shoots her a knowing look.

"Is that what's got your peaches in a pickle?"

"Well... yes. It's been on my mind for some time."

"Jenny, you're young. You do not have to limit yourself to a place because you feel like you have to be there. The world is out there for exploring and you will only be doing yourself a great disservice by not taking advantage of your youth. I understand the restlessness you feel so well. I once had it too ..."

"What changed?" Jenny butts in excitedly. "Oh, sorry. I should have let you finish."

"I didn't do anything about it," Dot says with a far away look. "I guess I was too scared to try."

"Oh." Jenny face falls.

"But, you shouldn't." Dot grips her arm firmly. "If you feel there's something out there for you, then by all means, please pursue it. You will understand better when you're my age."

"But you aren't too old, Dot. No one in this town has as much energy as you on a good day. I dare say even myself."

Dot face crinkles into a smile. "You're much too kind, Jenny. But flattery won't get you anywhere, so get back to work."

"There's no winning with you, Dot." Jenny grins, now rapidly packing the increasing orders with a light air.

"That reminds me!" Dot jerks up from her seat abruptly. "I need to visit Cliff. I'll see you later, Jenny."

"Alright, Dot. Don't be long."

CLIFF

Clifford Barnett deals with a different kind of Christmas cheer—or rather, the lack of it—at the Sip 'n Saw bar. Cliff is in his late forties, with a grizzled appearance that matches his gruff demeanor. He's a man of few words, preferring the company of his thoughts to idle chatter, but he has a heart of gold that the townsfolk have long come to rely on.

The bar is dimly lit, a refuge from the cold for those who prefer their Christmas spirit in the form of a stiff drink. The walls are lined with old photographs of Maplewood Grove, and the shelves behind the bar are filled with an eclectic mix of liquor bottles and dusty mementos from the past. A small Christmas tree sits on the counter, its lights blinking lazily as if even they are too tired to fully embrace the holiday.

Cliff wipes down the bar with a rag, glancing at the few regulars scattered across the room. Old Man Jenkins nurses his usual whiskey in the corner, muttering to himself about how Christmas isn't what it used to be. Cliff can't disagree. For him, the holiday has always been more of a chore than a joy. But still, he puts up the decorations, keeps the fire burning in the hearth, and even plays a few carols on the old jukebox, if only to keep the patrons from complaining.

As he works, the door swings open, letting in a blast of cold air along with a familiar figure. Dot Simmons strides in and a little jolt of pleasure shoots up his chest.

"Afternoon, Cliff!" she calls, her voice cutting through the quiet like a knife. "I thought I'd stop by and see how you're holding up this Christmas season."

Cliff grunts in response, which Dot takes as an invitation to continue. She slides onto a stool at the bar, her eyes taking in the sparse decorations.

"Now, Cliff, you can't tell me this is all the Christmas spirit you've got in you," she says, nodding toward the lonely tree on the counter.

Cliff shrugs. "It's enough for the folks who come in here. They're not exactly looking for festive cheer."

"Well, maybe they should be," Dot counters, her eyes narrowing in thought. "You know, Cliff, I was thinking the other day about that Christmas back in '92, when we had that terrible blizzard. The whole town was snowed in for days, and your place was the only spot folks could get to for warmth and a hot meal."

Cliff looks up, his expression softening at the memory. "I remember. We had half the town in here, and Loretta from the diner brought over pots of stew. We didn't even close for a week."

"Exactly," Dot says, her voice filled with conviction. "This place was a haven then, and it still is. You may not think it, Cliff, but this bar is part of what makes Maplewood Grove special. And at Christmas, more than any other time, people need a place like this—a place where they can come together and feel at home."

Cliff doesn't argue. He knows Dot is right, even if he won't admit it. Instead, he pours her a drink.

Dot takes the drink with a smile, raising it in a toast to Cliff before taking a sip. "Here's to Christmas in Maplewood Grove," she says, her voice warm and full of cheer. "I know it will only get better from here."

Cliff nods, a rare smile tugging at the corners of his mouth. "To Maplewood Grove," he agrees, his voice gruff but sincere.

ETHAN

"Pass me the lights there, will you, Ethan?"

The center of it all is the Maple Grove, where preparations for the annual Christmas Festival are in full swing. The grove itself is a winter wonderland, with towering evergreens draped in garlands, and a huge Christmas tree standing sentinel in the middle, its branches heavy with ornaments and memories from holidays past.

Ethan Parker, who owned the town's beloved auto repair shop, stood near the base of the tree. His steady presence was a comforting sight in Maplewood Grove, especially to those who remembered how he'd kept things running during past crises. Beside him, Noah Harrison, his business partner and long-time friend, chatted animatedly. Their combined efforts had been essential in past community events, making their participation today feel like a nod to the town's unity.

Noah Harrison, Ethan's best friend and business partner, had always been the more charismatic of the two. With a grin that could charm anyone and a knack for managing the business side of things, he was well-loved by the townsfolk. His recent involvement in town projects had made him an indispensable part of the community.

Liam Brooks, meticulous and driven, was a successful contractor and a familiar face at local events. His volunteer work at the animal shelter and dedication to town improvements revealed a softer side beneath his efficient exterior.

Tyler Reed, ever the joker, brought levity to any gathering. Known for his quick wit and infectious energy, Tyler's enthusiasm was especially appreciated during the holiday season, where he managed to make even the most mundane tasks fun.

"Ethan?!" The voice calls again insistently, jarring him out of his thoughts. He turns towards the direction of the voice with a startled look.

"Sorry, what?"

Noah Harrison, Ethan's best friend and business partner had been haggling with a vendor over the price of some Christmas wreaths before noticing Ethan's silence and approaching him. Now looking at him warily, he's puzzled by Ethan zoning out. It's unlike him to be so distracted during festivities.

"You've been out of it, man. What's wrong?" Noah asks.

"I'm okay, Noah. I'm thinking about something."

"Oh. Do you want to share?"

"Nah. I'll be fine. It's not a big deal."

"You sure? Yes, I am."

"You and Olivia okay?"

"Drop it, Noah. I told you I'm fine."

Noah raises his hand in surrender immediately. "Hey, easy tiger. Okay, if you insist."

Where Ethan is quiet and reserved, Noah is outgoing and charming, with a grin that could talk anyone into anything. He's dressed in his usual casual style, a wool hat pushed back on his head, and his hands animated as he gestures during his conversation. Noah has a natural warmth that makes him instantly likable, a quality that has served him well in his ventures—whether it's managing the business side of Parker's Wrench or in the other enterprises he's involved in around town.

Liam Brooks, the third in the trio is busy directing a group of volunteers who are setting up the stalls for the festival. His dark eyes flicker with purpose as he oversees the setup, making sure everything is just right. Liam is meticulous, almost to a fault, and he takes pride in ensuring that the Christmas Festival goes off without a hitch. His attention to detail is something the others have come to rely on, especially during the busy holiday season. But he suddenly looks at the two men sharply, overhearing their conversation.

"Are you two fighting again?" Liam's suspicious look flits between the two of them. Liam is tall and lean, with an air of quiet confidence that precedes his looks. An extremely successful contractor and volunteer at the local animal shelter in town, he's easily the softest person amongst them, even though he projects a gruff exterior. However, his calm demeanor and sharp mind makes him an invaluable friend.

"Don't ask me, ask him," Noah hastily interjects. "He's the one suddenly absent and not talking."

"Ethan?"

Liam's voice is softer. Ethan is the most reserved amongst them but easygoing too. Something must be eating him up for him to snap so easily at Noah.

"I'm fine, I'm fine. You both should stop looking at me like that."

"It's unlike you to be so short with us."

Tyler Reed, who's in the midst of decorating one of the stalls with a string of lights that seem to have a mind of their own, notices them. Tyler is the joker of the group, always quick with a quip or a smile to lighten the mood. His dark hair falls into his eyes as he struggles with the lights, but there's a playful glint in his gaze that suggests he's enjoying the challenge. Tyler is the life of the party, the one who can always be counted on to bring laughter to even the most mundane of tasks. His easygoing nature and infectious enthusiasm make him a favorite among the townsfolk, especially during the festive season.

"Yes, tell us," He drops a large arm on Ethan's shoulder, catching on to the conversation. "What's the big news. Trust us, we can handle it."

Ethan sighs, looking amongst the men, knowing he can't hide his mood anymore. "It's not really a big deal," he begins and falters.

"C'mon, man, it's unlike you to be at such a loss for words."

"Olivia is pregnant again."

There's a short silence, followed by loud excited exclamations. "You sly fox!"

"... Such a sharp shooter!"

"Congratulations, man. This is great news!"

They clap his back in excitement until Liam, who's been studying Ethan's face, breaks the conversation.

"But you're not happy?"

"Of course, I am." He sputters. "It's great news. More Christmas cheer…"

His voice trails away as he sees three pairs of eyes on him, nonplussed.

He sighs, running his hand through his hair.

"I don't know. We've not been having so much time to ourselves anymore. Liv is always exhausted and work has been taking me away more often. I don't know if a baby at this point would put a strain on our relationship further."

"Shit," Noah says quietly.

"Have you spoken to her about it, Ethan?" Liam asks.

"No. I… I don't want her to feel like I don't want the baby. I want the baby, truly I'm beyond excited. But I want us back first."

"Hey," Noah moves closer and places a hand on his shoulder. "Have that conversation with her first. I'm sure you will find a common ground. You know she loves you, right?"

"Yes, man. That's what makes it super difficult for me."

"You should, Ethan. Trust these women, most times all they need is just the thought that you are still present. I would know, after all. I'm living with one." Tyler quips with a hand over his heart, pretending to fall.

The others laugh, punching him playfully.

Ethan brightens up. "You're right, guys. I can't believe I was moping around when I could have talked about it sooner. That was so stupid."

"Hey, if you say so. Who are we to argue," Tyler adds.

"Smartass." Ethan slaps his arm and they both laugh.

"Thank you, guys."

"You know we got you, man." Liam squeezes his shoulder lightly while Noah grins.

Alex who is at the edge of the grove, carefully inspecting the ice rink that has been set up for the festival, walks into the display and looks at them, confused.

"What did I miss?"

"Your wedding party," Tyler rolls out to peals of laughter from the guys.

"That was a good one!"

Alex is a charming local high school teacher with an easygoing temperament. His blond hair is tousled by the winter wind as he carefully places the ice pack on the floor.

He is the outdoorsman of the group, the one who's most at home in nature. His rugged appearance and charming nature endear him to the townsfolk, especially the older women, who love having him around.

"Hey, I can't believe I'm saying this," Noah begins, looking at the men with a wry smile. "But I'm so glad to have you all. Even more glad because Christmas this year looks very promising."

"You can say that again!"

Unspoken Words Under the Stars

~∾⌒∾~

DOT

The evening shadows lengthen as the Christmas lights in Maplewood Grove blink softly, casting a warm, inviting glow over the town. Dot, having waited for Cliff to lock up for the bar, now sits on a weathered bench with him in the Maple Grove beneath the boughs of an ancient oak tree.

Dot's gaze is fixed on the Christmas tree in the center of the grove, its lights reflecting in her eyes like a constellation. Her silver hair is pulled back into a loose bun, a few strands escaping to frame her face. She wears a woolen coat that's seen better days but is lovingly patched up, hinting at years of wear. Dot's hands, though slightly gnarled with age, are warm and steady as she clasps them together.

Cliff, seated beside her, wears a leather jacket that has seen many seasons and a wool cap pulled snug over his graying hair. His hands, large and calloused from years of work at the Sip 'n Saw, rest on his knees, his fingers drumming a slow, absent-minded rhythm.

The silence between them is comfortable. Dot shifts slightly inhaling deeply the breath of the crisp night air. "Do you ever think..." Her voice trails away as she struggles to put her thoughts together.

"What's that, Dot?"

"That maybe we ought to do more?"

Cliff's forehead crinkles, as he turns to look at her. "I'm not sure I understand what you mean."

Dot sighs, placing her hands on Cliff's, feeling the warmth emanate from them to her soul. Cliff freezes immediately at her touch.

"I've been thinking, Cliff. We're old and we have fond memories of our life here. But are you truly happy? Do you think maybe we could have done more?"

Cliff's look focuses on something far away and his voice takes on a wistful quality.

"I like to think I'm happy. I spent most of my life here and I've not regretted any moment. But you're right. Lately, I've been feeling almost empty. Like there's something important I've missed out on–"

"Like love?"

Cliff reddens and tries to cover it up in an awkward chuckle. "Weird that you would say that. I've been thinking of my love interests over the years quite more often than usual."

"Naturally," Dot teases. "Amanda made quite an impression with her red hair and bright personality."

"And for some reason, you never liked her."

"C'mon, I did. I just thought she was too loud," Dot protests half-heartedly.

"And Anna? You lot almost went for each other's head at the Mistletoe party years ago."

"She was being insufferable, that one. I never did know what you saw in her."

"Really, Dot?" Cliff exclaims with a laugh. "Should we do this?

Because I have quite a list of your dating history over the years. Each one cringeworthy or just plain annoying."

Dot breaks into peals of laughter. "Not fair. You were purposely riling them all. It's no wonder that neither of them can stand you."

"It's the bond, my darling. They lacked the spine to break it," Cliff jokes.

Dot swats his arm playfully.

There's a long pause, filled only with the soft hum of the Christmas lights and the distant laughter of children still playing. Dot's eyes drop to her lap, where her fingers play with the edge of her coat. "We were so busy back then," she says, her voice barely more than a whisper. "And you were always around, but never really... around. We both had our things, I guess."

The air suddenly shifts between them. Where it had been filled with companionable silence, now it is thick. Dot inhales slowly, feeling waves and waves of memories rolling over her. The past opens up like a journal and she peers through each page, feeling nostalgic at the intimate moments they shared together.

They had been so close.

Cliff shifts, the old leather of his jacket creaking as he moves. "We did," he agrees, his voice tinged with regret. "I think we both missed our chance that year. I didn't have the courage to tell you..."

Dot looks up at him, her eyes catching the soft light from the nearby lamppost. "Tell me what?" she asks, her voice steady despite the tremor of emotion underlying her words.

Her heart, which she thought lacked to ability to feel something other than warmth, now begins to flutter. There's a heightened awareness of Cliff in this moment that feels different from what she knows.

Cliff's gaze meets hers, and for a moment, the years seem to melt away, leaving only the two of them as they once were.

Their innocence and youth almost regained. Cliff's eyes are shadowed by a warm gaze and his face reflective. His lips move slowly as if trying to form the right words to say, but nothing comes forth.

This moment freezes in time till it's just the two of them. Alone in Maple Grove, buried feelings rushing to the surface with brute force.

The transformation is instant and shocking.

Dot gasps, her hand reaching up slightly as if to touch his. After a while, he shifts his gaze and the moment disappears. "Nothing, forget about it." he says gruffly and Dot's expression falls.

She had been eagerly waiting to hear something. But the words she longed to hear never came, so she struggles to search for the right response. "Oh," she whispers, lost for words.

The disappointment is deep and profound.

Had she imagined it?

Was there something between them really?

Dot's gaze lingers on the shimmering Christmas tree in the distance, her breath forming tiny clouds in the cold air, her hands resting on her lap.

Cliff's gaze drifts to Dot's profile, and he notes the subtle way her breath hitches, the slight flush of color on her cheeks. It's a reaction that makes him question the boundaries he's set for himself, the ones that have kept him from acknowledging the feelings he's buried for so long.

The night deepens, and the sounds of the festival fade into the distance. Dot and Cliff continue to sit together, slightly apart now but still holding hands. The silence between them is filled with a shared history and a strong sense of longing.

With a sinking feeling, Dot knows that this will be a very long Christmas for them.

Festival Preparations and Hidden Fears

~⌒⌒⌒~

DOT

The snow continues to blanket Maplewood Grove in a pristine layer of white as Dot and Cliff stand in the middle of Maple Grove, the epicenter of the town's annual Christmas Festival preparations. It's early morning, and the sun is just beginning to peek over the horizon, casting a warm, golden light on the bustling scene. Vendors are setting up their booths, and volunteers are arranging festive decorations with cheerful determination. They had been recruited into organizing the Christmas festivities together by the mayor.

Neither of them had known until they met at the Maple Grove this morning. Dot glanced around at the grove, now a flurry of activity as volunteers hurried to hang garlands and set up the final booths. It was just a few hours until the festival would open to the public, and the pressure of time bore down on her. She exchanged a knowing look with Cliff, understanding that they were in the final stretch.

Dot adjusts her scarf, her breath forming small clouds in the cold air. She glances at Cliff, who is surveying the area with his usual gruff demeanor. Her heart beats slightly at the memory of last night's expe-

17

rience. Somehow, it feels like a dam of repressed feelings has been let open and it's hard to close it again.

Cliff glanced at the half-decorated tree and back at Dot, the weight of both the festival and his private troubles pressing on him. "You think we can finish this in time?" he asked, a rare note of doubt in his voice.

Dot's eyes softened, catching the shadow in his. "We always have, Cliff. But not without a little help." She paused, looking over at the busy crowd of volunteers, their laughter a balm against the cold air. "Let's call in some reinforcements."

With only hours left until the festival officially kicked off, Dot felt the pressure mount. The stage still needed trimming, and the main decorations were only half done. The sound of carolers practicing in the distance mixed with the shouts of volunteers, adding urgency to the scene. If they didn't push through now, all their efforts could fall short.

A stack of Christmas lights and a box of ornaments sit between them, waiting to be sorted.

"Looks like we've got our work cut out for us, Cliff," Dot says, her tone light. She kneels beside the box and begins untangling a mess of twinkling lights.

Cliff's gruff chuckle rumbles through the morning air. "You're telling me. They've got us decorating the entire park. I thought I signed up for a simple tree-lighting ceremony."

Dot's eyes twinkle with amusement as she lifts a strand of lights, her fingers deftly working to sort them out. "You know the town, Cliff. They always have grand plans. And you're always up for the challenge. Besides, it's not every day you get to work with me on this."

Cliff's gaze meets hers, a flicker of something unspoken passing between them. "Oh, so you're saying I'm lucky to have you as a partner?"

Dot chuckles, a soft sound that warms the chilly air around

them. "Something like that. But don't get too comfortable. I'm known for having strong opinions about these things."

He raises an eyebrow, his expression both skeptical and intrigued. "Strong opinions, you say? I'll believe it when I see it."

Dot takes charge of organizing the decorations, her eyes lighting up as she discusses the plans for the festival. "I was thinking we could hang these lights along the gazebo. It'll create a nice backdrop for the carolers. And maybe some wreaths on the lamp posts."

Cliff nods thoughtfully, his hands working alongside hers to hang the lights. "Sounds like a plan. I'll get the ladder. You're the expert in this, so I'll leave the design choices to you."

Dot grins, her cheeks flushed from the cold and her exertion. "It's a deal."

The two of them work together slowly, enjoying the pace. For a minute, it feels like old times.

"Pass the white balls, will you, Cliff?"

"Here," Cliff stretches out the pack containing the shiny ornaments and his hand brushes against Dot.

A sharp intake of breath follows, and Dot grabs the balls quickly, avoiding Cliff's eyes.

She felt it and she's sure he did too.

The slight zing of warmth when their hands touched.

Dot is puzzled. Cliff has been her friend for so long, and there's never been any inkling of an attraction between them. Yet, now...

She can't quite put the feeling in words, but it's there.

This slowly building emotion that makes her heart race madly when he's near. Or her nerves tingling when their fingers brush, like now.

Is this real?

What if it was? Is she willing to do something about it?

She focuses on her task, determined to put as much distance as she can between them until she can make sense of the new development within her.

Soon, the festival preparations slowly take shape. The park begins to sparkle with festive lights and decorations.

The afternoon sun casts a warm glow over Maplewood Grove as Dot and Cliff continue their preparations for the Christmas Festival. The park, now adorned with twinkling lights and festive decorations, hums with activity as townsfolk bustle about, adding their final touches. Cliff walks to the festival's main stage to check on the setup, and he is greeted by the town's mayor.

"Good afternoon, Cliff!" Mayor Eugene Beckett booms as he approaches, his voice as hearty as his jolly laugh. He's clad in a Christmas sweater adorned with reindeer and a tie featuring a row of dancing elves. "I see you two are hard at work. Everything coming together smoothly?"

Dot looks up at the sound of his voice and smiles warmly at the mayor, her eyes twinkling with amusement. "Afternoon, Eugene. Everything's looking great, thanks to everyone's hard work. But I'm sure you're here to add your special touch."

Mayor Beckett laughs, a sound that seems to echo throughout the park. "Of course! I've got some new ideas for the festival's grand finale. This year, we're going to have a synchronized light show and a choir singing Christmas carols. We're going to make sure this festival is the talk of the town for years to come!"

Cliff raises an eyebrow but can't hide his grin. "Sounds ambitious, Eugene. I hope you've got the logistics sorted out."

"Leave that to me!" Mayor Beckett exclaims with a dramatic flourish. "I've got everything under control. And if I don't, well, I'll just blame it on the Christmas spirit!"

As the mayor bumbles off to coordinate his grand plans, Agnes and Mabel Carlton make their entrance, a lively duo that immediately draws attention. The elderly twin sisters, dressed in matching holiday sweaters and oversized red hats, are an unmistakable sight.

"Hello, dear!" Agnes says as she and Mabel approach Dot and

Cliff, each of them balancing a basket overflowing with homemade cookies. "We've come bearing Christmas cheer—and cookies!"

Mabel nods in agreement, her voice carrying the same warmth as her sister's. "And we're here to help with the decorations. Nothing says Christmas like a little extra sparkle, right?"

Dot's eyes sparkle with delight as she accepts a cookie from Agnes. "Thank you, Agnes. And you too, Mabel. We can always use some extra hands."

"Oh, we're just here to make sure everything's perfect," Agnes says with a mischievous glint in her eye. "We've got a knack for spotting where a little extra ornamentation is needed. Isn't that right, Mabel?"

Mabel giggles. "Absolutely. We're practically professionals at this point. Just ask anyone."

As the sisters move off to add their personal touch to the decorations, Dot and Cliff exchange a knowing smile. The sisters' penchant for matchmaking is well-known in town, and their enthusiastic involvement in the festival is no different.

"Have you heard their latest matchmaking scheme?" Cliff asks, leaning closer to Dot as they watch Agnes and Mabel work. "Apparently, they're trying to set up Sheriff Colton with someone they met at the last farmers' market."

Dot chuckles softly. "I heard about that. I don't think the Sheriff stands a chance. Agnes and Mabel are relentless when they set their minds to something."

"Jingle bells, jingle bells, jingle all the way."

The Christmas music flows softly from the extended sound system placed at the center of the makeshift stage currently in the works. A large part of it is still bare, but the townsfolk, awash with excitement at the Christmas cheer, do not seem to mind.

Dot glances at Cliff, feeling her heart warm with tenderness as she looks at his gruff profile. It's almost like she's seeing him in a new light and a large part of her questions how true her feelings are.

In the town square, a towering evergreen tree stands. Bare for now, but Dot can picture how colorful it will be adorned by twinkling lights, tinsel, and hand-carved ornaments by this time tomorrow.

The storefronts are already decorated with wreaths, red ribbons, and strings of lights that frame the windows. There are displays of cozy sweaters, handcrafted toys, and festive treats which makes her mouth water. The scents of cinnamon, nutmeg, and fresh baked cookies from Agnes and Mabel waft through the air.

As if on cue, the mayor's voice booms again, this time from the stage where he's directing a group of volunteers. "Everyone, gather 'round! We've got a surprise for you! A special guest appearance!"

Curiosity piqued, Dot and Cliff make their way to the stage. The volunteers and townsfolk gather around, their faces lighting up with anticipation. Mayor Beckett steps aside to reveal a familiar figure in the center of the stage.

"Ladies and gentlemen," the mayor announces with a flourish, "please welcome our very own resident inventor, Jasper Finch!"

Jasper, dressed in a mismatched collection of clothing and sporting a pair of goggles perched on his head, waves sheepishly from the stage. His yard-sale creations and eccentric demeanor are well-known in Maplewood Grove, and his appearance always adds a touch of whimsy to any event.

"I've got a special treat for you all," Jasper says with a shy smile, "a Christmas-themed contraption that will bring a little extra joy to the festival."

The crowd murmurs with excitement as Jasper begins to demonstrate his latest invention—a mechanical reindeer that prances around the stage, its antlers twinkling with lights. The crowd's laughter and applause fill the air.

Dot and Cliff clap along in enthusiasm, all thoughts of work forgotten.

"You know we really need to get everyone back to work." Dot giggles, clapping excitedly at Jasper's next trick.

"I know," Cliff says warmly. "But you can't deny that we are having so much fun. Even you."

"Yes, but the decorations won't hang themselves. The festival is in a few hours. We still have to add a few touches to pine trees and complete the flowers for the stage–"

"Shhh, stop worrying." Cliff stops her midroll with a finger to her lips. Dot's heart races into overdrive. "Just enjoy the moment. We can complete the work later."

With a nod, she turns back to the show, unable to speak but aware of her pulse racing wildly.

She hasn't been imagining things. Her racing heart is enough evidence of this admission. There's an attraction between them–hot and heavy.

Oh dear.

The question is if Cliff feels the same way too.

Confronting the Past

CLIFF

The first hints of twilight begin to darken the sky over Maplewood Grove, casting long shadows across the Christmas festival grounds. The park, now empty, betrays the worry hanging over Dot and Cliff.

Dot's eyes flick over the empty space where a shipment of Christmas lights and decorations is supposed to be. She checks her phone for the umpteenth time, hoping for some reassuring news. The message she received earlier is clear: the truck delivering the crucial supplies has broken down, and the shipment won't arrive in time for the festival.

"This is a disaster," Dot mutters, her voice tinged with frustration. "We're running out of time, and this is the last thing we needed."

Cliff stands beside her, his brow furrowed in concern. His grizzled face, usually so calm and collected, now shows the strain of the situation. "What are we going to do? We can't have a Christmas festival without plates and napkins."

Dot's expression softens slightly. "We have to go get them

ourselves. The nearest town with a supply store is an hour away. We'll have to drive there and back if we want to salvage the festival."

She glanced at the list in her hand, double-checking the missing items. The decorations were already up, albeit sparse, but the plates and napkins were non-negotiable for the community feast that brought everyone together. "Without them, it's not just decorations we're missing—it's the whole heart of the event," she added, urgency sharpening her voice.

Cliff's eyes widen in surprise. "You think we can make it? It's already getting late."

Dot nods resolutely. "We don't have much choice. If we don't act quickly, we'll miss the festival altogether."

Cliff sighs, rubbing his chin thoughtfully. "Alright then. Let's do it. I'll grab my truck."

Dot's face lights up with a grateful smile. "Thank you, Cliff. I knew you'd come through."

They walk to Cliff's truck, the cold evening air biting at their cheeks. Dot's hands are full of a few leftover decorations she grabs in a last-minute attempt to salvage what she can. Cliff, ever the practical one, ensures that his truck is packed with essentials—flashlights, a first-aid kit, and a thermos of hot coffee.

The drive to the neighboring town is filled with the soft rumble of the truck and the steady rhythm of tires on asphalt. The sky darkens quickly, leaving the road illuminated only by the truck's headlights and the occasional glimmer of distant stars.

Cliff glances at Dot, who sits beside him, her gaze fixed on the road ahead. "You sure you're up for this? It's going to be a long night."

Dot turns to him, her eyes bright. "I wouldn't be anywhere else. This festival means a lot to everyone in town. It's worth every bit of effort."

Cliff nods, a hint of admiration in his gaze. "You've always had a way of making things better, Dot. I've seen it countless times."

Dot and Cliff bump along the uneven road, the rickety old pickup truck swaying with each twist and turn. Dot, bundled in a navy wool coat, adjusts her seatbelt and glances at Cliff. The dim light from the dashboard highlights the crinkles around his eyes as he navigates the winding road with a practiced ease.

She shifts in her seat, her eyes drifting over the snowy pines and the distant hills bathed in twilight. "You know," she says, breaking the silence, "this road hasn't changed much since I was a kid. I remember coming out this way with my family for a picnic. We'd make the drive, and then there was this spot, right by a big oak tree, where Dad would set up the grill. I thought that oak tree was the biggest in the world."

Cliff chuckles, his eyes crinkling further. "Sounds like you've got some fond memories of this place."

"I do," Dot replies, her tone softening. "But it's funny how time changes things. I bet that oak tree isn't as big as I remember. I haven't been out here in years."

He glances at her, a thoughtful expression crossing his rugged features. "I don't think time changes things so much as it just makes you see them differently. I remember this old fishing hole up north— used to be my favorite place. I went back a few years ago, and it was... smaller. Not the pond, but the experience. It wasn't quite the same as when I was a kid."

Dot nods, her gaze returning to the landscape. "It's like those places are frozen in time for us, but the world keeps moving."

The truck rumbles over a pothole, jolting both of them. Cliff slows down, his grip tightening on the wheel. "You know, I never thought much about things changing," he says after a moment. "Just figured you deal with what comes. But listening to you talk about that tree... maybe there's more to it than just moving on."

Dot looks at him, seeing a glimmer of vulnerability in his eyes that he usually hides behind his gruff exterior. "You ever think about what you'd want to change, if you could?"

Cliff hesitates, the silence stretching between them as he navigates a particularly rough stretch of road. "Maybe," he finally says. "Maybe I'd have taken more chances. Spent more time with people that mattered."

Dot studies him, feeling a pang of sympathy. "I think we all have things we wish we'd done differently. I've got my share of regrets, too. Like not telling people how much they mean to me when I had the chance."

Cliff's gaze meets hers briefly before he turns back to the road. "It's never too late, Dot. To say what you need to say. Or to take those chances."

She smiles softly, her heart warmed by his unexpected tenderness. "You've always had a way of saying things that make me think. Even if you don't always mean to."

Cliff looks at her, a faint smile tugging at his lips. "I'm not always good with words, but I guess I've been trying to find the right ones for a long time."

They drive in companionable silence for a while, the only sound being the steady hum of the truck's engine and the soft crunch of snow under the tires. Dot's mind wanders back to their shared history, the years of unspoken words and missed opportunities.

Cliff's voice breaks the quiet, gentle and almost hesitant. "You know, Dot, I was thinking about when we used to organize the festival together. We made a pretty good team back then."

She turns to him, a playful glint in her eye. "We did, didn't we? Even if you did always insist on making the biggest, most complicated float every year."

Cliff grins, the old spark of mischief returning. "And you were always the one who managed to pull it off. I guess we were a pretty good match, weren't we?"

Dot's laughter is warm and genuine. "We were. And we still are. Even if we've both gotten a little older and a little wiser."

Cliff's eyes soften as he glances at her. "Yeah, maybe so. But some things don't change. Like how easy it is to talk to you."

Dot feels a flush of warmth spread through her, touched by his sincerity. "It's easy to talk to you too, Cliff. Always has been."

"I remember when I first moved to Maplewood Grove," Dot continues, her tone nostalgic. "I was so eager to make a difference, to be involved in everything. It's funny how much this town has become a part of me."

Cliff chuckles softly. "You've always been one to dive headfirst into things. I remember the first time I saw you at the community center, organizing an event. I thought, 'Who is this woman and why is she so determined?'"

Dot laughs, a soft, melodic sound that warms the truck's interior. "And what did you think when you saw me?"

Cliff glances at her, a smirk playing at the corners of his mouth. "I thought you were a force of nature. You still are."

Dot meets his gaze, her eyes lingering on his for a moment longer than necessary. The atmosphere in the truck grows warmer.

They arrive at the supply store just as the last light of day fades. The store's neon sign flickers, casting an inviting glow over the parking lot. Dot and Cliff hustle inside, greeted by the cozy warmth of the store and the smell of fresh pine and artificial snow.

The store's aisles are filled with Christmas decorations in every conceivable color and shape. Dot and Cliff quickly find the section with lights and decorations, their movements synchronized as they select the necessary items.

"Do you think we have enough?" Dot asks, holding up a box of twinkling lights.

Cliff inspects their haul, his brow furrowing in concentration. "I think we've got it covered. We should head back before it gets too late."

They walk to the checkout counter and Cliff glances at Dot, his expression thoughtful. "You know, I never really got to say this, but I appreciate everything you do for Maplewood Grove. You've got a heart of gold."

Dot blushes slightly, her cheeks already flushed from the cold. "Thanks, Cliff. I couldn't do it without everyone's support, including yours."

They finish their shopping and head back to the truck, their arms laden with boxes of decorations. The drive home is quieter.

They near Maplewood Grove, and the festival's lights begin to sparkle in the distance.

"We made it," Dot says, slumping into the seat, her voice filled with relief. "Thank God."

The Heart of Maplewood Grove

DOT

The Christmas Festival is in full swing, and Maplewood Grove glistens under a blanket of snow. Twinkling lights drape from every storefront, casting a festive glow over the town. The scent of pine and cinnamon fills the air as Dot and Cliff work side by side, their breath mingling in the crisp winter air.

Dot, wrapped in a bright red scarf and mittens, hums a holiday tune as she adjusts a string of lights around the old oak tree in Maple Grove. Her face is flushed from the cold, but her eyes are bright with excitement. Cliff, dressed in his usual rugged attire, is perched atop a ladder, untangling a stubborn knot in a string of lights.

"Hand me that clip, will you?" Cliff calls down, his voice slightly muffled by the scarf he pulled up to ward off the wind.

Dot passes him the clip, their fingers brushing briefly. She feels a spark of warmth from the contact, but she quickly shakes it off. "You've got quite the knack for turning these lights into a puzzle," she teases.

Cliff chuckles, his rugged face breaking into a grin. "And you've got a knack for making everything look like it's straight out of a holiday card. I don't know how you do it."

She laughs, adjusting a stray strand of tinsel. "It's all in the magic of Christmas, Cliff. You just have to believe in it."

"Yea, whatever." He grins.

By noon, Dot and Cliff are joined by various townsfolk—Agnes and Mabel Carlton, who are busy setting up the rose garden-themed booth; Mayor Eugene, who is giving directions with his usual over-the-top enthusiasm; and Patty Sullivan, who is setting up a book stall adorned with travel trinkets from her many adventures.

The air is filled with the sounds of cheerful chatter and the occasional clink of festive decorations. Dot and Cliff exchange smiles and light banter as they work, their chemistry noticed by the rest of the townfolk, who share secret smiles.

During a noontime break, Dot catches sight of Cliff in a quiet corner of the park, deep in conversation with Noah Harrison. She approaches with a hot cocoa in hand, ready to offer Cliff one, but she overhears a snippet of their conversation that makes her stop in her tracks.

"I'm telling you, Noah, it's time for a change," Cliff says, his voice low and earnest. "I've been thinking about selling the bar for a while now. It's just not the same anymore."

Dot's heart skips a beat. She feels an icy pang of worry. Selling the bar means leaving Maplewood Grove—leaving her. Her mind races, piecing together the fragments of what she's overheard. She sets her cocoa aside on a bench, her hands trembling slightly.

Taking a deep breath, she collects her emotions together–disappointment, worry and hurt. She thought they were friends.

Why didn't he mention this last night? Or did he think it wasn't important enough for her to know?

The thoughts jostle for position in her head as she straightens and begin walking towards them.

Cliff notices her approach, his face showing a flash of surprise before it smooths into a neutral expression. "Hey, Dot," he says, his tone casual. "I didn't see you there."

Dot forces a smile, her voice strained. "Hi, Cliff. I was just, uh, checking in on how things were going."

"It's great, Dot. How about your end?"

"It's okay too."

Noah nods and offers a friendly smile. "Hey, Dot. Cliff's been telling me about some big changes he's been considering."

"Yeah," Dot says, trying to keep her tone light. "I heard. Must be nice that you thought to sell the bar but didn't think to let me know."

The conversation feels awkward now, tension hanging in the air. Cliff cleared his throat, shifting his weight as if the words were heavy.

"Dot, I wish you hadn't found out like this," Cliff said, his voice cracking under the weight of the words. "I kept it quiet because admitting it felt like failing. I thought if I could handle it alone, I could spare you the worry. But I was wrong, and I'm sorry for shutting you out."

Dot's heart aches at the sadness in his voice, but her pride gets in the way. "I see," she says coolly. "Well, if you're thinking about leaving, I guess it's none of my business."

Cliff's eyes widen in surprise. "Dot, that's not what I meant. It's just been on my mind. I love this town, but sometimes—"

Dot took a sharp breath, her fingers curling into her scarf as she steadied herself. "Cliff, you don't get it, do you? This bar isn't just a place—it's a heartbeat in this town, your heartbeat. And you've always been the one to hold it together, even when things felt fragile."

Cliff's jaw tightened as he looked away, eyes dark with understanding, a flicker of doubt in their depths. "I thought letting you in would make me weaker, make you see me as less."

The words settled heavily between them, and for a moment, the only sound was the distant hum of the festival preparations. Dot swallowed hard, feeling the weight of his confession pressing on her heart.

"Sometimes what, Cliff?" Dot interrupts, her voice sharper than she intended. "Sometimes it's too small? Or maybe you're too restless?"

Cliff looks taken aback. "No, it's not like that. It's just—"

"Just what?" Dot presses, her emotions boiling over. "You're thinking of moving on, and now's not the time to talk about it. Not when everyone's counting on us for this festival."

Cliff's frustration shows now, his face hardening. "I didn't mean to upset you. I'm just trying to figure things out. I didn't realize it would be such a big deal."

Dot's eyes flash with hurt. "Maybe if you'd talked to me about it instead of keeping it a secret, it wouldn't be such a big deal."

She turned away, eyes misting as memories of late nights spent at the bar, sharing laughter and stories, rushed back. The ache in her chest grew. How could Cliff think this place—and their friendship—wasn't worth fighting for?

He reached out, a rare desperation in his voice. "Dot, I kept it quiet because I didn't want to burden you. I thought it was my battle to fight alone."

The words hang between them, a heavy silence following the outburst. Cliff's shoulders slump as he looks away, clearly affected by her reaction.

Noah, sensing the tension, steps in. "I think maybe we all need a break. Why don't we grab some hot cocoa and take a breather? Dot, I'm sure Cliff didn't mean to upset you."

Dot nods, walking away, though her expression is still troubled. "Sure, hot cocoa sounds good. I'll get it myself."

"I'll join you both in a minute," Noah said, placing a hand on

Cliff's shoulder as Dot walked away. "Cliff, you've got to tell her everything. Keeping it inside is what's driving that wedge between you two, and trust me, she's tougher than you think."

Cliff's eyes flickered with something unspoken before nodding. "Maybe you're right, Noah. I just don't know if I can fix this."

CLIFF

The sun dips below the horizon, casting long shadows across the snow-covered town. The Christmas lights begin to shine brighter, but the festive spirit seems dimmed for Dot as she walks through the bustling festival grounds. Her cheeks are still flushed, but now it's from the sting of Cliff's words.

She busies herself with adjusting decorations, her movements quick and mechanical. The laughter and chatter of festival-goers feel like distant echoes. Her mind replays the conversation with Cliff, the way his words seemed to come between them like an icy wall.

Cliff, meanwhile, is visibly troubled as he helps Agnes and Mabel set up their booth. The twin sisters' lively chatter and playful bickering go unnoticed by him. His eyes frequently dart to where Dot is working alone, and he can't shake the feeling of guilt pressing down on him.

"Something on your mind, Cliff?" Agnes asks, eyeing him with a knowing look as she hands him a strand of holly.

He forces a smile. "Just a bit of a rough patch with Dot. I didn't mean for things to get so tense."

Mabel, her face creased with concern, chimes in. "Well, I heard there was some sort of misunderstanding. You two should talk it out. You've been dancing around each other for years. Don't let this be the thing that finally makes you stumble."

Cliff's gaze softens, but he nods in agreement. "I know. I'll try to sort it out. Thanks for the advice."

Dot stands at the refreshment stand, staring absently into her cup of hot cocoa. Her hands tremble slightly, not from the cold but from the conflict still simmering inside her. She tries to focus on the crowd's enjoyment—the laughter of children as they play in the snow, the warm glow of the festival lights—but it all feels distant and unreal.

Loretta, noticing Dot's distress, approaches with a concerned look. "You okay, hon? You've been looking a bit off all night."

Dot forces a smile. "Just a bit tired, Loretta. The festival's been a lot to manage."

Loretta's eyes narrow with empathy. "That's not it, and you know it. I've seen that look before. Something's bothering you. Maybe talking about it would help."

Dot hesitates, then sighs, her shoulders slumping. "It's Cliff. I overheard him talking about selling the bar. I know he didn't mean for me to hear, but... I can't shake the feeling that he's planning to leave Maplewood Grove. And if he does, it feels like everything we've done here... it just won't be the same."

Loretta nods thoughtfully, her gaze softening. "Cliff's been through a lot, Dot. Sometimes people talk about big changes when they're feeling uncertain. But he's always had a soft spot for you and this town. Maybe he just needs to sort out his feelings."

Dot looks at Loretta, her eyes reflecting a mix of sadness and confusion. "Maybe. But it's hard not to feel this way. This feeling of betrayal. We've been friends all our lives, why wouldn't he tell me?"

Loretta places a comforting hand on Dot's arm. "You've been a big part of his life for a long time. Don't underestimate the impact you've had on him. Sometimes, people need a little nudge to see what's right in front of them."

The conversation is interrupted by the arrival of Cliff, who has finally managed to approach Dot. His face is etched with concern, and he takes a deep breath before speaking.

"Dot," he begins, his voice hesitant. "Can we talk?"

Dot looks up, her expression guarded. "I don't know if there's much left to say, Cliff. I'm sorry but I don't think I want to talk about it."

"Dot, please..." Cliff begins but she's turned around to walk away, leaving a deep ache of loss in his heart and a sense of lost opportunity.

Under the Mistletoe

CLIFF

"You done messed things up now, Cliff."

Cliff sighs morosely, lost in his own world as he stands behind the bar, a worried expression etched into his features. He pours drinks mechanically, his movements lacking their usual enthusiasm.

Dot enters the bar, her eyes immediately seeking out Cliff. After the conversation last night, she felt like she needed to see Cliff. Maybe hear his side of the story as she didn't give him much chance to explain. After all, they are past that age to keep grudges.

The moment she walks in, she can tell something is amiss; the usual warmth that once filled the space is now overshadowed by a thick tension. Dot walks to the bar.

"Cliff, can I talk to you for a minute?" she asks, her voice carrying a note of concern.

Cliff looks up, forcing a smile. "Of course, Dot. What's up?"

Dot motions to the back room, where they can speak privately. Cliff nods and follows her, his movements slow and heavy with worry. Once they're in the small office behind the bar, Dot turns to him, her gaze steady.

"What's going on, Cliff?" she asks, her voice gentle but firm. "You've been off lately. I thought initially that it was the holiday spirit, but coming here again, I can't help but feel like something's wrong."

Cliff sighs, running a hand through his hair. "You're right. There's been a lot on my mind. The bar's been struggling financially. I've been trying to keep things afloat, but the bills are piling up, and I'm not sure how much longer I can keep this going."

Dot's eyes widen. "Wow. Is this why you wanted to sell it? Why didn't you say something earlier? We could have found a way to help."

Cliff shakes his head, his expression resigned. "I didn't want to burden anyone. I thought I could handle it on my own."

Dot steps closer, her eyes softening with empathy. "Cliff, you don't have to go through this alone. This bar is more than just a business; it's a part of our community. We can rally together and find a solution."

Cliff looks at her, his heart swelling with a mix of gratitude and relief. "I appreciate that, Dot. But I don't want to impose on anyone. I've always managed on my own, and it's hard for me to ask for help."

Dot places a reassuring hand on his arm. "It's not about imposing; it's about being there for each other. Maplewood Grove is a small town, but we have a big heart. Let me help you figure this out."

DOT

Determined to make a difference, Dot starts making calls and organizing a community meeting. The news spreads quickly through Maplewood Grove, and the town's response is overwhelmingly positive.

At the town hall, a gathering of concerned townsfolk buzzes with energy. Dot stands at the front, addressing the crowd with passion and sincerity.

"Thank you all for coming on such short notice," Dot begins, her voice strong and clear. "As you know, Cliff's bar has been a cornerstone of our community for years. It's where we've shared countless memories and celebrated milestones. Right now, it's facing some financial challenges, and we have a chance to show our support and keep this important part of our town alive."

The room erupts in murmurs of agreement. Agnes and Mabel Carlton exchange satisfied glances, while Mayor Eugene Beckett nods approvingly from his seat at the front.

"We can start by organizing a fundraiser," Agnes suggests. "A benefit night at the bar with local musicians and a raffle. That'll draw in a crowd and raise some much-needed funds."

Mabel adds, "And we could set up a donation box at the festival. People can drop in their contributions as they enjoy the festivities."

Mayor Beckett raises a hand. "I'll personally donate to the cause and see if we can get some local businesses to chip in as well."

The room buzzed with newfound energy as residents exchanged suggestions. "I can reach out to the local artisans," Agnes added, her eyes glinting with purpose. "They might be willing to donate part of their profits from the festival stalls." Mayor Beckett leaned forward, nodding thoughtfully. "And I'll see if we can get a few businesses to match donations up to a certain amount. That way, we can boost our total and encourage more people to give."

"What if we host a silent auction?" suggested Patty Sullivan, the town's travel enthusiast. "I can donate some rare trinkets from my adventures abroad." The idea sparked murmurs of approval. Jenny, the store's young clerk, raised her hand eagerly. "And I can organize a Christmas cookie sale with recipes passed down from my grandmother. People loved her gingerbread; it'll draw a crowd."

Even Old Man Jenkins, usually grumbling in the corner, piped up. "I've got some antique train sets that could fetch a good price. Always meant to sell 'em, but this seems like a better reason."

The room filled with energy as more suggestions were called out, each person adding their unique contribution to the growing list of fundraising efforts. Dot's eyes brimmed with gratitude as she saw the outpouring of support that went beyond the one-night event. This was the heart of Maplewood Grove—the community rallying to protect one of their own.

Dot's heart swelled with hope as she realized how many were willing to contribute, not just for a one-night fundraiser but to create a series of efforts that could continue until Cliff's financial troubles were behind him.

Dot's eyes shine with gratitude as she looks around the room. "Thank you all. Your support means everything. Let's come together and make this happen for Cliff."

Plans are put into motion and within hours, Cliff's bar is transformed into a festive haven, with twinkling lights, colorful decorations, and a stage set up for live music. The town's warmth and generosity are on full display as the community comes together to support Cliff.

By the end of the day, the bar is packed. The air is filled with laughter, music, and the clinking of glasses. Dot stands at the entrance, greeting guests with a beaming smile. Cliff approaches her, his eyes filled with emotion. "I don't know how to thank you, Dot. This means more to me than you can imagine."

Dot smiles warmly. "You don't have to thank me. This is what we do for each other in Maplewood Grove. We support our own."

"You know," Cliff says softly, "I never realized how much this town means to me until I saw everyone come together like this."

Dot looks at him. "It's amazing what we can do when we work together. And it's a reminder of why we're all here."

Cliff nods, his gaze lingering on her. "Thank you for reminding me of that. And for reminding me of what really matters."

"Dot," Cliff begins, his voice hushed but earnest. "I need to say something."

Dot meets his gaze, her heart pounding. "What is it, Cliff?"

Cliff takes a deep breath, his eyes never leaving hers. "All this time, I've been trying to keep things together, thinking I had to do it alone. I didn't realize that... that I've been holding back my feelings too."

Dot's eyes widen slightly, her breath catching in her throat. "Feelings? What do you mean?"

Cliff steps closer, his hand gently cupping her cheek. "I've been scared to admit it, even to myself. But it's clear now—I've been in love with you for a long time. And I don't want to hide it anymore."

Dot's heart swells with emotion. The weight of their misunderstandings and unresolved tension seems to lift as she looks at him. "I've felt the same way, Cliff. But I was too afraid to say anything. I thought the timing was wrong, or that you didn't feel the same."

Cliff shakes his head, his thumb gently brushing her cheek. "No, Dot. The timing was never wrong. I was just too stubborn to see what was right in front of me."

As the realization of their mutual feelings settles in, the air between them crackles with intensity. Dot's eyes shine with unshed tears, her voice trembling as she speaks. "I've always admired your strength, your determination. But seeing you vulnerable, seeing you let me in—it means more than I can express."

Cliff's gaze softens, his eyes filled with affection. "And I've always admired your kindness, your ability to bring people together. You've shown me that there's more to life than just keeping my head above water. You've shown me love."

The space between them closes as they lean in, their breath mingling. The twinkling lights above seem to brighten. Dot and Cliff share a passionate kiss, their lips meeting with a fervor that speaks of all the feelings they've kept hidden for so long. The kiss is tender yet intense, a perfect blend of their shared love and newfound understanding.

When they finally pull away, both of them are breathless and smiling, their foreheads resting together. The world around them seems to fade into a blur of sparkling lights and soft music.

"I've wanted this for so long," Dot whispers, her voice filled with emotion.

"Me too," Cliff replies, his hand gently holding hers. "I think we've finally found our moment."

Resounding claps soon surround them from the excited townsfolks and they realize that they are standing under a mistletoe.

"Oh wow, we are back here again." Dot chuckles. "We never could escape the mistletoe, could we?"

"At least it would be on record that we tried our best." Cliff leans in to claim her lips in another long, soulful kiss. "I love you, Dot. More than words can ever say."

"I love you, too, Cliff," Dot sighs.

CLIFF

The Christmas Festival in Maplewood Grove is a resounding success. The town square is alive with a dazzling display of lights and decorations. The twinkling lights on the giant Christmas tree reflect off the snow-covered ground, creating a magical, almost otherworldly ambiance. Stalls lined with handmade crafts, festive foods, and cozy drinks draw in crowds of smiling townsfolk. Laughter and joyful chatter fill the crisp night air, mingling with the sweet strains of holiday music.

Horse-drawn carriages with bells jingling softly transport visitors through the town's snow-dusted streets. The horses' breath puffs out in white clouds, and the sound of hooves crunching through the snow adds a calming sound to the cheerful chatter of the bundled-up families.

The centerpiece of the holiday season is the annual Christmas market, held in the town square. Booths made of timber and adorned with holly and twinkling lights offer handcrafted goods, everything from knitted scarves to wood carvings. Local musicians play festive tunes on fiddles and guitars, with the townspeople joining in to sing carols, their voice blending harmoniously into the night air.

Dot and Cliff stand together at the heart of the festival, their faces alight with happiness and pride. Cliff's bar, now adorned with a fresh coat of paint and festive decorations, stands as a centerpiece, drawing admiration from everyone passing by. Dot watches as children run past, clutching candy canes and toy animals, their faces aglow with delight. She turns to Cliff, her eyes sparkling with a mix of joy and love.

"You did an amazing job with the bar," Dot says, her voice filled with admiration as she leans in closer. "It looks incredible."

Cliff, his arm wrapped around Dot's shoulders, smiles warmly. "Couldn't have done it without you, Dot. You've really made a difference, not just for the festival, but for me."

Dot blushes slightly, her eyes meeting his. "And you've shown me that there's more to life than just organizing events. You've helped me see that sometimes, the best things are the ones we find when we're not looking."

As the festival winds down, Dot and Cliff stand in front of the Christmas tree, now surrounded by the glowing faces of the townsfolk. The crowd gathers around them, sensing that something special is about to happen. Loretta, Noah, Liam, Tyler, and Alex stand nearby, their expressions filled with warmth and anticipation.

Mayor Eugene Beckett steps forward, his novelty tie gleaming under the lights. "Ladies and gentlemen, before we close out this wonderful evening, I'd like to recognize two people who have worked tirelessly to make this festival a success."

The crowd cheers as Mayor Beckett gestures to Dot and Cliff. "Dot Simmons and Cliff Barnett! Their dedication and hard work have brought so much joy to Maplewood Grove this Christmas."

The applause is thunderous, and Dot's eyes well with tears of happiness. Cliff's hand tightens around hers, and he leans in to whisper, "Looks like we've made quite the impact."

Dot smiles, her heart swelling with pride. "We certainly have."

As the applause dies down, Cliff steps forward and, with a deep breath, addresses the crowd. "Thank you all for your support. This festival has been a dream come true for both Dot and me. But more than that, it's shown me that Maplewood Grove is where I belong."

"This has been incredible," Dot says softly, her eyes scanning the townsfolk. "I never imagined that coming to Maplewood Grove would lead to all this."

Cliff looks at her, his expression thoughtful. "Neither did I. But I wouldn't trade it for anything. This place, these people—they've become my family."

Dot nods, squeezing his hand gently. "And we've built something beautiful here. I'm excited about what the future holds for us."

Cliff gazes at her, his eyes filled with a mix of love and determination. "Me too. There's a lot we can do with the bar, with the town. We've got a fresh start, and I want to make the most of it—together."

Dot's heart flutters at his words, and she leans in to give him a tender kiss. The snow continues to fall gently around them, adding to the serene and magical atmosphere. As they pull away, Dot looks up at Cliff with a smile.

"So, what do you think? Are we ready for the next adventure?"

Cliff grins, his eyes twinkling with excitement. "I think we're a bit too old for that. Let's just focus on enjoying life together."

"That sounds like a plan." Dot giggles.

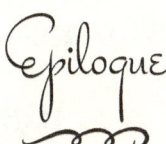

Epilogue

DOT AND CLIFF walk through Maplewood Grove. The town is a cozy, snow-covered wonderland, the lights of the Christmas Festival casting a soft glow on the streets. They enjoy the warm silence between them.

Cliff's gaze turns to the bar, his mind already working on ideas for improvements and new ventures. "I've been thinking about expanding the bar's menu, maybe even adding some live music nights. What do you think?"

Dot nods enthusiastically. "I love that idea! And maybe we can also host community events, like book readings or craft fairs. There's so much we can do to make the bar a hub for the town."

Cliff's eyes light up with excitement. "That sounds perfect. And with your support, I know we can make it happen."

"You can definitely count on me for that."

The End
Did you enjoy *Sweet Mistletoe*?
Please consider rating it on Amazon, Goodreads, Bookbub, or your favorite retailer. Reviews help me reach new readers.

If you enjoyed *Dot and Cliff's* story, you'll love *Eden and Rory's* story in Christmas Kisses, the next book in the Mistletoe Kisses series!

Find all the books in the Mistletoe Kisses series at:
MISTLETOE KISSES FULL SERIES

Sweet Mistletoe is also part of the *Maplewood Grove* series. Read *Sweet Rivals*, the first book in the series.

Join my newsletter for updates and giveaways!
www.daisylandishromance.com

Sweet Valentine

~ಶಾ~

Reluctant Hearts

PATTY

THIS TIME of day is one Patty Sullivan usually lives for. Just as Maplewood Grove starts revving to life, she opens up her beloved Whispering Willow for the day. Her bookstore doubled as a café, but Patty knew it was much more than just those two things. Immersed in the cocoon she's built piece by piece from her life wildly lived, the proof is everywhere: filled with postcards from countless countries, globes in sizes big and small, accurate and not, and more than enough souvenirs to satisfy a magpie.

The Whispering Willow isn't what one would expect to find in a small town in upstate New York, so rooted in its traditions that time couldn't modernize its charm. She loves it all the more for it. It is her pride and joy. It's a big part of why she carries a smile with her wherever she is in the store; it's her favorite accessory for any ensemble.

That day, when that accessory is nowhere to be found, it's bound to be unmissable.

She wipes down the counter with deliberate care, her bangles clanging together in sharp contrast to the quiet. Patty avoids looking up, not wanting to meet the red and pink hearts hanging from the ceiling. They were Jasmine's idea, of course, but Patty can't deny they fit right in with the town's Valentine's craze. It isn't that she hated the holiday. Well, not completely. But every time she sees those decorations, it stirs something deeper—a memory of promises once made and broken, of a time when love seemed like something she could hold onto.

Patty's distaste for Valentine's Day ran deeper than the commercialism or the overused symbols. Every red heart and pink petal reminded her of the love she'd once believed in—until it slipped through her fingers like cold coffee forgotten on the counter. It wasn't just the bitterness of past heartbreak, it was the fear that love, like that latté, would always cool, leaving nothing but an empty cup. She's the only one who seems to care.

The windchimes she had stuck to the door last fall, adorned with a delightful bouquet of peacock feathers, jangle merrily when it's pushed open. In bursts the pretty but fickle town gossip Betty Lou Hopkins. She enters arm-in-arm with the wife of the town mechanic, Liv Parker, the other town mechanic. "You're *so lucky*, Olivia," Betty Lou is gushing, her red hair bouncing. "He is *such* a good man!"

The dark-haired beauty doesn't gush back with the same girlish, giddy enthusiasm—but Patty only needs to look at Liv's face to see how smitten she is. Patty doubts the helpless grin tugging at the corners of her full mouth is attributed to her, though the mechanic greets congenially, "G'morning, Patty. Love the décor. Using that height to your advantage, are we?" Liv points a blunt-nailed forefinger ceiling-ward.

Patty has no choice but to look at the very decorations she'd been avoiding now. She isn't positive a smile could *taste* strained—but hers does. Fortunately, the girls don't pay much attention past Patty's strained return of, "Yeah. Good morning!" With her complicated sentiments taking up the room they do, there isn't any left to stow guilt over inadvertently stealing credit for Jasmine's labors. "What'll you have?"

At the inquiry, Betty Lou leans heavily into the display case. Her forearms stack, bracing her weight, as she looks down through the glass. "Mmm-mm-mmm," she harrumphs, bottom lip protruding in a pout that Patty can tell is meant to be cute. It is, until Betty Lou whines, "Patty, nothing *Valentiney?*"

Liv snickers, the arm that had been linked through her friend's slinging comfortably over Betty Lou's shoulders, tutting, "Not sure that's a word, Betts. And besides, there's still a week to go, right?" Patty isn't sure which one of them Olivia aims the question at. It doesn't matter.

Betty Lou bemoans, "Oh, as if you don't know it's six days till February fourteenth, Olivia Parker! You've got a Valentine for life. *Some of us—*" The words are pointed, in a way that unnerves Patty, "—are still looking for a Prince Charming." Her hopes that she'd dwindled to an insignificant spectator are extremely short-lived. Betty Lou looks to her for confirmation. "*Patty.* Patty, you get it, right? Us gals can't afford not to take the Love Quest seriously. It just *kills* me, thinking of dying alone. And it must be—gosh, it must be so much *worse* for y— *Ouch!*" Betty Lou looks down at a leg Patty can only imagine Liv has kicked to dislodge the foot she'd been jamming in her mouth. She doesn't know what makes her feel more pathetic: Betty Lou's earnest, albeit saccharine, compassion, or the sheepish pity in the other woman's face.

"Love Quest?" Patty echoes dubiously.

"The *Valentine's* Love Quest?" Betty Lou enunciates slowly. Patty's mouth purses into a hard line. She isn't a woman with much of a temper. Its fuse was beginning to feel shorter now, though. Betty Lou doesn't notice. "You should get involved, you know. The pairings will be random. And there's some fun surprises packed in this year!"

"It's a scavenger hunt in randomly assigned pairs," the mechanic clarifies. Patty finds it harder to be irate with her, given that Olivia had only moved to town a couple of years ago. She was still catching up on everybody's life stories; a task that wasn't as easy as it sounded, especially when one was both a newly-wed and a recent mother.

As Betty Lou prattles on, clearly oblivious to Patty's discomfort, the door chimes again, and in walks Jonah—Patty's ex, striding in like he owns the place. Her heart drops. Of all days. She hasn't seen him in months, but there he is, all charming smiles.

"Hey, Patty," Jonah drawls, his voice carrying easily through the noise of the crowd.

Betty Lou's elbow nudges Liv, missing the sudden tension that sucks the air out of the room. "Didn't expect to see you around," Jonah adds, his voice far too casual, eyes flicking toward the window.

Patty forces a polite smile, but her pulse quickens. Her gaze instinctively drifts to the glass, her heart skipping a beat. There, standing outside in the cold, is Colton, watching. His brown eyes— why hadn't she ever noticed how piercing they were?—meet hers, sending a wave of unease and something else entirely through her.

He doesn't come in. He just watches.

Betty Lou, clearly unaware of the rising tension, jabs Liv again. "I heard he's back in town for her," she whispers, just loud enough for Patty to overhear. Patty's heart drops further at the implication.

"Poor Colton," Liv replies, her eyes darting between Jonah and the window, where the Sheriff still stands, watching but silent. "He doesn't stand a chance if Jonah's in the picture."

Patty's breath catches. She wonders why, for the first time in so long, she cares about what happens next.

Belatedly, she identifies the sheriff. Colton Rhodes, his name is – but everyone just calls him Sheriff. *Sheriff Rhodes,* if one wanted to get more intimate about it. Nevertheless, it is impossible to divorce the man's occupation from his personality. She doesn't know him, not really. He isn't a very knowable creature, Sheriff Rhodes. He ensures it. Patty is certain it's on purpose, too. Not that she judges; that would make her a hypocrite, wouldn't it? Patty herself enjoys the occasional bout of beguiling with an enigmatic nature.

Yet, as his gaze latches to Patty's, she could swear she sees his soul echo the lament hers has been for years now. *Oh,* she thinks. Just *oh.*

COLTON

He is used to being a bystander. The spectator. The watchful eyes, keeping the halcyon innocence of this town safe. It doesn't really bother him the way the townsfolk sometimes watch him, effusing amusement over his staid determination. He's grown desensitized to it. Truthfully, Colton finds he is desensitized to most things.

When he'd been a young boy growing up in Brooklyn, he'd had bad teeth. He'd spent a lot of his adolescence in the dentist's chair—which was, in fact, his father's chair, though Colton didn't ever talk about that. He thinks, though. He thinks too much. The pinch before numbness spread was a familiar and seminal experience in his life. It wasn't a remarkable or original one.

But pain, Colton Rhodes was all too aware, did not have to be either of those things for it to still be painful.

He remains vigilant to the way several pairs of eyes linger on him as he walks down Maplewood Grove's main street. One could say his uniform is why he sticks out like a sore thumb—if they didn't know any better. It's Maplewood Grove, though, so everybody already does. Knowing everybody's (and their grandmother's) business was just part of small-town territory, and he had moved here knowing that. He may have once had more naive notions about this place... but Colton didn't ever talk about those, either.

There were a lot of things that permeated his life like that. Colton could live with them. He had been doing so for years, now. Besides, he had long since found his little ways to deal.

Like this: when he rounds the corner towards the Maple Grove, typically lush parkland that is covered in a picturesque dusting of snow where children shriek with laughter and play without inhibition, kicking about a football between them, boys and girls alike.

His brows are dark and severe, and his eyes naturally narrowed in menacing, serpentine slits; his mouth is the part that softens at the sight. A wind blows through town, biting, and he feels it so much more than any of the kids seem to.

"Sheriff! *Sheriff– Look!*" Young Jamie Green waves his hand with unbridled excitement there wasn't an adult in Maplewood who'd understand. When he has Colton's undivided attention, he kicks the ball with impressive intensity, especially since the little fella was only nine years old. Raised by a single mother who had grown up in this town and hadn't been back in years on top of it.

Wild horses couldn't have stopped him from soaking his winter-chapped mouth with his tongue before he pressed his fingers into it, blowing out a voracious wolf whistle that evolved into encouraging applause. "*You're doing great, bud!*" Colton hollers back, his chest aching at the broad grin that scrunches the kid's eyes shut.

He keeps it, the mental image he snaps of the sight—before he tucks it away like a business card slid one's way that had nothing to do with the life one was currently living, but felt like a bad idea to dispose of because of what it represented with its very existence.

Then he keeps patrolling, trudging onward.

Paces away on the other side of the Grove, he comes across another gaggle of kids—older ones, this time, middle schoolers on the precipice of adolescence they were mistakenly giddy over hurtling towards—gathered around picnic tables. He zeroes in on the glitter and markers that pass hands while they work tirelessly at cards with love hearts and lopsided handwriting and bad rhymes. They are all so young, Colton thinks mournfully. They don't know anything yet, and soon they will know too much. There was no way to stop it. It was the way of the world, no matter how much he couldn't stand it.

He doesn't linger at the sight for long. Can't. Won't.

Not just because the optimism with which they practically burst has his stomach roiling. He has a routine, too. A system. One he's cultivated over his handful of years in Maplewood Grove. One he will not fail for a stupid holiday that isn't even a holiday.

One that is heinously disrupted by the oodles of decorations that drip from every corner of the town. The chill worsens the farther he ventures down the streets. With the gray skies as his companion as he confronts all sorts of ridiculousness: not a local business in sight that isn't littered with cheesy puns or heart-shaped window decals; windows all over cluttered with twinkling strings of lights that would drive up electricity bills folks would bemoan later; not even lamp posts or benches were spared, sporting unnecessary paraphernalia like red and white ribbons and gaudy wreaths of flowers that will be dead before February fourteenth even shows up.

Colton's breath fogs in front of him with the heat of his aggrieved sigh. His head turns away from the cloud, his gloved palm wiping condensation that clings to his pallid cheeks.

Somehow, his eyes find another pair on the other side of window glass that was mostly obscured by something far more interesting than the same thematic doodads taken out of storage once a year. Postcards, as far as the eye can see. Strange and chaotic, except for how they seem to make total sense.

It isn't the first time they've stopped him short. Patty Sullivan's bookstore—though it wasn't just that, by far—was a rare gem. It had made it onto magazine listicles of one-of-a-kind places to check out in whimsical towns to get lost in when the city drained you for good reason.

Every time Colton saw her, though, *Patty*...

Well, he couldn't help but think it was her that was worth coming to see. She was a vision. Vibrant. Except, unlike the stinging red that lanced its way through Maplewood Grove, there was nothing off-putting about it. Her effect was the opposite. There is a balance between her willowy limbs draped in lustrous, flowy fabrics that rustled like an autumn breeze whenever she moved, her pores seemingly exuding warm cinnamon sweetness, like the woman was a baked good, wholesome as apple pie, even with those dark, delicate features that paired intriguingly with such a potent, passionate spirit. Colton hardly made it a habit of pontificating poetry about strange women. Only, he couldn't imagine whose eyes wouldn't have a hard time not lingering on Patty Sullivan. She is magnetic.

She looks like the keeper of an enchanted forest. There was a serenity to her movements, and a bravery in her grin whenever it sprawled, infectious and unnerving.

His heart stumbles in his chest when she looks back at him.

The Sheriff of Maplewood Grove had never before felt like the one caught red-handed.

The Love Quest Begins

PATTY

BY THE END of the week, as it turned out, Patty hadn't grown up quite as much as she had convinced herself she had. At least, not enough to be able to resist peer pressure any better than she had when she'd been the strange girl people laughed at more often than they laughed with in high school.

For all her adamance and well-reasoned copouts, all it had ultimately taken was the right person standing in front of her. When it was one of the only people who had been kind to her before she had learned how to be kind to herself to demand she participate in the name of town spirit, insisting it wasn't all about romantic coupling, Patty had caved like a house of cards in a snowstorm. It was some comfort, at least, to remember she'd never met a soul with the nerve to deny Dot Simmons.

The woman wasn't the mayor of Maplewood Grove, but Patty wasn't certain Dot didn't have more power than the stout, apple-cheeked sweetheart of an eccentric man who actually held the title. She believed in Dot's dominion—which wasn't political or authoritarian in nature—and she wasn't the only one. No one could deny it: if there was something to know in town, Dot Simmons was the first one to know it. She wore the title of the town's unofficial historian with pride. Patty also happens to consider her the implicitly official Absolem of their little Wonderland on top of it, though Dot isn't nearly as amused by that comparison as Patty remains.

"That's okay," Patty consoles serenely, motioning her on. "Just tell me who my random partner is, and let's get this show on the road."

Dot swirls her hand through what Patty can only describe as a gigantic fishbowl. From it, she plucks a white heart-shaped card that she opens. When she holds it up, it's Dot who looks amused and Patty who wears dismay. In sturdy, block lettering is written the name **COLTON P. RHODES**. The man put an initial down for his middle name. *That*'s how serious a person he was. The red heart-shaped card with her own name on it featured only her first name in a cursive, sprawling font. There are stars whimsically doodled around it.

"Oh, the *Sheriff*," Dot says, sounding impressed in a way that sounds... a touch too theatrical for the woman Patty understands her to be. Then she adds, "That'll definitely give you a leg up in the scavenger hunt, that's for sure." Rational, no-muss-no-fuss thinking. *That* is more the Dot she knows. Of course, there isn't too much time to appreciate it before Dot is announcing to the crowd of townsfolk all over the Sip 'n Saw bar they'd all gathered at, already paired off, or are waiting to be: "*Sheriff Rhodes!* Sheriff Colton P. Rhodes! You're with *Patty Sullivan!*"

Patty gapes at the other woman. Or rather, is left gaping in general. She can't comprehend it. Any of this.

Not that someone who was arguably the most sensible person Patty knew had talked her into this spectacle in the name of community advocacy. Not that she had just announced a man Patty spent most of the time feeling immensely wishy-washy in front of, was *with* her, resulting in titters and poorly concealed whispers spreading through the masses.

And not—*especially* not—that Colton Rhodes, Mr. Big Serious Cop from the Big Apple, would sign his name onto a heart-shaped card... subsequently signing his entire day away just to traipse between historic and scenic locations all around the fairweather town that was *all* they had in common. Not that he steps out of the crowd, in his uniform the way he always is, and holds his arm out to Patty, as if she is a princess about to descend the last step of a grand staircase and needs an escort for it.

She doesn't mean to laugh. It's an involuntary spurt that leaves her, mostly as air through her nose. Patty can see the tips of Colton's ears turn red.

"You're super gentlemanly, man," Patty is quick to say. She throws up a spontaneous peace sign he doesn't know what to do with. For some reason, it gets under her skin, the notion that he might twist her laughter into something meanspirited. Too many men, Patty had long since learned, let their pride get in the way of a swell time. Given everything she had tucked away to show up to Sip 'n Saw today, she wasn't about to let him make a hard day harder. When her arm hooks through his, it's with gravitas. He hasn't said a word. "I dig it," she assures, taking charge since the man has been rendered mute. "Shall we?" There is a lilt to the words. Theatrics are more her vibe than Dot's anyway.

Her heart may be bruised, but Patty Sullivan's *je ne sais quoi* remains an indefatigable force. All the more so when she suspects they're going to need it to power them through this hunt.

COLTON

In retrospect, Colton thinks ruefully, he should have known when Betty Lou Hopkins had walked up to his usual table at Loretta's Diner a few days ago and plopped down in the seat opposite him that something was amiss. It should have set off an alarm bell or two in his head when she hadn't had any tips to give him, none of the intel she typically served him with plenty of sauce on the side. Maybe, he had to consider, irked, he'd grown desensitized to his own detriment.

It had been too late when he hadn't thought anything of the vaguely impish glee shone in the young woman's eyes as she had prompted, apropos of nothing, "So, Sheriff, how come we never see you with a lady on your arm?" Colton had stared at her blankly. Befuddled. Non-reactive. It hadn't been as if it was the first time one the townsfolk had pried. What wouldn't fly in the city he'd come of age on the gritty streets of, was the norm in Maplewood. He'd grown accustomed to it.

He'd forked another bite of his pancakes into his mouth, and listened to her go on about how he was getting on in his years. With the salt and pepper streaking at his temples, Colton knew she was right. He felt nothing over it. Besides, he already knew nothing could have dissuaded the post office clerk from gabbing on. Unlike diners back in New York, there was no TV at Loretta's. This did the same job, in a way.

Yet he should have known better than to be lulled into submission due to the sheer familiarity of it. By the time *knowing better* had come around, he may as well have been waving a white flag in the air, signaling to racing cars revving to tear away from the starting line. By then, Betty Lou had already corralled over the two elderly twins, Agnes and Mabel Carlton, to join her makeshift brigade. Colton had long since stopped taking at the face value of their creaky knees and learned to recognize the menaces they were; the sight of them, and the concerning knowing gleam in their eerily bright eyes, had been what had finally raised his hackles. Too late.

Now, even days later, the sheriff felt swindled. Colton wasn't sure how he hadn't remained immune to it. The only way to get them to quit probing, it had felt, was to agree to be a part of some scavenger hunt Betty Lou had insisted the entire town was set to partake in. He could have left, of course, but that common sense hadn't chimed in at the moment of disaster.

It helped, at least, that this once, the town gossip's word was good as gold. The entire town jammed itself into Cliff Barnett's Sip 'n Saw bar – which he typically lent to the town for impromptu town meetings anyway, and wouldn't think of denying his other half, Dot Simmons, for the Love Quest.

Colton's attention zeroed in on the sea of townsfolk. It was his job to look after them, and he had shown up to do it—yet he can't shake the uncanny feeling that it's *them* watching *him*. Watching him tactlessly, and intensely, while he stands amidst them, as much of a sore thumb sticking out as ever. He almost misses his name being called. Dazed, Colton has no honorable choice but to step up to the plate for none other than Patty Sullivan herself.

His nostrils flare. There is something fishy at work here. The suspicion doesn't prickle just because, as a rule of thumb, Colton Rhodes is not a man who puts any stock in the notion of coincidence. He wasn't a charlatan who dismissed them in favor of devotion to newfangled, woo-woo explanations. He just understands the existence of a bigger picture.

All one had to do was zoom out. He tries...

Until Patty loops her arm through his. Colton had gotten used to the unnerved manner in which townsfolk tended to simultaneously seek him out and avoid his gaze. Now, they *watch*. Like they are waiting, with bated breath. It's far from the first time he's seen them all this way. He's always been an observer; not the main character in their tomfoolery.

He doesn't have to eye Patty for long to know she's as, if not more, in the dark as he is.

Colton breaks more than one of his rules when he only half-listens to Dot speaking, albeit it is while she elaborates on the details surrounding a scavenger hunt of all things. He typically prides himself on paying attention in ways most take for granted. Only, right then, Patty holds his focus hostage, standing beside him, growing stiffer and stiffer the longer they stand there.

Colton keeps his distance, not because he wants to, but because he doesn't know how to bridge the gap. Every now and then, as they walk, he catches himself watching the way Patty's hair danced in the wind or how her lips curved into a small smile when she thinks he isn't looking. It's small moments like these, the ones she never noticed, that make him feel the pull. But he doesn't let himself act on it—not yet. Instead, he lets the tension simmer, lets it build slowly, like a storm gathering on the horizon, content to wait for the right moment, whenever that might be.

"Everybody, be sure to grab a bag of *Sweethearts*!" Betty Lou chirps from the bar she's been parked behind since the unofficial town meeting had kicked into gear. It was where the Love Quest would begin; their starting line of sorts. "Get your *Sweethearts*, then grab your sweetheart's hand and go forth!" Colton can't help but cringe at the words, his body viscerally rejecting the cloying sentiment.

Ironically, it is the sight of Patty's palm meeting her forehead in an exasperated *thwack* that curbs the secondhand embarrassment.

"You all right?" He nudges Patty's side gently.

She freezes. He can see, plainly, the effort it takes her to nod her head, and tersely say, "I'll just go grab our candies, partner. Hang... Hang, uh, tight, huh?" Patty doffs an imaginary cowboy hat in his direction and weaves through the crowd before he can say another word.

Just as well, Colton thinks. He didn't have anything clever to say back either way.

Following the Trail

PATTY

WHATEVER CRUEL TWIST of irony that's to blame, Patty isn't sure. But the first place the pair of them are instructed to go is... right back to the Whispering Willow. Only this time, the clue wasn't just sitting on the counter. A riddle awaited them, hinting at something hidden within the maze of shelves. "The past holds the key to your future. Find the journey where it all begins," it read. Colton, ever practical, immediately began scanning the travel section, but Patty knew better. The journey, she realized, was about her, about the path she had walked. She moved toward the memoir section, pulling down a well-worn copy of *Eat, Pray, Love*. There, nestled between the pages, was their next clue. The only evidence against the dire straits Patty's formerly iron-clad guts are convinced they're in, is how content she is to be back in her space. Like sucking in that first deep breath after being underwater too long, her body relinquishes tension it had been harboring with a hard exhale.

To think, for most of her life, she's been the opposite of a home-body. From as far back as Patty's memory stretches, she can recall the unburdened fervency with which she'd leaped into life's waiting embrace. She'd even had those rebellious, borderline reckless years of adolescence where she'd lumped her identity in with what the town she'd been born to would say about her. She was so far beyond that now.

If she'd thought Colton Rhodes would have cared at all about those nuggets of intimate trivia, maybe she would have said it all out loud with the same heft she exhaled her sigh. As it is, all she says to the town sheriff is: "Do you even have a sweet tooth, Sheriff?" Patty teased, glancing sideways at him. Colton, without missing a beat, shot her a rare, crooked grin. "You can call me Colton, Patty. But no, not much of a sweet tooth." She raised an eyebrow, lips twitching into a playful smile. "Really? Because I could've sworn you were eyeing those heart-shaped cookies earlier. Must've been my imagination." Colton chuckled, shaking his head. "You sure you weren't imagining me eyeing something else?" Patty's laugh rang out, warm and bright. "Oh, so the sheriff *can* flirt after all."

No one would believe it based on the events of this week, and especially those of the day, but Patty has a history of being a pretty smooth operator. She's just off her game. Given the time of the year, she isn't necessarily surprised by that.

Colton, he offers. She isn't entirely sure she can just leap to that – or that she even *should* when the way he says it, stood pin-straight like she is his drill sergeant and he's prepared to drop and give her twenty at her faintest whim, flusters her. A little, the somewhat dormant wild child in Patty squirms with pleasure at the idea. After all, it wasn't everyone—or just anyone—who got a man so flinty as Colton Rhodes all riled up and affected.

"That isn't an answer," Patty quips. She doesn't bother being chastened by the flat look he shoots her. It stokes some of the moxie that's been missing in action this week, instead. She shoots him a saucy wink in return—only to burst into involuntary, uproarious laughter for the second time that day when he abruptly drops both bags of *Sweethearts* he had insisted on carrying for them. She may not know much about him, but she knows he isn't a clumsy person. She's happy to take the credit for reducing him to it. It makes her pride soar in a way she hadn't even known she'd needed.

She watches him drop down to grab them, clearing his throat. "I like them fine, Patty," he insists. "I'm just not wild about..."

"Valentine's Day?" Patty finishes for him. He hands over a bag, nodding. She moves it palm to palm, wrapper crackling against her skin. "Me neither," she admits.

Again, the sheriff just nods. He isn't a loquacious fellow, she'd already assumed that. She doesn't linger on it, adamant to let him be himself as vehemently as she's let herself be herself. It isn't as if they don't have more clues to look for. Their first of the scavenger hunt had already been waiting against the cash register. She holds out the tiny envelope to the man who investigates for a living, even if the clue is sealed with a heart-shaped sticker.

His face is inscrutable as he plucks out the card. His sigh, however, flares with frustration with energy that's shrouded in grays. Before Patty can question—or rather, decide if she wants to question it, he flips the card over, holding it out for her to read:

Among the pages, stories spin,
Where whispers of journeys once begin.
But if it's love that you now seek,
Take a path where hearts can speak.
Beneath a roof where stars turn aglow,
Kisses exchanged so long ago.
Find the place where vows were said,
By lovers lost, but hearts still wed.

Pure habit has her reading it aloud. Patty doesn't even realize it for a moment until she stumbles over the mention of *kisses,* startled – only for the man to exhale, "Exactly. What on earth?"

Patty's brows shoot up her forehead. Of their own volition, the corners of her mouth twitch upwards, almost smugly. "The old gaze-bo," she explains. "There used to be all kinds of lore around it – about it being a lucky place to get married. Anyone who did had a long, endlessly happy marriage." Here, she must bite down on her lip to keep from laughing again. "Until, of course, someone who got married there got a divorce, and that was that."

She watched him rub his palm over his face. He shoves his bag of candies into his pocket, muttering something under his breath, and she almost misses it—and even then, she isn't certain she hears him correctly. By the time she decodes it, his face is shuttered and he's already opening the door for them to step back into the February chill: *Yeah. Because divorce is evil.*

She's hung up on it, confounded, but willing to distract him out of the ornery mood he seems to have been propelled into. "Oh, there's something on the back of it, too," she chirps, locking up behind herself without even looking at the key.

Gruffly, he asks, "Another poem?" A sideways glance confirms he is bracing himself.

"Questions," Patty answers out of left-field. "It's questions for us to ask each other." She lets out a pleased hum when he plucks the card right out of her hands and reads in a blunt, no-nonsense prescription:

1. **Share with your partner three things you like about each other.**
2. **Share with your partner your biggest fear.**
3. **Share with your partner your ideal date.**

Pointedly, he clears his throat—and, by then, it's Patty who is already questioning: "How would they even know if everyone's answering these? You don't have to." If they didn't want to answer, who could stop them? She looks at him—his grouchy face—and can't imagine him wanting to partake in makeshift-interrogation. Or act like this is a real date.

Maybe it's that, that creases his forehead: having to honor something he's signed up for, but not because he wants to do it. "They're probably assuming we've got integrity, and I am a-okay with that." He puffs his chest out, following her lead around the street corner she leads them down. "Do you want me to go first?" he just offers.

She acquiesces with the skepticism smothering the, "Uh, sure," she answers with.

"Three things I like about you? I... like your imagination and drive. Seeing what you have built into such a unique experience born out of joy. It's inspiring. That's one. Two—" Colton holds out two fingers, clearing his throat again, "—I like how kind you are. A lot of folks can be nice, especially in this town, but not everyone is... Yeah. So. That." He risks a look at her out of the corner of his eye. Lamely, he settles for, "Also, your perfume. You smell good."

Sheriff Colton Rhodes may not be a loquacious man. But Patty Sullivan has always been a lover of words. There are many things she has struggled with in her life—no matter how memory or social media may attempt to distort that fact—but talking isn't one of them.

So why does he make her speechless?

How?

COLTON

Patty's laughter sounds like the ridiculous windchimes hanging from the Whispering Willow's door. "My perfume?" Her breath catches in her throat, and when he hears it, his brain short-circuits over it. That, Colton thinks, can't be good.

But it feels it. It *feels* good to just say—

"You smell like candy canes," Colton taps into the reserves for his audacity to tell her. Her laughter softens over it, past the hitch of a breath he wouldn't miss no matter what his profession was. He's still a man. "Your turn."

Patty is quiet—but it isn't a vacant silence. Colton couldn't put it into words if he'd tried. He isn't remotely a man prone to hyperbole—but he could swear he can *hear* her think. Yet, when Patty speaks, it's confidently, without pause, factual and straightforward, even in her dreamy voice: "One, I like your hair. It's thick and dark and fickle. Like it can't make up its mind between black and brown, with those grays encroaching already. Two, your sense of integrity. There aren't too many people I've met in the world who are so solid that their faith in what's right and good and honorable couldn't at least be tempted. And three, your uniform. I like it. You look dashing. Even if you walk around like Scrooge."

"*Scrooge?*" Colton barks a laugh.

Patty nods very seriously, before her nose scrunches. "McDuck. Donald Duck's uncle."

That elicits another chuckle from him. Colton isn't sure if he finds her unexpected reference more amusing, or that he immediately gets it. This time when he nudges her, she nudges back. He hands her back the card, already having memorized the prompts. "Biggest fear?" he asks.

"You first," Patty decrees.

Colton shoves his hands in his pockets, and considers it. "Maybe that it will always feel this way." He doesn't mean for it to be a vague answer. In fact, it happens to be the most honest thing he's said out loud in all his years, Colton thinks. But that doesn't mean he doesn't recognize it sounds like one. His mouth opens again, ready to add – to clarify, no matter the unease already creeping its way into his chest. Patty says, so softly, "I understand that one." He doesn't understand how, or why, but he doesn't doubt it.

"For me," Patty adds, after a beat, "it's probably the opposite, in a way. That the best days are gone, and I'll never feel that way again. Not so young. Not so carefree and still courageous enough that it's effortless to forget there's a cost for everything." Colton listens, riveted. An unease burgeons in his belly over her words. Constantly vigilant, he's always telling the townsfolk to be. And he, himself, doesn't even notice a few minutes after, that they've come to a standstill at a gazebo.

"The third," he says definitively. "I don't believe in a single ideal date. A date should be about the person you are with; whoever asks, makes the plan. Am I just old-fashioned?"

Patty shoots him a grin—and, for the most part, it still reaches her eyes. "Yeah," she teases. It's warm, though, so there's no offense to be taken. "But I am, too. Most people don't believe it. Understandably. It isn't easy to comprehend walking contradictions."

Colton considers her. "Are you sure you didn't write the poem?"

Patty turns on her heel, walking in a slow, perusing circle around the gazebo. "If I was a part of setting up the Love Quest shenanigans, I wouldn't bother to pretend to look for the next clue, would I?" She challenges. Then, undercuts it went she jumped two feet in the air, screeching: "*Under the bench! It's under the bench!*"

She rushes up the two narrow steps up into the gazebo a single, ornately-edged bench the color of a dove sits. Reaching beneath it, Patty plucks away another tiny envelope. This time, it's pink as a blush on a girl's cheeks. She nearly rips it out, beginning to read—or perform, to be honest—another poem:

You've found the spot where love once bloomed,

A sheltered space where hearts consumed.
But now the task is up to you,
To craft a verse both sweet and true.
Take your candies, let them guide,
And share the thoughts you keep inside.
When your words and hearts align,
Maplewood Grove will show its sign.

Patty is taken aback by another impromptu poem. Her brow arches, wrinkling. There is a dimple in her chin, he notes, not for the first time. She shoots Colton a look, combing his features for giveaway sentiments while his warm eyes rove over the text. He knows the roll of his eyes is caustic, abrasive. "That's what the candy is for? Are they just making everyone do this stuff?"

Her shoulders hunch in a shrug, frustratingly nonchalant. "Presumably. Let's open the packets," she declares, shaking her own packet over her head like a maraca. Colton drops down to sit on the bench, shifting uncomfortably in the seat, chill seeping in through his trousers.

It was the sudden heat creeping up the back of his neck that couldn't cool. Least of all when Patty, with a decisive jingle, drops to her knees while she rips open the package with her teeth. She hums to herself a tune he doesn't even try to place, sorting through tiny heart-shaped candies. He looks like she's enjoying herself, utterly oblivious to him slowly losing his mind.

"Aaaalrighty, Sheriff," she says, voice light as air. Despite the challenge she shoots through the space between them like Cupid's arrow. "Show me what kind of poetry you've got up your sleeve."

Colton grunts tersely. The playful glint in Patty's eyes threatens to distract him. His head ducks, self-conscious as the schoolboy he hasn't been in decades. "Poetry's not exactly in my wheelhouse."

Patty isn't offended—or deterred. She plucks out a little candy heart, and plonks it down like a chess piece. "Freak less. They kind of do the work *for* you." She holds up another; *Be Mine* the little heart reads. Patty considers it, then drops it into the pile.

"Easy for you to say," he mutters under his breath, sifting through his own bag. As he absorbs the pastel-hued phrases, Colton wishes he'd lucked out with a simple *Be Mine*. Each one in his possession was absurd and too much, saccharine, unbearable. Nothing that remotely resembles what he'd consider saying to her.

His fingers fumble with a heart stamped with *Kiss Me*. Nope! No. Not that one.

Patty doesn't push. No impatience to be found when she asks, "Any luck?"

"Just... trying to put together something that doesn't sound ridiculous. Which is *not* what these work for."

"It's supposed to be fun," Patty reminds delicately. "No one's grading us. Just me here."

Colton almost groans. As if he isn't *abundantly* aware of it. Like the fact makes this any easier, instead of possibly harder. He exhales heavily, and grabs a handful at random; from the mini-pile, he plucks the least embarrassing combination of words. Which isn't saying much, since the entire set-up is too much. Grades would have been the least of his problems. This is pressure. Pressure to give away something he isn't ready to.

It feels like forever before he straightens up, his stomach tight with nerves. "Okay. Okay, here goes." One by one, he lays four tiny candy hearts down.

Miss You.
Dream.
Be True.
Forever.

In what seems to be slow-motion, Colton watches Patty pale. She starts off speechless, blinking. Then, her brows knit together. The air shifts with more than just February's frost; her smile fades, turns wan and haunted. She just stares down at it. "Uh... wow," she coughs out. Her fingers pick up the heart reading '*Forever*' gently. "That's – unexpected."

"Too much?" Colton asks meekly. His heart hammers inside his chest. What had he been thinking with that? *Forever?* He wonders if he can just plead temporary insanity in his defense.

"No. No, Colton, it's just—" His mouth goes dry. He can see they realize it together: it's the first time she has ever said his name. Her eyes, lashes impossibly long, flicker up to meet his eyes. Uncertainty clings to every contour and lineation of her pretty face. "It's... kind of intense."

What an out of body experience, watching your fear be realized in real time.

"I mean – 'Forever'?" she questions. The furrow of her brow appears pained. Colton had known, on some level, this was a bad idea. His heart still sinks.

"It's just candy, Patty," he rushes to remind, downplaying the whole thing for both their sakes. It's too late, though. Obviously, they both know it. Awkwardness settles between them like an elephant. He watches her smile, and watches it not reach her eyes.

"Just candy," she echoes. Her thumb brushes the printed letters of the heart she chooses from her own little pile of them. "Well... maybe mine will make some sense." Carefully, she puts them down. She had chosen:

Nice Guy.
Smile.
LOL!
Wink.

One of the most passionate, eloquent women he had ever met and she gave him... "Wink?" Colton stares down, dumbfounded.

It's a needle to the balloon that had grown to suffocate him from within his body, when Patty bursts into another wave of laughter. Like air-conditioned air out the open window in July, the tension evaporates in seconds. "I guess I'm not much of a poet either!" she says cheerfully. "But hey, the honor is in the attempt, isn't it? We tried."

He manages a weak chuckle. His mind still reels from his mistake. The tension might evaporate, but Colton can't shake off as easily the way Patty's expression had shifted at the sight of the word *Forever*. He thinks: *too far, too fast, can't take it back.* Dread gnaws within.

Patty's already on her feet again, gathering the remaining candies. She's already chattering away about the next stop on the scavenger hunt: Maple Grove. His thoughts remain stuck like gum to the same piece of candy. *Forever* is too heavy; angrily, he thinks of how it has no business being stamped on a piece of candy.

Especially not at the behest of a broken man with a battered spirit, who can't even tell if he'd meant it as a last resort—or if, deep down, it's something he actually wants to say to Patty Sullivan. "Shall we?" She holds out her arm to him, the way he had done earlier that day.

Colton takes it, almost astounded he can walk with his stomach in such knots.

Sweet Confessions

PATTY

Patty's relief at seeing Maplewood Grove disappears the moment her eyes land on Jonah standing casually by the gazebo, his smile sharp and disarming. Of course, he shows up now, she thinks bitterly. He has a knack for appearing just when she's beginning to regain her balance, always knocking her back down. Her stomach churns, and her heart tightens. Without realizing it, she tightens her grip on Colton's arm, seeking an anchor as the familiar twinge of discomfort blooms in her chest.

"Patty," Jonah greets, stepping directly into her path. His voice is smooth, casual, but his eyes flicker with something sharper when they land on Colton. "Didn't expect to see you here for the Love Quest." His smirk widens as his gaze lingers on Colton. "And with company, no less."

Before Patty can reply, Colton shifts beside her, his shoulders tense as he steps slightly forward, placing himself just ahead of her. "Is there a problem here?" Colton's voice is even, but the tension is unmistakable. His hand brushes against her arm, a silent reminder that she isn't alone.

Jonah's smirk doesn't falter. "Just catching up with an old friend, Sheriff. Nothing wrong with that, right?"

Patty feels the weight of the unspoken challenge hanging between them. Colton's jaw tightens, his eyes locked on Jonah. "Maybe you should move along," he says, his voice calm but resolute.

Jonah chuckles, his gaze lingering on Patty longer than it should. "I guess we'll catch up some other time."

As he walks away, Patty's heart pounds—not with the excitement Jonah once stirred, but with a creeping nausea that settles deep in her chest. The scars Jonah left behind are still there, hidden beneath her confident exterior. But now, here he is, with that same arrogant grin still lingering in her memory, threatening to disrupt the future she's started to imagine with Colton.

Traversing the park, there's no missing the amount of people filling it up. Townsfolk meant to be invested in the Love Quest that had brought them all here slip their way instead. A shock of red hair in the peripheral view tugs at her attention. Patty looks over just to find Betty Lou whispering in Olivia Parker's ear again, the two of them peeking from beneath their lashes in a way that didn't manage to pull off inconspicuousness. Now, Olivia's arms hold a baby in them, swaddled in a butter-yellow blanket. The baby is the only one who manages to be discreet by a long shot.

Fabulous, Patty thinks sourly, her chest aching with a pang, *an audience.*

The way Jonah's grin spreads would have made her heart skip a beat, once. Now it turns her stomach. "Patty," he drawls smoothly. That pompous tone already has her jaw clenching. "Long time, no see, girl."

"Jonah." She keeps her tone even, battling the urge to look over her shoulder for prying eyes. As it is, she can feel them. They bore into her, from the back and then the sides too. Jonah claps his hands in front of her face, trying to jolt his attention back towards him. Like she hasn't learned anything at all in the last few years. Colton's presence beside her threatens to suffocate her.

Meanwhile Jonah doesn't notice a single thing amiss. Either that, or he doesn't care. Both sound too much like him. "Didn't expect to see you doing the Love Quest after all," he says. His limpid gray eyes flick between her and Colton. His tone is too casual when he claims, "I thought you'd be paired with me, you know." His tone makes Patty's hackles raise.

Her eyes narrow. "And why would I be paired with you?"

Jonah's full mouth is smug as he steps closer. His voice drops, lowering, conspiratorially, like they were shaping a secret, the two of them. As if they shared anything at all these days besides all the ways he had turned the taste of others' champagne sour in her mouth forever. "I asked the townsfolk to set it up. Maybe it's the season, but I've been thinking about you, Patty. Figured this could be the perfect chance to... you know," his tongue clicks against the roof of his mouth wetly, "connect again."

Patty's stomach threatens to crawl out of her gaping mouth. His *gall.* She's about to snap—just blow, in every way she hasn't let herself, being mature and conscientious. Mrs. Jarvis is lingering along the fence, holding her phone up to her ear convincingly enough muttering into it, except for how she's holding it upside down, and clearly listening in. Her frustration builds.

Out of the corner of her eye, Patty checks on Colton. The sheriff stands rigid as a pole—all her work loosening him up undone now, and his body is back in a tense fold, exhausted. His face, unreadable again. There is a livewire pulled taut inside her. Jonah's smarmy expression helps nothing. "Reconnect?" she echoes, choking on distaste. Her voice sharpens. Frustration burns the edges of her words like a letter burning to ashes. "You know, last time I checked, cheating on someone when they're halfway around the world isn't *exactly* the best way to build a healthy, loving, sustainable relationship. I could be wrong." It took someone really knowing Patty to grasp how wrong she knew she was not.

This time, Jonah winces. Only briefly, unfortunately. His charm doesn't falter for long. "That was years ago," he insists. "Patty. People change. You have to grow with them." Patty finds she doesn't even have the words to begin to respond to that. It isn't as though he listens in the first place.

"Jonah," she tries. "This isn't the time—"

He just talks over her. "Look, I *know* I messed up." His voice softens—and Patty thinks it's a scene from a movie she's seen more than enough times to get sick of it. She can practically quote the lines before they pour: "I can't stop thinking about you. About us. We should have another chance. Another try. We had something great once. Didn't we?"

Patty swallows thickly. Whatever Jonah sees in her face, he takes leave to reach for her. His palm brushes her arm, making her stiffen. "I've changed, Patty. I'm not... C'mon, I'm not that guy anymore. I'm just stupid. I'm a stupid guy who did a stupid thing. I didn't realize what I had until you were already gone."

Like she's taken a bullet to the chest, Patty recoils. "It's not that simple," she says forcefully, turning her voice charming. "You broke my heart. I'm supposed to—what, forget all that for a scavenger hunt on Valentine's Day?"

For a moment, Patty feels a momentary soar of victory. She watches Joah's face fall, the moment before his features turn determined. "I know, but maybe—" He doesn't finish. Colton's voice cuts through the haze, deep and intense. "We should get moving," he says succinctly. "We're behind schedule."

Startled by the switch in his tone, Patty whips towards Colton to find his jaw clenched and his eyes chilling. She doesn't have to look around to confirm townsfolk are discussing him.

When Patty turns, so too does Jonah. He shoots Colton a lazy smile. "Sheriff," Jonah says coolly. "Keeping tabs on civilians?"

Colton's words are clipped as he replies, eyes hard, "Just doing my job. Keeping things in order." It is a faraway dream already; a total departure from reality, all in her head. Panic flickers inside of her, the fickle flame. She feels her partner literally pull away from her. He mutters something, and Patty doesn't even catch it before he's scuttling to the side, away from her—and this, whatever Jonah is trying to pull.

Jonah doesn't miss it. He smirks, glancing pointedly at the new distance between them. "It looks like your partner's not too happy." He taunts her. It had been so long ago, when she had craved just that. "Trouble in paradise?" he mocks.

Patty glares viciously. "Leave me alone. Go away. Come back if they have those phrases on candy and I'll be happy to put them into your lying, cheating mouth," she spits out, turning her back on him.

Jonah stands there for a moment longer, his smirk widening. He doesn't walk away just yet, clearly relishing the discomfort. He glances pointedly at the space between Patty and Colton. "It looks like your partner's not too happy," he mocks, his voice dripping with condescension.

Only then does Jonah finally step back, his lazy smile lingering before he turns and strides away, leaving an unsettling tension in his wake.

COLTON

Whatever threshold he'd had for the drama he'd left behind in the city, was quickly spent in the span of minutes watching a man hit on Patty with him on her arm. Frustration scuffs the dirt as he strides away from the park. Colton's chest is tight. He can't help interrogating himself: What did you expect from this ridiculous Love Quest?

He hadn't expected anything. Definitely not some man smiling at Patty as this Jonah character had. She wasn't about to walk away though. Nor did she have any obligation to. An awkward exchange of stamped candies and a trade of earnest confessions didn't mean she was his. She isn't. Patty isn't anyone's.

Still, it's her he catches bounding towards him with big, thumping footsteps. "Colton, *wait—*" she demands. She doesn't wait for him, though. With a harsh handful, she grabs a fistful of his uniform with which she wrenches him around. For such a slight woman, she truly had impressive musculature. "Will you just *wait,* please?" He freezes. Her earnest demand is impossible to deny. Sheer determination boosts her spirit enough to ask him, "What's going on with you?"

"Nothing." It comes out sharper than Colton wants it to. He winces, his head shaking as her brows furrow, not buying what he's selling. Her eyes narrow quizzically. "Nothing doesn't look like this," Patty asserts, tender but unyielding. "I don't get what just happened. I was confronted by an ex I was sure had left town—and you just stormed out, leaving me in that, like I did something wrong." The words come out sounding raw from her lips. Wounded.

Colton's stomach churns. "You didn't do anything wrong."

Yet someone may as well have tossed a lit match into his sliced open chest, setting his insides on fire. Jonah's words, his easy grin, the way he'd reached over and just touched Patty, like he'd done it hundreds of times before, and likely because he had—it sticks in his mind like gum under a cafeteria table, refusing to get scraped away. How can he tell her that? How does he explain it without coming off as a whackjob? A *jealous* whackjob.

There's no opportunity to contemplate it any further. Patty punctures his bubble of personal space, stepping closer. Her eyes map his face. "What is it then?" she asks, tender and urgent. "Why did you just shut me out like that? This has been going swell, I thought."

Never before has he seen this wild, wonderful woman look so forlorn. He exhales a sharp, miserable breath. The day keeps dwindling to a nightmare. Between the conversation pulling his teeth out, and this exposure to how ill-prepared he is to be close to another human being beyond the one dynamic he's managed to hack, he's about ready to give up on this entire endeavor. Except Patty isn't letting him off the hook. She doesn't look away, no matter how hard the intensity of her imploring gaze made it for him to breathe.

"I don't know," Colton mutters, looking anywhere but right at her. He's seldom felt this exposed in years. "I don't like that guy."

"Jonah?" Patty frowns. "Colton, I just told you—"

"I heard. I—" His teeth grind together, his jaw clenching until it begins to ache.

"I didn't know he was even in town. He doesn't mean anything to me."

"Someone who doesn't mean anything to you wouldn't affect you like that," Colton retorts coarsely.

Patty's fists plant at her hips as she stares him down, face-to-face with him. "Fine. Then he means a lesson it hurt to learn. Not something I am interested in repeating. Something I am still healing from. I *didn't* know he was going to be here."

A part of him itches to argue with it. His instincts are made for it, playing Good Cop, Bad Cop till he's blue in the face. It wasn't much of a thrill when he was playing both sides, though. He doesn't want to play with Patty anyway, not that way. But his head is a mess. How does he even begin to explain it to her?

He says the first thing that comes to mind: "It's Valentine's Day."

She stumbles back a step, taken aback. "Uhhh, yes. Yeah. Hence the hoopla. So?"

His mistake, Colton thinks with a grim smile, to think she'd make this easy on him. He could add it to the list of things he liked about her. "I don't like Valentine's Day," he grinds out, the confession sour in his mouth. Metallic dust. "Never have." His hands clench to fists in his pockets, fighting every instinct not to turn around and walk away in the opposite direction as fast as he can.

It helps, seeing her features soften for the truth. The confusion in her gaze doesn't dissipate though, and Colton knows this conversation isn't through. "Why? What happened on Valentine's Day?" Patty prompts without self-consciousness.

There may as well be a literal can of worms in his hand. This, right here, is nothing he's wanted to deal with again. This part—peeling back layers of himself until he felt flayed, and doing so in a leap of faith, letting someone see beneath the surface, not knowing if they'd leave him to turn septic before he'd stitched it all closed again. Could it still be his biggest fear if it had already been realized? "It's complicated," he says. "I— Back when I lived in the city, I was married."

Patty's eyes widen to saucers. Colton sees it, her mouth opening, before she snaps it back shut, thinking better of it and deciding to nod instead, encouraging little bobs of her head telling him to keep going.

He nods back. Colton's throat tightened before the words finally escaped him. The memory clung to him like a stubborn wound that refused to heal. "We were married... young, naïve. I thought love was something you could hold onto if you just fought hard enough. But one day, she was gone. She didn't even leave a note, just vanished into someone else's life the day before Valentine's Day." Colton's voice faltered, the raw edge of betrayal still fresh, even after all these years. "I still can't figure out how someone you trust that much could leave you like that."

If her step backward had been involuntary, her step back forward is the opposite. When Patty steps towards him, her arms uncrossing and falling to her sides, it's like a barrier comes back down. It's like she considers it hard, before she reaches for him. She murmurs, "Colton..."

He can't stand the pity all over her gorgeous face. It stings to look at. With a shake of his head, he cuts her off. "No, don't. I'm over it. My point wasn't throwing a pity party, Patty. I just keep my distance from all of it, and I'm answering why. Valentine's Day. Romance. All the talk, it's cheap—it's a *joke*." He is over it. As over it, he knows, as he will ever be. When his voice cracks at the end, he hates himself for it at least half as much as he hates the woman who had broken his heart. "I've made peace with it."

Patty only looks at him. She doesn't try to reach for him again— and for that, Colton finds himself immensely grateful. He stays put, despite her gaze lingering on him. There is no judgment there. Instead, he finds the same look she had given him the week before, from the other side of a window papered with postcards: knowing. Understanding. A kind that needed no words. That left him reeling; exposed, but inexplicably close to relieved.

"You're scared," she murmurs. It isn't a question. He doesn't answer it. "That's human, Colton. You were hurt, so now you're scared of getting hurt again."

Every muscle in his body tenses with the impulse to deny it. But how can he? It is all over his face, already. All over his words. Still, she's looking at him like this—with calm understanding, that cuts right through him. No voyeurism or looking away from the gristle and blood; her palms cradle his heart. It smarts, the vulnerability that claws at his chest from within.

"I don't do this, Patty," he repeats. His voice is a hoarse whisper now. "I don't do any of it. I've kept my head down for a long time—changed almost everything about the life I had once. I just do my job, and mind my business, and try to help as best I can. But you..." His heart thrums to life, hammering frenetically behind his ribs. "You make me feel. It does scare me."

Her palms are a cool relief against his hot cheeks. "Don't be afraid of me. Please. You don't have to be," Patty cajoles, her forehead flat against his. He would bet she can taste the bitterness in his laugh. "You say that... but people leave. They don't keep their promises. They just go. No forwarding address sometimes."

"Not everyone," Patty pushes back, gentle – but firm, fierce. "Not me."

He swallows hard, and the lump in his throat goes nowhere. Something inside him unspools, however—something Colton has no name for. For the first time in a long time, he can't deny that he wants to believe. Wants, despite many instincts, to *trust*. The locks and chains around a heart he'd boarded up have grown rusted over the years.

A palm drops to his chest as if it's a thought she can read all over his face. "You are a good man with a good heart and it would kill me to hurt it," she breathes. "I'm not asking you to change who you are today, right now, right here, because I've got sweet nothings to ply your trust with. That isn't how trust works. I don't expect it to. But I've been here – I've been shattered. I'm not your ex-wife. You're not Jonah." Honesty, so often, was confused for obnoxious bluntness. Those people, Colton thinks, should make Patty Sullivan an acquaintance.

He looks at her, and the sincerity that brims in her tender gaze is nearly too much to bear. He looks into those pools, and he may as well be standing at the edge of a cliff, looking down into the unknown. Yet, somehow, Patty—with a literal store oozing evidence to the contrary, boasting of her worldliness and spontaneity—feels steady. She makes it detrimentally hard, looking at him as she is, to believe that he may hurtle towards the ground but it wouldn't be without a parachute.

A hefty breath, and he allows, "Okay."

Patty's mouth sprawls in a wide, wild grin. "*Okay,*" she agrees.

Trust and Vulnerability

PATTY

When Patty finally pulls back from Colton, color blooms in her cheeks. None of the copious pairs of eyes on them bother with tact. Their mouths don't either—some tittering here, some whispering there. It doesn't render her as irritable as it has been. For the relief that finally smooths out the lines marring Colton's forehead, she stumbles back; when she does so, though, it's with nary a regret.

It's nice to be reminded, no matter by what circumstances, that she's still someone who can make someone feel less alone. To feel better. Symbiotically, she feels better too. She turns over another card, to read the way it says: *Follow the trail, Sweethearts.*

As they step forward, she notices a subtle change in the atmosphere. The familiar scent of her bookstore drifts on the air, but something catches her eye. Tiny heart-shaped candies are scattered along the path, each one carrying a different message. Patty bends down to pick up a few, reading the words with a mixture of amusement and confusion. *Be Mine. True Love. Second Chances.*

Colton stands beside her, watching her reaction closely. "This isn't just any trail, Patty," he says softly. "It's *our* trail." Her heart pounds as they follow the path of candies, the faint glow of twilight making everything feel dreamlike.

At first, she thinks it's a coincidence, but then Colton gently nudges her forward. "This trail leads to something important." Her breath catches as they approach the Whispering Willow, where the entire town stands gathered, each person holding a small handful of the colorful candies.

And standing at the center is Colton, holding out the final candy just for her. She reads the words on it, her heart swelling. *Forever Yours.*

Laughing under her breath, Patty bends down to pick up the next piece of candy. Her fingers brush against the faint layer of snow clinging to it. As she straightens, Colton steps closer, his voice low. "I wanted to remind you that wherever you go next... I want to be there with you."

Patty's heart flutters, a warmth spreading through her chest. She opens her mouth to respond, but before the words can form, a sudden cheer erupts from the crowd. The sound jolts her from the intimate moment, and she glances around, realizing just how much attention is on them. The townspeople are grinning, some snapping photos, others whispering excitedly.

Colton squeezes her hand, his smile soft but knowing. "Looks like we've got an audience," he whispers, his breath warm against her ear. Patty chuckles, feeling the weight of the moment lighten.

As the crowd begins to disperse, she tugs Colton's hand gently, leading him away from the gathering. "I think we've given them enough to gossip about for one day," she says, her voice teasing. But as they walk, her mind races with the words she wants to say, the emotions bubbling to the surface, waiting for the quiet moment they can share again.

At first, she thinks it is a coincidence, but then Colton gently nudges her forward. "This isn't just any trail, Patty. It's *our* trail."

Her heart pounds as they approach the Whispering Willow, where the entire town stands gathered, holding up books from her shop, each with a personalized note written on the inside cover. And standing at the center is Colton, holding out the final note just for her.

Laughing under her breath, Patty bends down to pick up the next piece of candy. She has to blow hard, getting rid of the faint layer of snow clinging to it. On the trunk of the enormous maple tree she spots the piece with another card: This time, a bright, giddy red envelope. There isn't a poem, just a reiteration of the last card, slightly altered:

Keep the candy. Create the poems.

Patty flips over the candy heart in her palm. The tiny red letters spell out, 'BE MINE.' When she holds it up for Colton to see. "Look, another one. You think this trail will take us to something real, or are we being messed with?"

Finally, it's an easier smile he slips her. "Maybe both," he allows. With a hint of a smile tugging at the corners of his mouth, Colton shrugs. Patty, meanwhile, tucks the little heart into her pocket. She adds it to the small collection they've already accumulated. She brushes her palms off on her thighs right after.

The trail was more and more obvious, the more to the right they leaned. Patty is quick to deduce it means they're nearing the end. It looks a lot like a sign that someone gave up being as tricky as possible. Giddily, she skips towards another piece, closer to a different cluster of trees, no longer as skeletal the farther they get from the depths of winter.

Colton walks beside her, more accompanying her than participating himself. Whether he's sapped of energy or not, it doesn't feel like it. There's something in the air he's no more impervious to than she is. He chases her chasing a whimsical candy trail, and it's young and silly and ridiculous, but Patty can't help but feel like they're on the cusp of something deeper than fun.

Not that it keeps Patty from pushing her luck, and prompting, "Any theories on the meaning of these candies, Sheriff?"

Colton raises a brow. His breath fogs palpably, the chill even brisker now that afternoon's begun to melt into twilight. "Besides the obvious?"

Laughing lightly, Patty suggests, "No, like... The deeper meanings. People just toss things like this out. 'Be Mine' and 'True Love' — and words are just words. Obviously. Harmless. Until they aren't. Then they *mean* something." She pauses, and pivots to catch him looking at her with such raw reverence she forgets what to do with her hands. It's thickly that she adds, "Maybe I'm just old fashioned too, I don't know. I overthink, as if there's such a thing. All I know is – every time I pick one up, it just makes me wonder how many people have traded an identical one in different parts of the world and not meant it. Or cared about meaning it."

Colton pauses for a beat. He approaches slowly, silently. His eyes scan the ground as they walk. "It's not overthinking. It's true," he says finally. "Though I'm hardly the poster child for normal takes on loyalty, for obvious reasons. The fact is that people do toss out those things. People can give things to other people without realizing the weight of what they're handing over sometimes. A lot of the time, maybe."

"Like what?" she questions, fascinated.

Colton is quiet again. She wonders if his mouth would taste like blood if she kissed him, given how often he bites his tongue. But it means something to her, when he still tells her, "Stuff like 'forever,' I guess."

"You really think that's just a word?" Patty asks.

Colton nods to the snowy path their boots imprint across. "Depends on who's saying it," he allows. "Not everyone understands a promise when they make it. Not everyone cares."

It's a callous view of the world, Patty thinks. She wasn't a cynic—but she finds it fascinating that he is one, though perhaps not incurably. Patty smiles, her hand lingering by the scattered candy. She doesn't toss another piece this time but instead turns to Colton, intrigued. "Trust, huh? More important than love?"

Colton's gaze doesn't waver as he answers. "Yeah. Trust is everything. I don't give it easily. It would be stupid to, after being burned." His voice softens as he adds, "But that's where I am."

Patty hums in agreement. "Same."

Patty nods along, humming agreement. "Same."

"Jonah?" Colton asks. She bites her lip, confirming. "Yeah. Jonah." There is no pang when she says his name. At least, the pain isn't piercing. It's a duller throb of a bone that's healed, but still aches every time it rains. Patty finds herself wanting to say more—not because Colton pushes for it, but because he leaves her room to fill if it is her prerogative to do so—and when he's already poured out so much to her today; how can she not pour back? "I wasn't always this confident cool chick. You know the weird girl who ate her hair in the back of class in the Breakfast Club? That was more my territory. And then high school was over and I grew into myself. It's all good. It was better than good when the once upon a time captain of the football team asked me out. I loved him. And I really thought we had something very evolved and real. But when it came down to it, if I wasn't always there, always catering, it wasn't enough. That's a – love I'm not interested in. It's flimsy."

"You deserve any kind of love you want," Colton says firmly. Patty beams at him. Almost, she adds something snarky, willing to offer him levity in exchange for his bravery today. She's surprised when he continues, "No, seriously. If he couldn't see what he had, that's on him. It should never be an out of sight, out of mind thing. Look at you– how could you ever be out of mind in the first place?"

Her beam softens to a candlelight intimacy. For a moment, Patty is perfectly glad to walk beside him in silence. It's unmissable, the sharp hitch of her breath when the back of his hand grazes her—and Colton is the one who leaps, reaching out and tangling their fingers together for real. He adds in a squeeze for good measure. Patty squeezes back.

This time, it's him who bends down to grab a piece of candy. "Call Me," Colton reads out the message.

"Think one's too outdated, Mr. Old Fashioned?"

"No ma'am," he snorts. "Still counts so long as phones exist."

Nodding seriously, she holds open her pocket for him to drop it into. It clacks like a seashell with the others. "So," Patty falls back into step with him, matching him stride for languorous stride, "which one would you choose? Out of all of them."

Colton comes to a standstill, not answering right away. But he looks at her in a way that makes her certain he has an answer. It's just one he's afraid to say out loud. Patty reminds him again, "You don't have to be afraid of me." Only a few words, and she can see the way they make him braver. They let him admit, tenderly, "'Trust Me.' Not because I'm asking you to, but... Because *I'm* trying to."

Her heart takes hope and runs with it, picking up the pace as the rhythm turns jump rope levels of skipping. "I'd pick that one too," she admits.

They squeeze each other's hands at the same time, startling a laugh out of both their mouths.

COLTON

Eventually, the trail leads them to a picnic table. With a checkered blanket spread across it, and to-go boxes with Loretta's Diner's symbol on top, and candles lit in the middle, all the brighter in the last dregs of afternoon light—there's no way to miss that this isn't an accident. "I think," Colton announces, deadpan, "we are being set up."

Beside him, Patty bursts into laughter. Her hand doesn't relinquish its grip on his, and he turns into her shaking; her body leans into his with an ease neither expect yet both welcome. She smells divine, he thinks. "You don't say," she chokes out between giggles, wiping at her eyes with the back of her free hand. "The fancy vintage candelabra wasn't the instant giveaway? How about the way Betty Lou's been stalking us for the past week?"

She could get as sassy as she wanted with him. He remains caught up in the free, easy tide of her laughter; just the sound of which had unbundled the bundle of tension in his chest. Whether it was the absurdity of the townsfolk, or the exhaustion from their wandering and arguing and wandering some more, Colton doesn't know. He just thinks that sound softens the world in their vicinity. He knows it heals something inside of him every time he earns it.

"I'm glad you're enjoying being a town puppet," Colton sasses back, without any bite to the words. He sits down, crossed arms stacking on top of the table.

Happily, Patty agrees, "Oh, I totally am. But, I'm starving, too, so... Now, I'd like to be a well-fed puppet. Please tell me that there's a cheeseburger in here and nothing that actually requires us to use silverware?" Colton didn't know how she had to ask. He can smell the rich, meaty smell of the burger bun already. Besides which Loretta's menu was small and targeted; it didn't do too much, so whatever it did, it did extremely well.

Patty picks up the thermos to the side, shaking it experimentally.

The liquid sounds too thick and viscous to be a beverage. Not water, or even coffee. "*Soup*," Patty says, uncapping and taking a big whiff of the decadent steam that wafted off the dishes.

"They really went all out with this, didn't they?" Colton huffs, his eyes settling on the envelope precariously attached to the dramatic and ornate candelabra.

She leans her own elbows on the table, brows wagging up and down in succession three times. "Let's open it? Last one."

Colton unsticks it, then slides it over. "Let's do it."

Without any further ado, she rips it open. From inside, she pulls out one last small, folded card. Her eyes scan over the words that widen her eyes all over again, triggering, too, a flicker of something crossing her face. *Wonderment,* Colton things.

"What does— What does it say?" he asks.

With gravitas, Patty sits up even straighter, pushing the long tendrils of her dark hair back, and reads aloud: "Your final task is to tell each other how you feel. Using *only* the words from the Sweethearts candies you've collected."

Colton, none too surprisingly, freezes. "Are you kidding?"

Patty genuinely has to bite down on her lip again to keep from dissolving into laughter again. "They're pushing their luck, or putting it on the spot – I don't know. But I don't have a problem with it. Both of our candies pooled together couldn't be so bad, could it? It can be a redo for earlier since that..." She makes a face, mostly to mess with him, "Uh, well, that was awful. Especially since this is now officially a first date."

It surprises her a little, but very pleasantly, when he gamely leans into it. She empties her pockets; first one, and then the other, until a chunk of the table is more or less covered. "Let's see," he starts. He doesn't pause. In the end, he just props a few into a row, side-by-side, with the diagonal slants of the sides of the hearts pressed together: *Call Me, Trust Me, Kiss Me.* "Yeah?" he checks with her, looking up after.

Out of his pile, it's 'Trust Me' that Patty picks to tap with a fore-finger. "Hard one."

Colton swallows thickly. "But worthwhile, hopefully."

For a prolonged beat, Patty holds his gaze. The air between is thick, charged with the unspoken. Slowly, she lays down the candy then considers the rest of the options. Inquisitively, she sifts through the pile. She curls it into her palm before he can see it. "Let's," Patty says, eyes breathtakingly bright, "try this..." Her forefinger taps on top of his third choice. "And we'll see about my addition after."

There are a lot of things Colton believes about himself, and a lot more he doesn't. Yet his genuine care and burgeoning desire for Patty Sullivan challenge everything he had decided to settle for when he'd moved into Maplewood Grove.

When Colton stands to round the picnic table, his eyes latch to Patty's the way they had the week before—this time, it isn't just the lack of window between them that renders their connection so potent. All people feel; all of them put feelings into words. Most made promises, and few, in Colton's experience, actually kept them. It was rare to connect with someone—to feel for them—in a way that transcended speech. It's connection. A collision of souls, if one believes in such a notion.

It is about action, he thinks, in the breath before he bows over Patty, his palm cradling the soft line of her jaw to bring her supple lips to his. His hand covers hers, clenched with her secreted piece of candy. In between the waves his lips make over hers, he asks without needing to see it: "Be Mine?"

Words Unspoken, Hearts Revealed

MUCH, much later, after a romantic twilight had been spent wrapped up in the warmth of one another's company, Patty Sullivan and Colton Rhodes meander back into the thick of their little town's melee. The glow of the string lights is bright, making it seem earlier than it is—but it doesn't blind them. It feels right. With laughter permeating the air, turning crisp chill warmer when the molecules are traded between their warm bodies, it's only right.

As they look around—Colton, vigilant, and Patty, curious—she nudges the sheriff with her elbow, a playful glint dancing in her eyes. "You know," she chirps, "we owe a little birdie a visit."

Colton smirks. Her stomach flip-flops over the brash way he drawls, "Oh, I haven't forgotten, doll."

Across the square, Betty Lou Hopkins stands nursing a styrofoam cup of cocoa by the refreshments corner. Her eyes dart around enviously, a hunger in them that too-obviously morphs into satisfaction that radiates from her. The new couple exchange a knowing glance as they close in on their pretty, troublesome target.

"Oh, Betty Loooooou," Patty hollers sweetly, a lilt of mischief almost undetectable. Not to the man whose hand she holds, though.

"We need to have a word with you," Colton adds, cocking a severe brow. His expression is more daunting than Patty's; it has the town gossip's eyes widening comically, her hands nervously primping up her hair.

Betty Lou releases a theatrical gasp. "Don't tell me you're going to give me grief for working for the greater good, folks!"

Colton steps closer to the other side of the refreshments table. His tenor staid and his features the picture of utmost authority. "We know what you've been up to. You orchestrated this whole thing, didn't you? Start to end." Patty nods besides him somberly, her eyes narrowed, and her hands on her hips in her best imitation of a stern mother. Her lips helplessly twitch with amusement she tries her damnedest to rein in.

Betty Lou is impervious. Her nose in the air, she huffs, indignant and defensive, "Well! Idle minds wander!" She raises her cup in a toast—and it isn't altogether clear whether it is to the happy couple or her own masterminding. Either way, Betty Lou insists: "Can you even blame me? Someone had to give you two crazy kids a push. The Sheriff's been making eyes at you for months. And you're a darn fine lady, Patty. I won't apologize. You *can't* make me."

Silence hangs heavily. Colton blinks at the young girl like he's considering how true her claim is. A beat passes, before his face breaks into a grin. "Well, we just wanted to say..."

Patty joins in, happily finishing the sentence, "*...thank you.*" Her giggles don't stem from amusement, but rather, pure contentment.

Betty Lou lets out a triumphant cackle, her grin widening. "I knew it! I knew you two were a match."

Patty shoots her a pointed look she may have stolen from Colton. "You didn't exactly give us much choice."

Colton pulls Patty closer to his side, his arm draping over her shoulders. "I guess we can let you off the hook this time."

As they part ways with Betty Lou, Colton leans down and whispers, "How about we escape all this matchmaking for a bit?"

Patty smiles up at him, warmth flooding her chest. "You have something in mind?"

"A quiet weekend," he suggests, "just the two of us. Away from the town and Betty Lou's prying eyes."

Patty grins. "I like the sound of that."

Just before they head out of the square, they catch sight of Rachel Green standing with her son Jamie. Rachel waves, a soft smile on her face as she chats with Max Bennett, the local craftsman, who's eyeing her with interest. Patty glances at Colton. "Looks like someone else might have been set up tonight."

Colton chuckles. "Looks like Betty's magic works on more than just us."

Hand in hand, they make their way into the night, ready to begin their own quiet adventure.

The End

Did you enjoy Patty and Colton's story?

Consider reviewing it on Amazon, Goodreads or Bookbub. Reviews help me reach new readers.

Read *A Heart in Bloom*, the next story in the **Valentine's Sweethearts** series.

Sweet Valentine is also part of the Maplewood Grove series. Start the series with *Sweet Rivals*!

Join my newsletter for writing updates, new releases, sales and promotions!

Sweet Hope

Previously published as: Rule #2 Expect the Unexpected

Morning Routine

GENE

"Where's my tie, Amanda?" I call out, rummaging through the drawers in my office.

Amanda, my thirteen-year-old daughter, pokes her head around the doorframe, a smirk on her face. "Dad, you've got like fifty ties. How do you even lose one?"

I groan, holding up my prized collection of novelty ties, each one more ridiculous than the last. My favorites include a tie with little UFOs, a giant rubber duck one, and today's pick—the one with dancing cows. But it's gone.

"You don't understand," I say, pointing at the empty hook where it should be. "The town's expecting this, Amanda. You can't kick off the annual Maplewood Grove Farmers Market without the cow tie."

Amanda rolls her eyes but ducks into the office, helping me search through the clutter. "Maybe if you cleaned this place up, you wouldn't lose things so easily," she says, giving the stacks of papers a judgmental glance. She's a lot like her mother, organized and always two steps ahead of me. But I'm determined to get this summer right.

Amanda's staying with me for the next few months, and it's been too long since we spent this much time together.

"Dad, this is why Mom gets annoyed with you," Amanda continues, pulling open another drawer. "You make everything such a big deal."

I wince a little, then force a smile. "It's because I care. People come to the Farmers Market for the local produce, sure, but they stay for the Mayor's novelty ties."

Amanda hands me a plain green tie, clearly unimpressed. "How about this? It's simple. And maybe a little less embarrassing."

I gasp, clutching my chest theatrically. "Amanda! No. The cow tie is tradition." But before I can protest further, there's a knock at the door.

It's Betty Lou Hopkins, and from the look on her face, I know exactly why she's here. "Gene," she says with a smirk, "don't tell me you've lost that hideous cow tie again."

Betty Lou

Honestly, Gene is a walking disaster.

I tap my foot, watching as he fumbles around his office, papers flying and ties scattered everywhere. This is exactly why he needs my help—not that he'll ever admit it. Mayor Eugene Beckett, the man who can give the longest speeches on earth about nothing, yet somehow manages to forget the simplest things. Like his own wardrobe.

"Gene," I say again, more pointed this time. "Just wear the duck tie or the one with UFOs. No one cares about the cows."

He looks up, his expression a mix of panic and determination. "Betty Lou, that cow tie is tradition."

I roll my eyes. "The only tradition in this town is you making a big deal out of everything." I cross my arms, leaning against the door-

frame of his tiny office. "Besides, aren't you supposed to be organizing for the market instead of having a fashion crisis?"

Gene waves me off, clearly not listening. "I am organizing. I
just—"

"Lost your tie?" I finish for him. "Again?" I glance over at
Amanda, who looks just as exasperated as I feel. "Amanda, honey,
you should just give up. Your dad's never going to change."

Amanda sighs, holding up a plain green tie. "Tell him. He won't
listen to me."

Gene narrows his eyes at both of us. "Traitors, the both of you."

I laugh and start walking back to my post at the Maplewood
Grove Post Office, which, conveniently, shares a building with the
town hall. Small-town life means you're never more than a stone's
throw from anyone else. The mail needs sorting before the market
starts, and I've got my own routine to keep up with—one that
doesn't involve Gene's endless drama.

But as I pass by Amanda, I catch her giving me a strange look. It's
the kind of look teenagers give when they're trying to figure something out. "You okay, sweetie?" I ask, softening my tone.

She shrugs. "Yeah. Just... it's funny seeing you and Dad bicker
like that. You're like an old married couple or something."

I stop dead in my tracks, heat creeping up my neck. "Married
couple? Please. Your dad's a pain in my side. Always has been, always
will be."

Amanda giggles, glancing between me and Gene. "Sure, Betty
Lou."

I glance over at Gene, who's still muttering something about
tradition and cow ties, oblivious to the conversation. The thought of
us as a couple is ridiculous... isn't it?

Gene

Betty Lou thinks she can get the last word in, but I'm onto her. That woman's been running her mouth for as long as I've been Mayor, always with a comment, always ready to remind me of every little thing I forget. And okay, maybe I forget a lot. But that's not the point.

I watch her walk away, a smirk still playing on her lips, and something about it makes my heart skip a beat. Not that I'll ever admit it. The truth is, Betty Lou and I have been bickering for years, ever since she took over the post office. She knows exactly how to push my buttons, and I... well, I'm just trying to keep up.

"She's right, you know," Amanda says, snapping me out of my thoughts.

"About what?" I ask, still trying to wrestle my thoughts back to reality. "The tie?"

"No, Dad." She shakes her head, grinning at me. "About you two. You and Betty Lou argue like an old married couple."

I chuckle, waving it off. "That's just how we are. She gives me a hard time, I give it right back. It's part of our routine."

Amanda narrows her eyes at me, like she's trying to figure something out. "Sure, Dad. If you say so."

I don't know what she's getting at, but I push the thought aside. There's too much to do before the market. "Come on, Amanda. Let's get down there. We've got to make sure everything's ready."

Amanda grabs her bag, still giving me that look, like she knows something I don't. I shrug it off. She's probably just tired of my fussing.

As we head outside, the early morning sunlight filters through the trees, and I can already see the vendors setting up for the market. It's one of my favorite events of the year, where the whole town comes together to celebrate Maplewood Grove's local farmers, crafters, and businesses.

And yes, the cow tie is important. Tradition matters, even if Betty Lou can't see it.

I spot her at the post office window, sorting mail with her usual efficiency, but her eyes flicker toward me as we walk by. I don't know what Amanda's thinking, but there's no way Betty Lou and I... that's just ridiculous.

Right?

Summer Plans

AMANDA

I'm sitting on one of the rickety benches at the town hall, waiting for Dad to finish up his millionth speech about the Farmers Market, when I spot a flyer pinned to the community board. Maplewood Grove Theater Camp—Mid-Summer Play, Looking for Help with Costumes and Decorations!

My eyes light up. Perfect. I've been looking for something fun to do while I'm stuck here in Dad's world of novelty ties and long-winded speeches. I grab the flyer, folding it neatly and tucking it into my bag. As much as I love my dad, this summer needs a bit more excitement.

When I finally catch up with him outside, he's chatting with Betty Lou again. Surprise, surprise. They're bickering like usual, but today, it seems more... intense. Their voices are a little louder, their faces a little more flushed.

I stand off to the side, waiting for them to finish whatever argument they've got going on today. I've seen them go at it before, but there's something about the way they're standing that feels different

—closer, like neither of them is willing to back down. Or maybe they just enjoy pushing each other's buttons.

It's funny. All the kids in town have been whispering about them. Gene and Betty Lou are basically an old married couple without the marriage. That's the running joke, anyway. I didn't see it at first, but now... maybe they're onto something.

As soon as Dad's free, I hold up the theater camp flyer. "Hey, Dad. Can I join the theater camp? They need help with costumes and decorations for the mid-summer play."

His face lights up with enthusiasm, the way it always does when he gets the chance to get involved in anything town-related. "That sounds great! I could help organize the decorations."

I grin, knowing he'll probably overdo it with his usual enthusiasm, but that's exactly what I need. "Perfect. And Betty Lou could help with the costumes."

Dad blinks at me, confused. "Betty Lou? Why would she—"

"She's great at stuff like that," I say with a shrug, even though I'm totally guessing. But I've seen her around town enough to know she's always got a sharp eye for details. Plus, it wouldn't hurt to get her and Dad working together on something that isn't just arguing over post office hours or the Farmers Market schedule.

Dad looks skeptical, but I can tell he's considering it. "I suppose I could ask her..."

I smile to myself. This could be interesting.

Gene

I don't know how I got roped into this.

One minute, Amanda is showing me a theater camp flyer, and the next, I'm standing here with a clipboard in my hand, trying to organize decorations for a bunch of pre-teens. How did this happen? I'm supposed to be spending the summer reconnecting with Amanda, but instead, I'm knee-deep in streamers and paint samples.

And of course, Betty Lou's here too, because Amanda thought it'd be a great idea to get her involved in the costumes. Why? I don't know. Maybe my daughter thinks she's some kind of matchmaker. Kids have funny ideas sometimes.

I glance over at Betty Lou, who's sorting through a pile of fabric swatches with her usual no-nonsense attitude. She's muttering something under her breath about "cheap fabric" and "no proper budget," but she's already making progress. I have to admit, she's good at this stuff.

Amanda bounces over, grinning. "Dad, do you think the streamers should be blue or red?"

I blink at her, then at the sea of decorations she's laid out. "Uh... both?"

Amanda giggles and shakes her head. "Betty Lou, what do you think?"

Betty Lou barely looks up from her fabric. "Red. The blue clashes with everything else."

"See, Dad?" Amanda teases, giving me a wink before dashing off to find more supplies.

I narrow my eyes at her, but she's already gone. Something tells me she's up to something. I know how teenagers think—they've always got some kind of plan in the works. And if I didn't know better, I'd say she's trying to push me and Betty Lou into some kind of... situation.

Ridiculous.

I turn back to my clipboard, trying to ignore the fact that Betty Lou is standing just a few feet away, close enough that I can hear her muttering about thread counts and stitch work. And okay, maybe I'm starting to see why Amanda thinks we argue like an old married couple. But that doesn't mean anything. We're just... colleagues. Sort of.

Betty Lou glances up, catching me staring. "What?"

"Nothing," I mutter, looking away quickly. "Just... decorations. I'm organizing."

She snorts, shaking her head. "You call that organizing? Look at this mess."

She's right, of course. The decorations are everywhere, and my system is already falling apart. But I'm not about to admit that.

Betty Lou

This theater camp is a disaster. I've worked in a lot of chaotic environments, but this? This is a whole new level.

"Gene, those streamers are tangled," I point out, watching as he struggles with a bundle of red ribbons that somehow turned into a knotted mess in his hands.

"I'm working on it," he mutters, clearly flustered. His clipboard is tucked under one arm, his face red with frustration. "It's... part of the process."

I roll my eyes, stepping over to untangle the mess myself. Honestly, for someone who runs this town, you'd think he could handle a few decorations. But no. I have to step in, as usual.

As I sort out the ribbons, I glance over at Amanda, who's watching us with a mischievous grin on her face. She thinks she's so clever, getting me and Gene involved in this theater camp nonsense. But I see through her little plan. She's trying to play matchmaker, the same way kids in town have been teasing us for years.

"Your daughter's up to something," I say quietly to Gene, leaning in so Amanda can't hear.

He looks at me, confused. "What do you mean?"

I nod toward Amanda, who's currently tying together a banner with a group of her theater friends, whispering and giggling. "She's trying to set us up."

Gene's eyes widen. "What? No, she's not. She just wanted help with the play."

I raise an eyebrow. "Gene, please. You really think this whole thing is about streamers and costumes?"

He frowns, glancing between me and Amanda, clearly trying to piece it together. I don't know why I bother. Men like Gene never see these things coming.

"Look," I say, straightening up and crossing my arms. "We'll get through this play, we'll bicker like we always do, and then we'll go back to running the post office and town hall like nothing ever happened. Got it?"

Gene stares at me, his face slightly pink, but he nods. "Right. Of course. Just... normal bickering."

I smirk, turning back to the ribbons. "Exactly."

But as I continue working, I catch Amanda watching us again, her eyes twinkling with that teenage matchmaking spark. And for the first time, I wonder if maybe... just maybe... she's onto something.

The Theater Challenge

BETTY LOU

I swear, if I have to listen to Gene go on about "optimal streamer placement" one more time, I'm going to lose it.

We've been at this for hours, trying to put together the set for Amanda's mid-summer play. I'm stuck on costume duty, sewing endless ruffles onto skirts and tying ribbons onto hats, while Gene stands in the corner, bickering with me over every little detail.

"The streamers are too low," Gene says, staring up at the hanging decorations like they're some kind of math problem. "They need to be higher, so they don't block the view of the stage."

I raise an eyebrow, barely glancing up from the costume I'm working on. "Gene, they're fine. It's a kids' play. Nobody's coming for the streamers."

He frowns, clearly not satisfied. "But it's about presentation, Betty Lou. You know, first impressions matter."

I stifle a sigh. "If you want them higher, then go grab a ladder and move them yourself."

Gene hesitates, glancing at the ladder propped against the far wall. "Fine. I will."

I watch him march over to the ladder, determined to prove me wrong. As he climbs up, muttering something about streamers and angles, I try to focus on the stitching in my hands. But I can't help but glance over at him, shaking my head at how serious he's taking all this.

Then, as he stretches to adjust the streamer, there's a loud *snap*, followed by a *crash*.

The ladder wobbles beneath him, and before I can blink, Gene topples over, landing in a pile of streamers and set pieces.

"Gene!" I jump up, rushing over to where he's sprawled out on the floor, looking dazed and tangled in ribbons. "Are you okay?"

He groans, sitting up slowly. "I'm fine... I think."

I reach down, helping him untangle himself from the mess. As soon as he's free, I can't help it—I burst out laughing. Gene looks up at me, confused, then a little sheepish.

"Are you laughing at me?" he asks, rubbing his shoulder.

"Yes," I manage between giggles. "Yes, I am. Only you would manage to fall off a ladder while adjusting streamers."

Gene starts laughing too, his face turning red. "Well, you told me to do it!"

"I didn't mean for you to take a nosedive in the process!"

We're both laughing now, and for the first time in... I don't even know how long, it feels like we're on the same page. No bickering, no tension—just two people laughing at a ridiculous situation.

Gene

I'm still laughing as I sit on the floor, surrounded by a mess of streamers, ribbons, and fallen set pieces. Betty Lou is standing over me, hands on her hips, a smile tugging at the corners of her mouth. For a second, I forget that we've spent the last week bickering over every little thing.

"Are you sure you're okay?" she asks, still grinning.

I nod, standing up and brushing off my pants. "Yeah, yeah. Just my pride that's bruised."

Betty Lou shakes her head, but there's something different in her smile today—something softer, more playful. For once, she's not throwing another snarky comment my way. It's... nice.

Before I can think too much about it, the sound of giggling reaches us from the other side of the auditorium. I glance over to see Amanda and a couple of the other kids from the theater camp, huddled together, watching us.

"They've been at it again," one of the kids whispers, elbowing Amanda.

"They're so obvious," another girl adds, grinning.

Amanda gives me a wide-eyed look, then quickly waves the other kids away, clearly embarrassed. But I can't help but overhear what they said.

I frown, walking over to where they're working on the play's banner. "What's obvious?" I ask, trying to keep my voice casual.

Amanda shrugs, avoiding my gaze. "Nothing. Just... you and Betty Lou. You're always fighting. The kids think it's funny."

"Funny?" I raise an eyebrow. "Why's it funny?"

One of the other girls giggles, clearly enjoying this more than she should. "Because you guys act like you're married."

I blink, completely caught off guard. "Married? We don't... we're not..."

Amanda rolls her eyes. "Dad, it's not a big deal. It's just... everyone in town knows you and Betty Lou argue all the time. It's kind of your thing."

"Our thing?" I repeat, glancing over at Betty Lou, who's still untangling the mess I made of the set. I feel a flush of heat creep up the back of my neck. Is this really what people think?

"Yeah, your thing," Amanda says, smirking. "It's like a running joke."

Great. Just what I needed—the whole town thinking I'm Betty Lou's grumpy husband or something. I open my mouth to argue, but before I can, Betty Lou calls out from across the room.

"Gene! Stop wasting time over there and help me fix this mess you made."

I groan, rubbing my face. Yep. Definitely a running joke.

Betty Lou

Once we get the streamers and set pieces sorted out, the kids head off to rehearse, leaving Gene and me alone with the final touches on the decorations. The bickering has died down—for now—but there's something else in the air now, something I don't quite know how to handle.

Gene's standing on the other side of the stage, straightening one of the backdrops. He glances over at me every few minutes, like he's waiting for me to make a comment. Normally, I'd have something snappy to say, but today... today I feel weirdly quiet.

Maybe it's because of what Amanda said earlier. Maybe it's because we spent the last ten minutes laughing together like two idiots who fell off a ladder. Or maybe it's because, for the first time in years, I'm starting to wonder if there's something more to this whole Gene and Betty Lou thing than just banter.

I shake my head, trying to push the thought away. It's ridiculous. I've known Gene forever. We've always been like this—bickering, arguing, and getting on each other's nerves. But lately, it's been... different. Softer, somehow.

I glance up as Gene steps down from the stage, wiping his hands on his pants and giving me a sheepish look. "You okay?" he asks, his voice quieter than usual.

"Yeah," I reply, clearing my throat. "Just... thinking."

Gene frowns, taking a step closer. "About what?"

I open my mouth to answer, but the words get stuck. I don't know what to say. Should I tell him what Amanda said? Should I admit that I've been thinking about us—about what it would be like if we weren't just bickering all the time?

I glance up at him, my heart doing a weird little flip, and suddenly, I realize how close we're standing. Close enough that I can see the faint creases around his eyes, the slight flush in his cheeks. Close enough that I can smell the faint scent of his cologne, something warm and woodsy.

I take a step back, trying to put some distance between us. "Nothing important," I say quickly, turning back to the costume I've been working on.

Gene watches me for a moment, then nods, like he knows I'm avoiding something but isn't going to push it. "Right. Well, we should probably finish up here."

"Yeah," I agree, not looking at him. "Let's finish up."

But even as I say it, I know that something between us has already changed. And I don't know how to change it back.

Past Hurts Revealed

GENE

It's the night before the Mid-Summer Play, and the town is buzzing with excitement. I'm running around town hall, trying to make sure everything is in order for tomorrow. Amanda's been rehearsing nonstop, the kids are ready, and the set looks incredible thanks to Betty Lou's sharp eye for detail.

But something feels off.

I can't quite put my finger on it, but as I glance over at Betty Lou, who's adjusting one of the last backdrops, I notice she's been quieter than usual. She's been working just as hard as ever, but the playful banter between us has faded into something... different. Something heavier.

I grab the last stack of programs from the table and walk over to her, clearing my throat. "Hey, uh, Betty Lou? You got a minute?"

She glances at me, then back at the backdrop. "What is it, Gene?"

I shift awkwardly, running a hand through my hair. "I just wanted to say... you've been amazing. This whole thing, the play, the costumes—it wouldn't have come together without you."

She raises an eyebrow, her lips twitching like she's trying not to smile. "Is that your way of saying thanks?"

"Well, yeah," I admit, chuckling nervously. "You deserve it."

She sighs, dropping her hands from the backdrop and turning to face me fully. "I'm not in this for the compliments, Gene. I'm here because Amanda asked me to help, and... well, because it's important for the kids."

I nod, my stomach twisting. I've been feeling out of sorts lately, like I'm missing something when it comes to Betty Lou. She's been a constant in my life for years, but I've never stopped to ask her about herself—about her past, her life outside of Maplewood Grove.

Something pulls at me, and before I can stop myself, I ask, "Why do you stay in Maplewood Grove, Betty Lou?"

She blinks, caught off guard. "Why do you care?"

"I don't know," I say, feeling the weight of the question hang between us. "I guess I'm just curious. You've lived here your whole life, right? But you never talk about your family or... anything outside the post office."

Betty Lou shifts uncomfortably, crossing her arms. "What's there to talk about? I like my life the way it is."

I frown. "But do you? You seem... I don't know. Like maybe there's more to it."

Her eyes narrow, and for a second, I think she's going to snap at me. But then she sighs, her shoulders slumping slightly. "You don't get it, Gene. I've seen what happens when people take risks. When they go after things they think they want, only to have it all fall apart. I've seen it too many times. I'd rather stay where I know I'm safe."

Her words hit me harder than I expect, and I realize there's more to Betty Lou than I ever imagined. I've always seen her as the sharp-tongued post office clerk, always ready with a comment, always in control. But now, standing here in the dim light of town hall, I see something else—someone who's been hurt before, someone who's scared of stepping outside the life she's built for herself.

I open my mouth to respond, but before I can, Amanda comes running over, her face flushed with excitement.

"Dad! You've gotta see the costumes. Betty Lou finished the last ones, and they look amazing!"

Betty Lou takes the opportunity to step back, her usual expression back in place. "Go on, Gene. Check the costumes. I'll finish up here."

I hesitate, torn between wanting to push the conversation further and knowing that she's already retreated behind her walls. I nod, giving her a small smile. "Thanks, Betty Lou. For everything."

She doesn't respond, just waves me off as I follow Amanda toward the costumes.

Betty Lou

I watch Gene walk away with Amanda, my chest tight with something I can't quite name.

Why did he have to ask about my past? About my reasons for staying in Maplewood Grove? I've spent years keeping those questions at bay, staying busy with the post office, focusing on the little details of everyone else's lives, so I wouldn't have to face my own.

I grab the edge of the backdrop, tightening the ties as my mind wanders back to what he said. Do you like your life the way it is?

Of course I do. Don't I?

But then I hear his voice again, quiet but insistent. Is there more to it?

I shake my head, frustrated that Gene, of all people, is the one making me think about these things. He's always been so bumbling, so clueless when it comes to anything deeper than his speeches or his ridiculous ties. And yet... here we are.

I walk over to the pile of leftover fabric and begin folding it, trying to push the thoughts away. But it's no use. Gene's questions hang in the air like a storm cloud I can't shake.

I know why I've stayed in Maplewood Grove. I've seen people leave, chase dreams, take risks, and then come crawling back with nothing. I've seen heartbreak firsthand, and I swore to myself a long time ago that I wouldn't be one of those people. I'd stay here, keep my life simple and predictable, and avoid the hurt that comes with taking chances.

But now... now I'm not so sure.

I glance over at Gene, who's inspecting the costumes with Amanda, his face lighting up with that goofy, proud smile of his. He's a mess, sure. But there's something about the way he looks at Amanda, the way he cares about this town, that makes me wonder if maybe—just maybe—I've been too cautious. Too closed off.

"Betty Lou?"

Gene's voice snaps me out of my thoughts. I look up to see him standing in front of me, his expression softer than usual. "You okay?"

I nod quickly, avoiding his gaze. "Yeah. Just... tired."

He doesn't push, but I can tell he doesn't believe me. He just stands there for a moment, like he's waiting for me to say something more. But I can't. Not yet.

Finally, he nods, taking a step back. "If you ever want to talk... I'm here."

I swallow hard, the weight of his words settling over me. I nod, offering him a small, tight-lipped smile. "Thanks, Gene."

He gives me one last look, then walks back to the costumes, leaving me alone with my thoughts—and the strange feeling that maybe, just maybe, I'm ready to let someone in.

Gene

Betty Lou's been quiet all evening.

I watch her from across the room, folding fabric and adjusting the backdrops, but she's not her usual sharp-tongued self. Something's different. She's holding back.

I think about what she said earlier, about staying safe, about not taking risks. I never would've guessed that Betty Lou—of all people—was the type to play it safe. She always seemed so confident, so sure of herself. But now I'm starting to wonder if there's more to her than I realized.

Amanda runs up to me, tugging on my sleeve. "Dad! Look at the costume I'm wearing tomorrow. Isn't it awesome?"

I smile down at her, admiring the intricate details Betty Lou put into every stitch. "It's perfect, Amanda. You're going to be the star of the show."

Amanda beams at me, her eyes sparkling with excitement. "And you and Betty Lou are gonna be there, right?"

I blink, taken aback by the way she said it. Like me and Betty Lou are some kind of package deal.

"Of course we'll be there," I say, trying to keep my tone light. But Amanda's words stick with me.

Me and Betty Lou.

I glance back over at her, still folding fabric, her movements slower now, more deliberate. She looks... vulnerable. And for the first time in all the years we've been bickering, I wonder if maybe I've been looking at her all wrong.

Maybe there's more to her than the town gossip and the quick wit. Maybe there's a reason she stays behind those walls she's built around herself.

And maybe—just maybe—I want to be the one to help her tear them down.

Mid-Summer Play

GENE

The whole town is buzzing with excitement as the kids prepare for the mid-summer play. The auditorium is packed, the lights are dimming, and the set looks incredible. All those hours of bickering and ladder-climbing disasters were worth it. I glance around the room, catching sight of familiar faces—Mrs. Thompson from the bakery, Mr. Monroe from the hardware store, even old man Jenkins is here, sitting in the front row with his usual grumpy expression.

But I'm not focused on them. My eyes keep drifting back to Betty Lou.

She's sitting in the front row too, her hands folded in her lap, watching the kids backstage. She's wearing this simple navy blue dress that I've never seen her wear before. And I'm noticing things I shouldn't—like the way her hair curls softly around her face, or the way her lips twitch like she's trying to hold back a smile.

I shake my head, forcing myself to focus. This isn't the time to be getting distracted. The kids have worked hard on this play, and I'm here for Amanda, not to gawk at Betty Lou.

Amanda appears next to me, bouncing with excitement. "Dad, it's almost time! Are you ready?"

I smile down at her, proud as can be. "I'm ready, sweetheart. You're going to be great."

She beams at me, then glances over at Betty Lou. "Isn't she great too, Dad? She's really helped me a lot."

"Yeah," I mutter, watching Betty Lou again. "She has."

Before Amanda can say anything else, the lights go down and the music starts. She hurries backstage, leaving me standing in the shadows. I sit down in my seat, trying to shake the strange mix of nerves and excitement swirling in my gut.

But as the curtain rises and the kids take the stage, I can't help but sneak one last glance at Betty Lou.

Betty Lou

The play is going off without a hitch, and I should be relieved. The kids look adorable in their costumes, the set looks perfect, and everything is running smoothly. But instead of feeling satisfied, I feel... out of place.

I can't stop thinking about what Gene said earlier. Why do you stay in Maplewood Grove? He didn't mean it as an insult, but it stung all the same. It felt like he was questioning my entire life, the choices I've made. And it's not the first time I've felt that way around him lately.

I glance over at Gene, watching him watch Amanda on stage. He looks so proud, so... happy. And something inside me twists painfully. I know I'm being ridiculous, but I can't shake the feeling that whatever's between us—this flirting, this banter—it's temporary. Just like everything else.

I hear someone whispering behind me, and I catch bits of the conversation. "Gene's probably going to leave town... Amanda doesn't even like it here... I heard he's thinking about moving back to the city."

My heart skips a beat. Leave Maplewood Grove? Gene?

I glance back at the stage, trying to keep my expression neutral, but my mind is racing. Is that what he meant? Is he just passing through town, using me for a little small-town entertainment before he goes back to his real life?

I feel a lump forming in my throat. Of course that's it. People like Gene—they don't stick around. Not for people like me.

I lean back in my chair, crossing my arms tightly. I've been so stupid, letting myself get caught up in this... whatever this is between us. I should've known better. Gene's always been full of big ideas and grand gestures, but when it comes down to it, he'll go back to his real world, and I'll still be here.

I glance over at him again, but this time, my heart feels heavy. This was never going to last.

Gene

As the play moves into its final act, I can't shake the feeling that something's off with Betty Lou. She's sitting a few seats down from me, her arms crossed, her posture stiff. She hasn't looked at me once since the play started, and every time I glance over at her, her face is like stone.

I don't get it. We were doing fine earlier, even laughing together. But now it's like a switch flipped, and I'm back to being the town idiot in her eyes.

The kids take their final bow, and the applause fills the room. I clap along with everyone else, proud of Amanda and the work all the kids put into this, but my mind is stuck on Betty Lou.

As the crowd starts filing out, I make my way toward her, trying to figure out what I could've done wrong. "Betty Lou," I call out, stepping up beside her as she stands to leave. "Hey, can we talk?"

She barely glances at me, her jaw tight. "There's nothing to talk about, Gene."

I frown, taken aback by the sharpness in her voice. "What do you mean? Did I do something—"

"I heard what you said," she interrupts, her eyes flashing. "About leaving. About Amanda not liking it here."

I blink, confused. "What? What are you talking about?"

She crosses her arms tighter, looking away from me. "It doesn't matter, Gene. We were just having fun, right? Bickering, playing along... But I know you're not going to stay in Maplewood Grove forever. You've got your real life to get back to."

My heart sinks. She thinks... she thinks I'm leaving? "Betty Lou, that's not—"

"Save it," she says, cutting me off. "I'm not interested in being some temporary amusement while you figure out your next move."

I open my mouth to protest, but the words don't come. I can't believe she thinks that. After everything we've been through, all the time we've spent together, does she really think I'm just going to leave?

"I'm not going anywhere," I finally manage, my voice low. "I never said that."

She shakes her head, still refusing to look at me. "It doesn't matter. This was never going to work, Gene. We're too different."

"Betty Lou," I say, stepping closer, my chest tight. "I'm not leaving. I'm here. I'm right here."

She takes a deep breath, finally meeting my gaze. For a second, I see something flicker in her eyes—something vulnerable, something real. But just as quickly, it's gone, and she turns away, walking out of the auditorium without another word.

I stand there, watching her leave, my heart pounding in my chest.

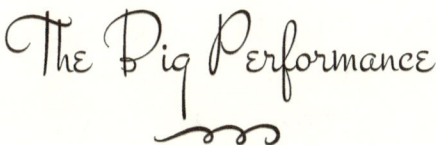

The Big Performance

BETTY LOU

The night air is cool as I step outside the auditorium, my heart still pounding in my chest. The play was a success—everyone's saying so—but I can't stop thinking about my conversation with Gene. Or, rather, the argument.

I shake my head, trying to push it all down. I knew this was a bad idea. Letting myself get close to Gene was a mistake. He's just like all the others, passing through Maplewood Grove on their way to somewhere bigger, somewhere better. He doesn't belong here. He doesn't belong with me.

I walk down the quiet street, my arms crossed tightly over my chest, trying to hold myself together. But then I hear footsteps behind me. His footsteps.

"Betty Lou, wait!" Gene calls out, his voice loud in the stillness of the night. I don't turn around. I can't. If I look at him, I'll break, and I can't afford to do that right now.

"Betty Lou, please." His voice is closer now, and I feel a hand on my arm, gently pulling me to a stop.

I turn, and there he is, standing in front of me, his eyes wide with concern. There's something in his expression that makes my chest tighten, something that makes it impossible for me to look away.

"What do you want, Gene?" I ask, my voice sharp even though I don't mean it to be.

"I want to explain," he says, his voice low but urgent. "You misunderstood what you heard. I'm not leaving Maplewood Grove."

I shake my head, trying to pull away, but he doesn't let go. "You don't have to explain, Gene. It doesn't matter. None of this matters."

"It does matter," he insists, stepping closer. "It matters to me. You matter to me."

My heart skips a beat at his words, but I force myself to stay strong. "Don't do this, Gene. Don't pretend like you're going to stay here forever. You've got a life outside of this town, and I'm not going to be some... some placeholder while you figure things out."

Gene's grip on my arm tightens, but his voice softens. "You think I'm just passing through? That I'm going to leave? Betty Lou, I've spent my whole life trying to figure out where I belong. And the more time I spend here, with you... the more I realize that Maplewood Grove is where I'm meant to be."

I blink, completely taken aback by his words. "What?"

"I'm not leaving," he repeats, his voice steady now. "I want to stay. Here. With you."

I stare at him, my heart racing, and for the first time, I feel my defenses start to crumble. But I can't let him in. I can't risk getting hurt.

"Why?" I ask, my voice trembling. "Why would you want to stay in this small town? Why would you want to stay with me?"

Gene's eyes soften, and he takes another step closer, so close I can feel the warmth of his breath on my skin. "Because I've never met anyone like you, Betty Lou. And I've never felt like this before. I'm not here for a fling. I'm not here to waste time. I'm here because I care about you."

His words hit me like a ton of bricks, and suddenly, all the walls

I've spent years building around myself start to crack. I care about you.

I swallow hard, blinking back the tears that threaten to fall. "Gene... I don't know how to do this."

He smiles, a soft, understanding smile that makes my heart ache. "Neither do I. But we can figure it out together."

Gene

I've never been good with words. I can talk about town events, I can give speeches that go on for days, but when it comes to saying what really matters—when it comes to telling someone how I feel—I get tongue-tied.

But standing here, looking at Betty Lou, I know I can't mess this up. I can't let her walk away thinking she's just some passing amusement to me, because she's not. She's so much more than that.

"I've been a fool," I admit, running a hand through my hair. "I've spent so much time arguing with you, bickering over the smallest things, and all this time, I didn't realize what was right in front of me."

Betty Lou watches me, her eyes wide, her breath catching in her throat.

"You're right," I continue, my voice steady now. "We do bicker. We argue. But I've realized something, Betty Lou. We do it because we care. You challenge me. You keep me on my toes. And you're the only person in this whole town who isn't afraid to call me out when I'm being ridiculous."

She lets out a soft laugh, but there's still a hesitation in her eyes, like she's not sure if she can trust what I'm saying.

"I know I'm not perfect," I say, taking a deep breath. "I know I can be a bit... much sometimes. But I care about you, Betty Lou. I care about you more than I've ever cared about anyone."

Her lips part, but she doesn't say anything. She just stands there, staring at me like she's waiting for me to say the one thing she needs to hear.

"I love you," I say, my voice quiet but firm. "I love you, Betty Lou Hopkins, and I don't want to spend another day pretending like I don't."

The words hang in the air between us, heavy and real. For a moment, everything is still—like the whole world is holding its breath, waiting for her to respond.

And then, slowly, she steps forward, closing the distance between us. Her hand reaches up to cup my cheek, her touch gentle but sure.

"I love you too, Gene," she whispers, her voice trembling. "I've been trying to ignore it, trying to pretend like it didn't matter, but... it does. You matter."

My heart swells, and before I know it, I'm pulling her into my arms, holding her close like I've been waiting my whole life for this moment. She melts into me, her arms wrapping around my waist, and for the first time in a long time, I feel like everything is exactly where it's supposed to be.

Betty Lou

I don't know how long we stand there, wrapped in each other's arms, but for the first time in years, I feel... safe. Like I can let my guard down, like I don't have to keep pushing people away to protect myself.

Gene holds me close, his warmth surrounding me, and I rest my head against his chest, listening to the steady rhythm of his heartbeat. It feels right—like this is where I'm supposed to be.

I take a deep breath, lifting my head to look up at him. "So... what now?"

He chuckles softly, brushing a strand of hair behind my ear.

"Now? Now we stop pretending like we don't care about each other."

I smile, a small, shy smile that feels foreign on my face. "And the bickering?"

"Oh, we'll still bicker," he says with a grin. "But it'll be different now."

I laugh, the sound light and easy, and for the first time in a long time, I feel... happy. Really, truly happy.

Gene leans down, pressing a soft kiss to my forehead, and I close my eyes, letting myself enjoy the moment. For years, I've been so focused on staying safe, on keeping everything in my life neat and controlled. But with Gene... I feel like maybe it's okay to let go. To take a risk. To trust that not everything will fall apart.

"I love you," I whisper again, the words feeling easier this time.

Gene tightens his arms around me, his smile warm and real. "I love you too."

And for the first time, I believe it.

Happy Ending

The sun is setting over Maplewood Grove, casting everything in a warm golden glow. I'm standing in the middle of the town square, where the annual End-of-Summer Festival is in full swing. Kids are running around with balloons, vendors are selling homemade pies and lemonade, and the familiar buzz of conversation fills the air. This is what small-town life is all about.

But tonight, it feels different. Tonight, I'm not standing here as just the town's bumbling mayor, known for my novelty ties and long-winded speeches. Tonight, I'm standing here with Betty Lou Hopkins by my side.

I glance over at her, and she's laughing at something Mrs. Thompson from the bakery just said. Her eyes crinkle at the corners when she smiles, and I can't help but feel a swell of pride that this incredible woman is standing next to me—*with* me.

"Dad!" Amanda's voice snaps me out of my thoughts. She comes running up, her face flushed from excitement. "Look! I won one of the games!" She's holding up a little stuffed bear like it's the greatest prize in the world.

I grin, ruffling her hair. "That's amazing, sweetheart. Keep it up and you'll have a whole collection by the end of the night."

Amanda beams at me, then glances at Betty Lou. She gives me a knowing look—one I've seen a lot lately. "You two having fun?" she asks, her tone mischievous.

I chuckle, wrapping an arm around Betty Lou's waist. "We are," I say, catching Betty Lou's eye. She raises an eyebrow, but there's a soft smile playing on her lips. "How about you?"

Amanda nods, but before she can say anything, her friends call her over to the pie-eating contest. "I'll be right back," she says, already running off, leaving me and Betty Lou standing together in the middle of the bustling festival.

I turn to Betty Lou, my heart feeling lighter than it has in years. "You know," I say, leaning in closer, "I think we make a pretty good team."

She laughs, shaking her head. "Is that your way of saying you finally admit I'm right most of the time?"

I grin, squeezing her waist. "Maybe."

She smiles up at me, her eyes twinkling in the fading light. "We do make a good team, don't we?"

"Yeah," I murmur, pressing a soft kiss to her temple. "We really do."

Betty Lou

I don't know when it happened—this shift between Gene and me—but standing here at the festival, surrounded by the town we've both called home for so long, I feel... content. More than content, really. I feel happy.

I glance around at the familiar faces of Maplewood Grove, all of them going about their business, enjoying the festival. There's a comfort in knowing everyone here, in being part of this community.

But there's something even more comforting in knowing that I'm not standing alone anymore.

Gene's arm is wrapped around my waist, and even though we're not making a big deal about it, I can see the looks we're getting. People are noticing. There are whispers—quiet conversations between vendors, knowing smiles from Mrs. Thompson and Mr. Monroe.

And I don't mind.

For years, I kept people at arm's length. I didn't want to be the subject of the town's gossip, didn't want to be vulnerable, didn't want anyone to get too close. But now, with Gene at my side, I feel like I can finally let all of that go.

I glance up at him, and he's beaming down at me like I'm the only person in the world. His goofy, proud smile makes my heart skip a beat, and before I can stop myself, I rise up on my toes and plant a soft kiss on his lips.

It's a small gesture, nothing grand or dramatic, but it's enough to make the people around us take notice. I can feel the stares, hear the whispers, but for the first time, I don't care.

Gene blinks, clearly caught off guard by the kiss, but then he laughs, wrapping both arms around me and pulling me close. "What was that for?" he asks, his voice warm with amusement.

I shrug, smiling up at him. "Just felt like it."

"About time!" someone calls out from the crowd, and I glance over to see Mrs. Thompson giving us a thumbs-up, her face beaming with approval.

Gene laughs, shaking his head. "Looks like we've become the talk of the town."

I smirk, leaning into him. "Guess we're not so different after all, huh? The mayor and the town gossip, finally giving them something to talk about."

He chuckles, pressing a kiss to the top of my head. "Let them talk. I don't care."

And, for the first time in my life, neither do I.

Gene

The festival is winding down now, the sun dipping below the horizon, casting the town square in a soft glow. Most of the vendors are packing up, the kids are yawning and heading home, but I'm not ready to leave just yet. I want to savor this moment—this feeling of being right where I'm supposed to be.

Betty Lou is still standing next to me, her hand resting comfortably in mine. Amanda is running around with her friends, laughing and carefree, and I can't help but feel a sense of peace wash over me.

"I've been thinking," I say, turning to Betty Lou.

She raises an eyebrow. "Uh-oh. That's usually dangerous."

I laugh, nudging her playfully. "No, seriously. I've been thinking about what comes next."

Her smile softens, and she tilts her head, watching me with those sharp, curious eyes that always seem to see right through me. "And what did you come up with, Mayor Beckett?"

I take a deep breath, letting the weight of the moment settle over me. "I think I'm finally ready to stop overthinking everything. To just... be here. With you. With Amanda. With this town. No more worrying about whether I'm doing things right. No more trying to prove myself."

Betty Lou's expression softens, and she squeezes my hand. "Gene... you've always belonged here. We all knew it. You just had to figure it out for yourself."

I smile, feeling a warmth spread through my chest. She's right. I've spent so much time second-guessing myself, wondering if I was doing enough, if I was being enough. But standing here, surrounded by the people I love, I realize that this is all I need. This town. This life. This love.

"I love you, Betty Lou," I say softly, my voice barely more than a whisper.

She smiles up at me, her eyes twinkling. "I love you too, Gene."

And with those words, everything falls into place. The past, the future—it all fades away, leaving just this moment.

We stand there together, watching the town square empty out, the stars beginning to twinkle overhead. It's quiet now, peaceful, and for the first time, I feel like I'm exactly where I'm supposed to be.

"Come on," I say, pulling her close as the last of the vendors pack up. "Let's go home."

And for the first time, that word—*home*—feels right.

The End

Did you enjoy Betty and Gene's story?
Consider reviewing it on Amazon, Goodreads or Bookbub. Reviews help me reach new readers.

Read ***Rule #3 Dad Knows Best***, the next story in the **Rules for Dating a Single Dad** series.

The book is also part of the ***Maplewood Grove*** series, known as *Sweet Surprise*.
Start the series with ***Sweet Rivals***!

Join my newsletter for writing updates, new releases, sales and promotions!

Sweet Patience

∿

Previously published as Rule #7 Patience is Key

A New Face in Town

ISABEL

"Sí, mamá, ya sé," I say into the phone, shifting a tray of empanadas onto the counter. My mother's voice on the other end is a steady hum of concern.

"You're always working, Isabel. What about you? Are you eating properly? Resting?"

I glance out the window, watching Mia play with her friends in the backyard. "Mamá, I'm fine," I reply, the same as always. "Business is good, and I've got everything under control."

"Hmm," she murmurs, but I know her well enough to hear the skepticism in her tone. "That's what you always say, mija, but you're doing everything by yourself. You need to take care of yourself, too."

I press my lips together and take a deep breath. It's hard for her to understand. Ever since we lost Mateo, it's been just me and Mia. I've had no choice but to keep going, to build this life for us. No one else is going to do it for me.

"I'm fine," I repeat, gentler this time. "Really. I've got help." I glance at the clock. Rosa will be here any minute to assist with the event prep, and I still need to finish a few things before heading out.

As I begin arranging the pastries for the evening event, a loud knock interrupts my thoughts. The door swings open before I can respond, and Dot Simmons strides in with all the subtlety of a tornado.

"Isabel! Have you heard the news?" she exclaims, not waiting for an answer as she leans against the counter. "Richard King, that billionaire, just moved into the old estate outside town. Everyone's talking about it!"

I stifle a sigh. The last thing I need right now is gossip. "Dot, I'm sure the town has more important things to focus on," I say, keeping my voice light. "What does that have to do with me?"

Dot raises an eyebrow as if I've missed the obvious. "What do you mean, what does it have to do with you? He's a billionaire, Isabel! A man like that is bound to throw some big events. And who's going to cater them?"

I glance down at the trays of empanadas I've been preparing, wiping my hands on a towel. "I'm sure he'll hire someone from the city. People like him don't usually look local for these things."

Dot waves me off, undeterred. "Nonsense. You're the best caterer in Maplewood Grove! Who else is he going to trust? It's worth keeping an open mind, don't you think?"

I pause for a moment, considering her words. More business wouldn't hurt, especially if it means securing Mia's future. But a billionaire? That's not my world. I've worked hard to build my little catering business from the ground up. I don't need someone sweeping in and changing things.

Before I can respond, Mia bursts into the kitchen, her face flushed with excitement. "Mamá! Can we make cupcakes later?"

I smile at her. "Of course, mija. After I finish work."

Dot gives me a knowing smile, patting my arm. "Just think about it, dear. You never know. Life has a way of surprising us." She leaves the kitchen as suddenly as she appeared, her words lingering in the air.

I watch her go, shaking my head. Richard King may be the talk of the town, but I have more important things to focus on. Like making sure Mia is happy, and this business keeps running.

Richard

I step onto the porch, looking out over the sprawling lawn of the estate. The wind rustles through the trees, carrying a sense of quiet that I haven't felt in a long time. It's exactly what I came here for—peace.

I turn back toward the house, half-expecting to hear Beverly's footsteps, but there's only silence. She hasn't left her room since we arrived two days ago. I can't blame her. She's been through hell in the past year—losing her mother and having to deal with the press hounding us constantly.

I pinch the bridge of my nose, trying to shake off the weight that's been pressing on me since we moved. This town, Maplewood Grove, is supposed to be our fresh start. A place where Beverly can grieve in peace. A place where I can finally breathe.

"This is it," I murmur to myself. "A fresh start for both of us."

The estate is far too big for just the two of us, but I needed something this secluded. No more flashing cameras, no more tabloid headlines. Just space and quiet, away from everything that reminds us of the life we left behind.

As I walk down the steps and onto the lawn, I spot two women standing by the gate, chatting. I catch their quick glances in my direction, and I know immediately what they're talking about. It's the same look I've seen a thousand times.

"Why is a billionaire moving to a small town like this? What's he running from?"

I exhale slowly, burying my hands in my pockets. Let them speculate. It doesn't matter what they think. All I care about is Beverly. She deserves a chance to heal, away from the chaos that our lives have been.

I glance back toward the house. If this place can give her that, it's worth it. If it can give us both a chance to heal, maybe we'll be able to move forward.

But right now, I'm not even sure what moving forward looks like.

Isabel

"Mamá! Did you hear?" Mia's voice bursts through the kitchen as she runs inside, breathless. "There's a fancy new man in town. Everyone's talking about him!"

I laugh softly, wiping flour off my hands. "I know, mija. His name is Richard King, and yes, he's new to town. But that doesn't change anything for us."

"But he's a billionaire!" she says, eyes wide with excitement. "Maybe he's like those people on TV."

I shake my head, smiling at her enthusiasm. "Maybe. But that doesn't mean anything for us, does it?"

Mia crosses her arms, a frown creeping onto her face. "Why don't we ever go see the big houses or meet anyone new? What if he's nice?"

I crouch down to her level, gently brushing a strand of hair behind her ear. "We've got a nice life here, don't we? Our house is plenty big enough, and we have everything we need. You don't need to worry about people like Richard King."

"But it would be fun," she insists, her lower lip jutting out in a pout. "Maybe he has a big yard for us to play in."

I chuckle, standing back up. "We have plenty of space to play in our own yard. And I'm sure Mr. King doesn't want strangers bothering him while he settles in."

Mia sighs, clearly not convinced, but she doesn't argue. "Can we make cupcakes later? Please, mamá?"

"Of course," I say, ruffling her hair. "But after I finish work, okay? We've got a busy day ahead."

She runs back outside, and I turn my attention back to the kitchen, focusing on the tasks at hand. The catering business keeps me busy, and that's how I like it. It keeps my mind off the past, off things I can't change.

Richard King may have the town buzzing, but I have a life to manage, a business to run, and a daughter to raise. That's where my focus needs to be.

An Unexpected Proposal

RICHARD

I walk into the community center, feeling the low hum of energy that always accompanies these small-town events. It's a far cry from the high-profile galas and corporate dinners I'm used to. Here, everything feels... simpler. Easier to breathe.

As I scan the room, my eyes land on a small buffet table near the back. The smell of freshly baked bread and roasted vegetables pulls me in, reminding me how long it's been since I've eaten anything homemade.

Isabel Martinez is busy setting up the final details of her catering spread, moving with the kind of efficiency that only comes from years of experience. Her long dark hair is pulled back into a loose braid, and there's a quiet determination in her movements. I find myself watching her longer than I mean to.

She doesn't seem to notice me, too focused on adjusting the trays and making sure everything looks perfect. The kids are running around, parents chatting in clusters, but she's locked into her own world, balancing her work with the occasional glance over at her daughter, Mia, who's playing by the entrance.

I grab a plate, mindlessly loading it with food. I didn't plan on attending this event. It's just a simple gathering for the community— exactly the kind of thing I came here for. But standing here now, I realize it's more than just a distraction from my own thoughts. It's a chance to start integrating into this place.

Isabel looks up and spots me. I nod, trying to offer a smile, but I don't miss the guarded look in her eyes. She knows who I am. Everyone in town knows. But I can tell she's not impressed by wealth or status. And for some reason, I find that... refreshing.

The food is incredible, far better than anything I've had in recent months. I make a mental note to find out more about her business. Maybe I can help—maybe it could be beneficial for both of us.

I take another bite of the empanada, my mind already turning with ideas.

Later in the evening, when the crowd has thinned, I see my chance. Isabel is packing up her supplies, stacking trays into the back of her van. I walk over, keeping my steps slow and non-threatening. I've learned that approaching people too quickly usually ends in awkwardness or suspicion.

"Isabel, right?" I ask, leaning slightly against the van door.

She looks up, surprised to see me standing there. "Yes... Mr. King, right?"

"Please, just Richard," I say, offering a smile. "I wanted to compliment you on the food tonight. It was exceptional."

"Thank you," she replies, though her tone is polite and distant. She's wary. I can see it in her eyes.

I decide to get straight to the point. "I've been thinking... I recently moved here, as you know. I've got a few charity events coming up that I'd like to host at my estate. I was wondering if you'd be interested in catering them."

Isabel blinks, caught off guard. "Charity events? At your estate?"

"Yes." I fold my arms across my chest, trying to gauge her reaction. "I thought it would be a good way to get involved with the community. I'd like to support local businesses, especially one as good as yours."

Her brow furrows, and I can tell she's hesitant. "I... I don't know. It's a generous offer, but—"

"There's no pressure," I interrupt, sensing her reluctance. "It's just a proposal. You'd have full control over the menu, and I'll make sure everything is up to your standards. I've seen how well you balance your work and your family. It's impressive."

She's quiet for a moment, clearly weighing the idea. I can see the wheels turning in her mind, but she's still unsure.

"I understand if you need time to think about it," I add. "No rush. Just something to consider."

Isabel looks up, her eyes narrowing slightly. "Why me? You could hire any high-end caterer from the city."

I chuckle, shaking my head. "I'm done with that life. I want something different now. Local, personal. You're clearly talented, and I think it could be a great partnership. But, like I said, no pressure."

She exhales, glancing back at the trays in the van. "I'll... think about it. That's all I can promise for now."

"That's all I'm asking for," I reply, giving her a nod. I take a step back, sensing the conversation is over for now. As I walk away, I feel a flicker of hope that maybe—just maybe—this town might finally be the fresh start I've been looking for.

Isabel

I watch Richard walk away, my mind spinning with a million thoughts.

Catering for a billionaire? It sounds ridiculous, but then again...

the money could be good. It would definitely help with Mia's schooling, and I could finally upgrade some of my equipment.

Still, there's something about the whole thing that doesn't sit right with me. I've worked too hard to build this business on my own terms. I don't need some wealthy outsider coming in and throwing money around like it's the answer to everything.

I pack the rest of the trays into the van, my movements automatic, but my thoughts are far from the task at hand. Why would someone like Richard King want me to cater his events? He could afford the best, hire the most exclusive chefs from the city. What's his angle?

It's not like we run in the same circles. I'm a single mom trying to make ends meet in a small town. He's... well, he's a billionaire. His world couldn't be more different from mine. And yet, here he is, asking me to be part of his plan to "get involved" with the community.

I'm not naive. I know how people like him operate. Money talks, and they expect people to listen. But I'm not about to let someone dictate how I run my business, no matter how big the paycheck might be.

I shut the van doors, leaning against them for a moment. Maybe I'm being too cautious. Maybe this is exactly the opportunity I need to take my business to the next level. But what if it's more than that? What if getting involved with Richard King complicates everything I've worked so hard to build?

My phone buzzes in my pocket, pulling me from my thoughts. It's Mia, asking if I'm on my way home. I glance at the clock—it's later than I thought.

With a sigh, I slip my phone back into my pocket and climb into the van. As I drive through the quiet streets of Maplewood Grove, Richard's offer keeps playing in my mind. I need time to think this through, to figure out if working for him is worth the risk.

But as I pull into my driveway and see Mia waiting on the front porch, a small smile on her face, I know one thing for certain: whatever decision I make, it'll be for her. It always is.

Behind Closed Doors

~∾∾⌒

ISABEL

The estate is even bigger up close than I imagined. I stand in the driveway, staring up at the enormous stone house that looks more like a castle than a home. It's almost intimidating, the kind of place you'd expect to see in a movie, not right here in Maplewood Grove.

Mia tugs on my sleeve, her eyes wide as she takes in the sprawling lawn and towering trees. "Mamá, this place is huge! Can we live here too?" she asks with a giggle, clearly impressed by the sight.

I smile down at her, shaking my head. "We're just here to work, mija. Let's not get any ideas."

She pouts but skips along beside me as we walk toward the front door. I remind myself for the hundredth time that this is just a job. It's good money, a step toward growing my business, but nothing more.

I knock on the door, and within seconds, Richard opens it. He's dressed more casually than the last time I saw him—no suit and tie today, just jeans and a simple button-up. He gives me a quick smile, stepping aside to let us in.

"Welcome," he says, his voice warm. "Glad you could make it. Is this Mia?"

Mia beams up at him, completely unbothered by his status or wealth. "Hi! Your house is like a castle."

Richard chuckles, crouching down to her level. "Thanks, Mia. It's a bit big, huh?"

She nods enthusiastically, and I can't help but smile at the exchange. It's strange seeing him like this, relaxed and... almost normal. But I remind myself to stay professional. This is a business arrangement. Nothing more.

"I've got the kitchen set up for you," Richard says, straightening up and motioning for us to follow him. "If there's anything else you need, just let me know."

I nod, walking behind him as we enter the massive kitchen. It's spotless, with gleaming countertops and appliances that probably cost more than my entire business. Mia gasps, running over to the double-door fridge and opening it like it's a treasure chest.

"Whoa! There's so much food in here!"

I laugh softly, shaking my head. "Mia, don't touch anything, okay?"

Richard watches us with a small smile, leaning against the counter. "Feel free to make yourself at home. I trust your judgment when it comes to the food."

I nod, setting down my supplies and pulling Mia away from the fridge. I've worked in some fancy kitchens before, but this one takes the cake. Still, I know what I'm doing, and I'm not about to let the grandeur of this place throw me off.

"Thanks," I say, keeping my voice steady. "I'll get started right away."

Richard gives me a quick nod, watching us for a moment longer before excusing himself. "I'll be in the office if you need me. Good luck."

As he leaves, I let out a breath I didn't realize I was holding. This is it—my chance to prove myself. No distractions. Just focus on the work.

Richard

I lean back in my chair, rubbing the back of my neck as I try to focus on the emails in front of me. The charity event is coming up fast, and there are still a dozen details to finalize, but my mind keeps wandering back to the kitchen.

I can hear the faint clatter of dishes and the low hum of Isabel's voice as she talks to her daughter. It's a sound I haven't heard in this house in... I don't know how long. For the first time in months, the silence feels less suffocating.

I stand up, pacing the length of the office. I wasn't expecting her to bring Mia with her, but seeing them together makes me realize how different their world is from mine. Isabel is so focused, so determined to make this work for her daughter, and I can't help but respect that.

After a while, I decide to check in on how things are going. When I enter the kitchen, Isabel is at the stove, stirring a pot of something that smells incredible. Mia is sitting at the counter, drawing on a napkin with a pen she must have found.

"Smells amazing in here," I say, leaning against the doorway.

Isabel looks up, startled, but quickly composes herself. "Oh, thanks. I'm just testing a few things for the event."

I walk further into the kitchen, noticing the way Mia watches her mom with admiration. It's clear that Isabel's world revolves around her daughter, and that kind of love is... well, it's something I haven't experienced in a long time.

"How's everything going? Do you need anything?" I ask, trying to sound casual, but there's something in the air between us that feels different tonight.

Isabel hesitates, then shakes her head. "No, everything's fine. We're on track."

I nod, but instead of leaving, I linger by the counter, watching her work. After a few moments of silence, I decide to speak up. "I admire what you're doing."

She glances at me, frowning slightly. "What do you mean?"

"This," I gesture toward Mia and the kitchen. "Balancing your business and your family. It can't be easy, but you make it look effortless."

Isabel lets out a small laugh, shaking her head. "It's far from effortless. But I do what I can. Mia comes first, always."

I nod, understanding more than she probably realizes. "I get that. Beverly—my daughter—she's... she's everything to me. But after her mother died... things have been difficult."

There's a pause, the weight of my words hanging in the air. Isabel looks up, her eyes softening. "I'm sorry. I didn't know."

I shrug, trying to brush it off, but the truth is, talking about it feels like lifting a weight I've been carrying alone for too long. "It's been a rough year. Moving here was supposed to give us a fresh start. But I'm not sure it's working."

Isabel is quiet for a moment, then she sets down the spoon and turns to face me fully. "It takes time. Grief... it doesn't follow a schedule. You just have to be there for her, even if it feels like you're not doing enough."

Her words hit deeper than I expected. She understands. More than most people would.

"I guess that's what I'm trying to do," I admit, my voice quieter now. "But I keep wondering if I'm just messing everything up."

She shakes her head. "You're here, aren't you? That counts for something."

For a moment, we just stand there, the warmth of the kitchen surrounding us. There's a connection here, something I didn't see coming, but it feels... real. Like I'm not the only one trying to figure all of this out.

Isabel

I don't know what just happened in the kitchen, but something shifted. For the first time, Richard didn't feel like some distant, untouchable billionaire. He felt... human. Like someone who's struggling just as much as I am.

As I turn back to the stove, I can feel his presence still lingering, even though he's left the room. Mia is humming quietly to herself, completely oblivious to the strange conversation that just took place.

"Mom, can I go outside? I saw a big garden when we came in!" Mia's eyes are bright with excitement.

I smile, nodding. "Just stay where I can see you, okay?"

She grins and runs toward the back door, throwing it open and dashing out into the garden. I laugh to myself, shaking my head. That kid has more energy than I know what to do with.

I step outside after her, leaning against the doorway as I watch her explore. She's running her hands through the tall grass, picking flowers and holding them up to the sky like they're some kind of treasure. Richard appears a few moments later, standing beside me.

"She's got a lot of energy," he says, chuckling softly.

"She keeps me on my toes, that's for sure."

We stand there in silence for a moment, watching Mia as she runs around the garden. And for the first time since I took this job, I feel like maybe... maybe this isn't just about business anymore.

Clashing Worlds

RICHARD

I stand on the phone, pacing the length of the library in my estate. "Yes, I want them to meet with her. She's talented. Local, yes, but trust me, she has potential." I pause, listening to the voice on the other end.

The people I've been talking to aren't from Maplewood Grove—they're my old contacts from the city. Clients I used to do business with in a world far removed from this small town. But that's exactly why I think this will work. Isabel deserves more exposure, and if I can help her business expand, why not?

I've already given them her contact information, set up a meeting between her and a few big-name clients. She doesn't know yet. I thought it would be a nice surprise.

When I hang up, I feel good about it. This is exactly what she needs. More visibility, more opportunities to grow her business beyond the limits of Maplewood Grove. She's too talented to be stuck in one place. I want to help her succeed, and this is the first step.

Satisfied, I head downstairs. Isabel is in the kitchen again, prepping for the upcoming charity event. The smell of her cooking fills the room, a warmth that cuts through the usual stillness of this house.

She's at the counter, focused, and I approach quietly, not wanting to interrupt her flow. But she looks up as soon as I walk in, wiping her hands on a towel.

"Hey," I say with a smile. "How's everything coming along?"

"Good," she replies, her voice neutral. She's in work mode. All business.

I step closer, leaning against the counter. "Listen, I've been thinking... I made some calls to a few clients of mine, high-end people who I think would be interested in your work. I've set up some meetings for you. I think it'll help take your business to the next level."

For a moment, Isabel just stares at me, her expression unreadable. Then, slowly, her brows knit together, and I realize something's off.

"You... did what?" Her voice is sharp, laced with disbelief.

"I called some people I know," I say again, a little more carefully this time. "They're interested in working with you. I figured it could be a good opportunity."

Her jaw tightens, and she shakes her head. "You called people behind my back? Made decisions for my business without even talking to me first?"

I blink, taken aback. This isn't the reaction I expected. "I was trying to help," I say, confused. "I thought it would be a good surprise."

Isabel drops the towel onto the counter, her movements tense. "I don't need you to make decisions for me, Richard. This is my business, my life. I've worked hard to build it from the ground up. You don't get to come in and decide what's best for me."

Her words hit me like a punch to the gut. I didn't mean it like that. I wasn't trying to control her—I just wanted to help. But I can see now that I've crossed a line.

"I'm sorry," I say quickly. "I didn't mean to undermine you. I just... I wanted to give you more opportunities. You're too talented to be limited to this town."

"That's not your call to make," she snaps. "I don't need you—or anyone else—deciding what I can or can't do."

Her eyes flash with anger, and I realize I've made a huge mistake.

Isabel

I can't believe he did this.

I stand there, my heart pounding in my chest as Richard stares at me, clearly confused. How could he think that making decisions for my business without even asking me would be okay? Does he think I can't handle it on my own? Does he think I'm not capable of making those decisions for myself?

"I don't need your charity, Richard," I say, my voice trembling with frustration. "I've worked too hard to get where I am. I built this business from nothing, and I've done it on my own. I don't need you stepping in and trying to fix things that aren't broken."

"I'm not trying to fix anything," he says, running a hand through his hair. "I just thought—"

"That's the problem, Richard. You thought. You didn't ask. You didn't consider how I might feel about it. You just assumed that I needed your help, that I couldn't handle it on my own. And that's not fair."

He opens his mouth to respond, but I cut him off. "You don't know what it's like to be in my shoes. You don't know what it's like to lose everything and have to rebuild from scratch. You think because you have money, you can solve everyone's problems, but that's not how it works."

The words spill out before I can stop them, but I don't regret saying them. I've kept too much bottled up for too long. It feels good to finally let it out.

Richard stands there, his expression a mixture of guilt and frustration. "I'm sorry," he says again, but this time, his voice is quieter. "I didn't mean to overstep."

I shake my head, turning back to the stove. "It's not just about overstepping. It's about control. I've spent too long trying to gain control over my life after losing Mateo. I won't let anyone take that away from me again."

For a long moment, the kitchen is silent. The tension between us is thick, and I don't know what else to say. I know I'm not being entirely fair—Richard was just trying to help—but the anger won't go away.

"I'll cancel the meetings," he says quietly, his voice heavy with regret. "I'll fix it."

I nod but don't respond. The damage is done, and I don't know how to undo it.

Isabel

After Richard leaves, I feel a knot of guilt twist in my stomach. I know he didn't mean any harm, but that doesn't make it okay. I can't shake the feeling that getting involved with him will only complicate things for me and Mia.

Mia. She's the reason I've been so protective of everything I've built. Ever since I lost Mateo, I've been doing this alone, and I've been fine with that. I had to be. For Mia.

If I let someone like Richard into our lives, what happens if it all falls apart? What happens if he decides one day that he's had enough of small-town life and leaves? What happens to us then?

I close my eyes, pressing my palms against the cool countertop. I don't want Mia to get attached to him, to start seeing him as some kind of father figure, only to have him disappear when things get difficult.

I can't take that risk. Not for her.

I glance out the window, watching Mia play in the backyard, completely oblivious to the turmoil inside me. She deserves stability.

She deserves to have a life free of drama and complications. And I've promised myself that I'll protect her from anything that threatens that.

And right now, Richard King feels like a threat.

I have to keep my distance. For both of us.

Moments of Vulnerability

RICHARD

The charity event is in full swing. The estate grounds are filled with people from Maplewood Grove, all here for a good cause. But I can't focus on any of it. My mind is stuck on the argument I had with Isabel days ago.

I keep replaying it in my head, wondering where I went wrong. I thought I was helping, giving her opportunities, but clearly, I overstepped. And now I'm standing here, hosting an event I don't even care about, surrounded by people I don't really know, all while Isabel stays distant, doing her job with a professional smile, keeping me at arm's length.

I lean against one of the large oak trees on the edge of the lawn, watching her move through the crowd, greeting people and ensuring everything runs smoothly. She's incredible at what she does, but I can see the stiffness in her posture, the careful control in every word she says to me.

She's keeping herself closed off, and I can't blame her. I messed up, trying to fix things with money and contacts, thinking I knew what was best for her. The truth is, I didn't understand what she needed. I still don't.

I push away from the tree and wander toward the back of the estate, away from the crowd. I need space to think. I thought moving to this small town would give me a fresh start, help me find some clarity. But all I've done is complicate things.

I glance back at the people milling about, all of them here for a cause that's supposed to matter. I've donated money, organized events, done everything I could to make a difference. But none of it feels real.

The only thing that feels real is her.

I look at Isabel one last time, then head further into the garden, needing to escape the noise, the expectations. I've spent my whole life throwing money at problems, thinking I could fix everything with a check or a phone call. But none of that works here. Not with her.

I don't know what I'm doing anymore.

Isabel

The charity event is going smoothly—at least, on the surface. I'm moving through the crowd, keeping everything in order, making sure the guests are happy, the food is perfect, and the donations are flowing in. But my mind is elsewhere.

It's been days since the argument with Richard, and things have been... strained, to say the least. He's been polite, keeping his distance, but I can feel the tension every time we're in the same room. He doesn't push, but it's clear he wants to say something.

I've thrown myself into work, keeping the distance between us. It's safer that way—for me and for Mia. I don't want to get any closer to him than I already have. It's too risky. But the truth is, I haven't been able to stop thinking about him either.

I spot him across the lawn, standing alone near the back of the estate, watching the crowd. There's something about the way he's standing, something off. He looks... lost. For the first time, he doesn't seem like the confident, in-control billionaire I've come to know. He looks like a man who doesn't know what to do next.

Without thinking, I find myself walking toward him. Before I realize what I'm doing, I'm standing next to him in the quiet corner of the garden.

"Richard?"

He turns, surprised to see me, but quickly hides it with a smile. "Isabel. Everything's going well."

I cross my arms, studying him. "Is it?"

He hesitates, and for a moment, I think he's going to brush it off. But then, his shoulders sag slightly, and he looks away, out at the crowd.

"I'm trying," he says quietly. "But I don't know if it's enough."

I frown, taking a step closer. "What do you mean?"

He sighs, running a hand through his hair. "All of this... the events, the donations, the charity work... it's what I'm supposed to do. But it doesn't feel like it's making a difference. It doesn't feel real."

There's a rawness in his voice I haven't heard before, and it hits me in a way I didn't expect. He's always seemed so sure of himself, so in control. But now... now he just looks tired.

I take a deep breath, feeling my walls start to crack. "It's hard to make a difference when you're not sure what you're really fighting for."

He glances at me, his eyes searching mine. "What are you fighting for, Isabel?"

For a moment, I don't know how to answer. I've spent so long fighting for Mia, for our future, for this business. But right now, standing here with him, I realize there's something else, too. Something I haven't been willing to admit.

"Control," I finally say. "I'm fighting to stay in control of my life. Of everything. But it's exhausting."

Richard nods, his expression softening. "Yeah. I know the feeling."

The silence between us is heavy, but it's not uncomfortable. For the first time since I've known him, we're not at odds. We're just two people, standing in a garden, admitting that neither of us has it all figured out.

Isabel

The quiet stretches between us, and I don't know how to explain the pull I feel. Maybe it's because we're both trying so hard to hold onto things we can't control. Maybe it's because, for the first time in a long time, I don't feel like I have to be strong every second.

Richard looks at me, and there's something in his eyes that makes my breath catch. Vulnerability. And something else—a longing, maybe. Whatever it is, it makes my heart race in a way that scares me.

"I've been thinking about what you said," he says quietly. "About control. About... what I've been doing. I'm sorry, Isabel. I didn't mean to make things harder for you."

His apology is genuine, and it cuts through the walls I've tried to build. I shake my head, looking down at the grass beneath my feet. "I know you didn't. I just... I've had to be in control for so long. It's hard to let that go."

We're standing close now, closer than we've ever been, and I can feel the tension between us. But it's not the kind of tension that comes from anger or frustration. It's something else, something deeper.

Before I can stop myself, I look up at him, and for a moment, everything else fades away—the crowd, the noise, the expectations. It's just us.

"I don't want to mess this up," Richard whispers, his voice low and full of uncertainty.

"You won't," I reply, though my voice is barely more than a whisper. "I don't want to either."

The space between us shrinks, and before I can think about it, we're leaning closer, drawn together by something we can't control. His hand brushes my arm, sending a shiver down my spine. My heart pounds in my chest as I realize what's about to happen.

But just as our lips are about to meet, I pull back, my breath catching in my throat.

"I... I can't," I whisper, stepping away. My mind is spinning, my heart racing. This is too much, too fast. I can't let myself fall for him —not when everything is still so uncertain.

Richard blinks, surprised, but he doesn't push. He steps back too, nodding slowly, his expression soft. "I understand."

We stand there in silence for a few moments, the tension still thick in the air, but it's different now. Softer. There's no anger, no frustration. Just... uncertainty.

"I should get back to work," I finally say, my voice shaky.

"Yeah," he replies, his voice just as unsteady. "Me too."

I turn and walk away, my heart still pounding in my chest. I don't know what just happened between us, but I know one thing for sure: nothing between us will ever be the same.

The Family Crisis

ISABEL

The charity event is winding down, the last of the guests filtering out. I'm finishing up in the kitchen, packing up the leftovers and making a mental note of what needs to be cleaned in the morning. Mia has been playing in the garden for hours, running around the vast estate grounds, and I'm grateful she's had such a good time.

As I wipe down the counter, a strange feeling creeps over me. The house feels quieter than it should. The sounds of the event have died down, but there's something else—a sense of unease that makes me pause.

I glance out the window, expecting to see Mia's bright pink jacket darting around the yard, but I don't. The garden is still. Too still.

"Mia?" I call, my voice carrying out into the night air.

No response.

My heart skips a beat. I drop the dish towel and rush to the door, stepping outside and scanning the grounds. The garden stretches far beyond where I can see, but I can't make out her small figure anywhere.

"Mia!" I call again, louder this time.

Still nothing.

Panic starts to bloom in my chest. She's always stayed close when we're at events like this, and she knows not to wander off, especially at night. I rush down the stone steps and into the garden, my eyes darting around, my breathing growing quicker with every second that passes.

"Mia!"

I turn the corner of the estate, my heart hammering in my chest. The dim lights that line the path are barely enough to see by. Where could she have gone? My mind races with worst-case scenarios, and a cold sweat breaks out on the back of my neck.

Out of the corner of my eye, I see Richard approaching from the other side of the garden, his expression changing the moment he sees the look on my face.

"Isabel, what's wrong?" he asks, immediately concerned.

"Mia," I gasp, struggling to keep my voice steady. "I can't find Mia. She was playing in the garden, and now... she's gone."

Richard

As soon as I hear the panic in Isabel's voice, my chest tightens. Mia's missing.

I don't hesitate. I step closer, placing a hand on her shoulder. "We'll find her. She can't have gone far."

Isabel nods, but I can see the fear in her eyes, the barely-contained terror of a mother whose worst nightmare is unfolding. I've seen that look before. I've felt it myself when Beverly went missing for an hour after her mother's funeral, hiding away from the chaos. That fear never leaves you.

"Let's split up," I suggest, already moving toward the far end of the garden. "I'll check the back near the trees. You take the front by the fountain."

She hesitates, torn between wanting to search everywhere and staying close. "Okay," she finally says, her voice trembling.

I take off at a jog, scanning the shadows under the trees. My heart races as I call out Mia's name, my voice echoing through the still night air. She has to be here somewhere. This estate is massive, but it's fenced in. There's no way she could have gone far.

As I move further into the garden, I hear a faint sound—something soft, like crying. I stop, my breath catching in my throat.

"Mia?" I call gently, stepping toward the sound.

I round a tall hedge and see her, sitting on the ground, her knees pulled up to her chest, tears streaming down her face. Relief washes over me like a wave. She's safe.

"Mia," I say again, kneeling down in front of her. "Hey, it's okay. We've been looking for you. Your mom's worried sick."

She looks up at me, her little face tear-streaked. "I... I got lost. I didn't mean to."

I smile softly, reaching out to wipe away her tears. "I know. It's okay. Let's get you back to your mom, all right? She's been worried about you."

Mia nods, sniffling, and I stand, holding out my hand. She takes it, her grip tight, and I walk her back toward the house, my heart finally starting to calm down.

As we approach the main part of the garden, I see Isabel running toward us, her eyes wide with panic. The moment she sees Mia, her entire body sags with relief.

"Mia!" she cries, rushing forward and scooping her daughter into her arms. "Oh, thank God. I was so worried."

"I'm sorry, mamá," Mia sobs into her shoulder. "I got lost."

Isabel holds her tightly, kissing the top of her head, her tears mixing with Mia's. "It's okay, baby. It's okay. You're safe now."

I stand back, watching the scene unfold, feeling a strange mix of emotions—relief, gratitude, and something deeper. Something I can't quite put into words.

Isabel

I hold Mia so tight I'm afraid I'll never let go. The fear that gripped me when I couldn't find her is still thrumming through my veins, but now it's mixed with overwhelming relief. She's safe. She's here. And that's all that matters.

But as the adrenaline starts to fade, something else starts to bubble up inside me—guilt. Guilt for letting her out of my sight, for not paying closer attention. And... fear. Fear that I can't protect her from everything.

I glance up at Richard, who's standing a few feet away, watching us with a look of concern. He was the one who found her. He was the one who brought her back to me. And as much as I hate to admit it, I don't know what I would have done without him.

I take a shaky breath, still holding Mia, and look up at him. "Thank you," I say, my voice barely above a whisper. "Thank you for finding her."

He nods, his expression soft. "I'm just glad she's okay."

I swallow hard, the weight of everything pressing down on me. "I... I can't do this," I blurt out, surprising even myself with the admission.

Richard frowns, stepping closer. "What do you mean?"

Tears well up in my eyes again, and I can't stop them this time. "I can't keep pretending I've got it all together. I can't do this alone, Richard. I thought I could, but..."

I trail off, my voice breaking. It's all too much—raising Mia, running the business, trying to stay strong when all I want to do is fall apart.

Richard steps closer, his hand gently resting on my arm. "You're not alone, Isabel," he says quietly. "You don't have to do it all by yourself."

I shake my head, the tears falling freely now. "I don't know how to let anyone help me. I've been doing this on my own for so long, and... I'm afraid."

He looks at me, his eyes filled with understanding. "You don't have to be afraid. I'm here. And I'm not going anywhere."

His words cut through the fog of fear and guilt, and for the first time in a long time, I feel like maybe—just maybe—I don't have to carry the weight of the world on my shoulders anymore.

Without thinking, I step forward, wrapping my arms around him in a tight hug. He doesn't hesitate—he hugs me back, his warmth and strength grounding me, steadying me.

And in that moment, everything shifts. The walls I've built around myself start to crumble, and I realize that maybe, just maybe, I can let him in.

Building a Future Together

RICHARD

I sit in my office, staring down at the small wooden box in front of me. Inside is the gift I've been working on for the last few days, something that feels more personal than anything I've ever done. It's not the kind of gift I usually give. There's no price tag, no brand name attached to it. Just something from me.

I run my fingers over the smooth wood, feeling the weight of it. It's a simple thing, really—something I made for Mia. I've spent hours in the workshop, carving, sanding, and painting. It's a small toy chest, customized with her name and little flowers etched along the sides. I wanted to give her something that shows I'm not just here for Isabel, but for her too. That I want to be part of their lives, not with my money, but with my heart.

I take a deep breath, picking up the box. It's time.

Isabel and Mia are outside, sitting under the large oak tree in the garden. The evening sun is casting a warm glow over the estate, and there's a calmness in the air that I haven't felt in a long time. As I approach them, Mia looks up and waves excitedly, her face lighting up when she sees me.

"Hi, Richard!" she calls out, running over to meet me. "What's that?"

I kneel down, holding out the box. "This is for you, Mia. I made it myself."

Her eyes widen as she takes the box from my hands, running her fingers over the carved flowers. "You made this? For me?"

I nod, feeling a lump form in my throat. "Yeah. I thought you might like a place to keep your toys or your treasures. Something just for you."

She grins up at me, and I can see the joy in her eyes as she opens the box and peers inside. "It's beautiful! Thank you, Richard!"

Isabel watches us from where she's sitting under the tree, her expression soft but thoughtful. As Mia runs off to show the box to one of her friends, I turn to Isabel, feeling the weight of the moment settle between us.

"That was sweet," she says quietly, her eyes meeting mine.

"I wanted her to know that I'm not just here for you," I reply, my voice soft. "I'm here for her too. I want to be part of both your lives —if you'll let me."

Isabel's gaze holds mine for a long moment, and I can see the uncertainty, the vulnerability, but also the hope in her eyes. She takes a deep breath, nodding slowly. "We've come a long way, haven't we?"

"Yeah," I murmur, sitting down beside her under the tree. "And I don't want to stop now."

Isabel

I sit next to Richard under the oak tree, watching Mia run around with her new toy chest. It's small, just a simple wooden box, but it means so much more than that. It's Richard's way of saying he's not trying to buy his way into our lives. He's here for real—for me, for Mia, for whatever comes next.

I glance over at him, feeling the weight of the past few months pressing on me. So much has changed since he came into our lives. I never imagined I'd let someone in like this, never imagined I'd trust someone with my heart again after losing Mateo. But here we are, sitting under this tree, with the future stretched out in front of us like a blank canvas.

Richard's gaze is steady, his expression open, and I know he means what he says. He wants to be part of our lives, not by controlling things or throwing money at problems, but by being here, being present. And for the first time, I think I'm ready to let that happen.

"You know," Richard says after a moment, his voice low, "there's something else I've been thinking about."

I raise an eyebrow, curious. "Oh?"

"I want to help you grow your business," he says carefully. "Not by taking over or changing anything you don't want to change. But... what if we used the estate's grounds to host more events? You could expand the catering business, offer outdoor weddings, community gatherings, whatever you want. You'd have complete control."

I blink, surprised by the suggestion. I've been so focused on keeping things small, manageable, that the idea of expanding—especially using his estate—never crossed my mind. But now that he's mentioned it, I can see the potential. The estate's grounds are stunning, and it would be the perfect place to grow my business, all while staying true to what I've built.

"You're serious?" I ask, my voice soft.

"Completely," he replies, his gaze never leaving mine. "I want to support you, Isabel. I believe in what you're doing. And I want to do this the right way—on your terms."

A small smile tugs at my lips, and I feel the tightness in my chest begin to ease. He's not trying to take over or control anything. He's offering me the chance to grow, to take the next step. And for the first time, I realize that I'm ready to do that—with him by my side.

"I think that could be a good idea," I say, feeling a warmth spread through my chest. "But I want to take it slow. No rushing into anything."

"Of course," he agrees, his smile gentle. "We'll go at your pace."

I take a deep breath, feeling lighter than I have in a long time. This isn't just about the business or the estate. It's about the future we're building together—one step at a time.

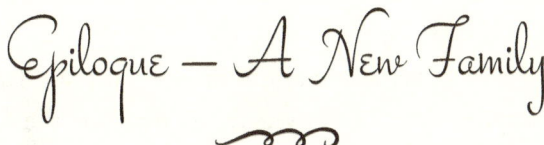

Epilogue — A New Family

ISABEL

The sun is setting over the estate, casting everything in a soft, golden light. Richard, Mia, and I are sitting on the back patio, surrounded by a small group of close friends and family. It's not a big gathering—just a simple, intimate dinner to celebrate the new chapter we're starting together.

Mia sits next to Richard, laughing as he helps her put together a small model airplane. She's been so happy these past few weeks, her smile coming more easily, her laughter filling the house. It's amazing to see how much she's changed, how much we've both changed.

I lean back in my chair, sipping a glass of iced tea, and glance over at Richard. He catches my eye, smiling that warm, genuine smile that always makes my heart skip a beat. There's something so peaceful about this moment, something that feels... right.

I never thought I'd be here—never thought I'd find someone who could love me, love Mia, and help us build a new life together. But Richard has proven, time and time again, that he's not going anywhere. He's here for the long haul, and I'm ready to take that step with him.

As the evening stretches on, the conversation quiets, and we all sit in comfortable silence, watching the stars begin to appear in the sky. Mia leans against Richard, her eyes growing heavy with sleep, and I smile at the sight.

This is what I've been searching for. Not perfection, not control, but peace. A family. A future.

Richard glances over at me again, his eyes soft and full of something I can't quite describe. Love. Trust. And for the first time, I don't feel the need to question it.

We've built something here—something strong, something real. And I know, deep in my heart, that whatever comes next, we'll face it together. As a family.

The End
Did you enjoy Isabel and Richard's story?
Consider reviewing it on Amazon, Goodreads or Bookbub. Reviews help me reach new readers.

Read **Rule #8 Love Isn't a Playbook**, the next story in the **Rules for Dating a Single Mom** series.

The book is also part of the **Maplewood Grove** series. Start the series with **Sweet Rivals**!

Get **bonus recipes** inspired by the characters — including empanadas, cupcakes, and small-town lemonade magic — delivered straight to your inbox!
Get it them here!
https://BookHip.com/CAZGFNQ
It's free, cozy, and tastes like love.

Sweet Return

A SMALL TOWN SECOND CHANCE ROMANCE

Coming Home

SHEILA

The silence hits me first.

Not the absence of sound—there's plenty of that in Maplewood Grove, where the streets are lined with trees and houses that actually have space between them. It's the absence of *urgency*. No helicopter rotors cutting through dawn. No radio static crackling with coordinates I need to memorize in three seconds flat. No boots hitting linoleum at a dead run because someone's dying and I'm the one who has to keep them breathing.

Just quiet. And my sister Grace humming something off-key in the kitchen while she makes what smells like her terrible attempt at cornbread.

I drop my duffel bag on the hardwood floor of her guest room—*their* guest room, I correct myself—and immediately feel guilty about the thud it makes. Grace and Tyler have been married eight months now, and I'm still getting used to the idea of my perpetually single sister being half of a couple. Especially a couple that seems genuinely happy, which shouldn't surprise me but somehow does.

Everything feels too loud when you've been living on high alert for two years straight. Even my own breathing sounds amplified in this space that smells like vanilla candles and the lavender detergent Grace has always been obsessed with.

The bed looks enormous. Queen-sized, with about six pillows arranged just so and a quilt that probably took someone's grandmother months to make. In Afghanistan, I slept on a cot that was barely wide enough for my shoulders, with a pillow that had seen better decades and the constant awareness that mortar fire could wake me at any moment.

This feels like luxury. It also feels wrong.

There's one face I still see every night when I close my eyes—a nineteen-year-old kid from Ohio who bled out faster than I could work. But I don't let myself think about that. Not here. Not in Grace's perfect guest room with its soft lighting and peaceful quiet.

"Sheila?" Grace's voice drifts down the hallway. "You settling in okay?"

I should answer. She's been nothing but kind since I called her three weeks ago and asked if I could crash at her place for a while. Didn't ask questions, didn't push for details about why I was suddenly discharged or why I couldn't face going back to Fort Belvoir to deal with my belongings in storage. Just said yes and started making plans to feed me, which is very Grace.

"Yeah," I call back, though my voice comes out rougher than intended. "Just unpacking."

Except I'm not unpacking. I'm standing in the middle of this perfect guest room staring at my duffel bag like it might explode. Everything I own fits in there—three sets of civilian clothes, my dress uniform I'll probably never wear again, a toiletry bag, and the medication bottles I'm trying not to think about.

Two years of my life, and it all fits in one bag.

Grace appears in the doorway, flour dusting her hands and that newlywed glow she's been carrying since the wedding. She's wearing Tyler's old Columbia University sweatshirt over leggings, her dark hair swept back in a messy bun. She looks settled in a way that makes something in my chest ache with longing.

"Tyler's picking up groceries for tomorrow," she says, leaning against the doorframe. "Maggie's coming for dinner, and Sam, and..." She pauses, studying my face. "Actually, there might be one more. Maggie mentioned something about her friend needing company for the holidays."

I manage a small smile. "You don't have to manage my social life, Grace."

"I'm not managing anything. I'm just... hoping you might want to be around people who care about you." She steps into the room, her eyes taking in my unopened bag and the way I'm standing like I'm still waiting for orders. "You don't have to perform for me, Sheila. You're home now."

Home. The word sits funny in my chest. I haven't had a home in so long I'm not sure I remember what it's supposed to feel like. The Army gave me purpose, structure, places to be useful. But home? Home requires something I'm not sure I have left to give.

I move to the window, drawn by the sound of a child's laughter from the yard next door. A little girl is raking leaves with her father, both of them bundled up in coats and scarves. Normal life happening at normal speed. The kind of scene that used to feel foreign but now just feels... impossible.

"Grace," I start, then stop. She's looking at me with those patient brown eyes that have been seeing through my bullshit since I was twelve. "I don't know how to do this."

"Do what?"

"Be here. Be still. Be normal." I turn away from the window and the happy family outside. "For two years, every single day was about keeping people alive. Making split-second decisions that meant someone got to go home to their family or they didn't. And I was good at it, Grace. I was really good at it."

She moves closer, and I catch the scent of vanilla and flour that clings to her clothes. "I know you were."

"But I can't anymore." The words come out in a rush, like they've been building pressure for months. "The last month over there, I couldn't sleep. Couldn't eat. Couldn't make my hands stop shaking during procedures. And I kept thinking, what if I mess up? What if someone dies because I'm falling apart?"

The kid from Ohio flashes through my mind again—Jeremy Martinez, age nineteen, who wanted to be a teacher when he got home. I force the image away.

Grace is quiet for a long moment, just watching me with that steady attention that makes me feel seen without feeling judged.

"So you came home," she says finally.

"So I came home." I sit down hard on the edge of the bed, and it's so soft I almost bounce. "Except I don't know how to be a person who's not needed every second of every day. I don't know how to care about things like what to have for dinner or whether I should buy new shoes. It all feels meaningless when I know what real stakes look like."

Grace moves to sit beside me on the bed, her presence warm and solid. "You're not an asshole for feeling that way, Sheila. You're tired. And you're allowed to be tired."

I want to lean into her, to let myself be the little sister for once instead of the one who's always had to be strong. But I can't seem to make my body relax enough to accept comfort. Everything in me is still braced for the next emergency.

"Tell me about married life," I say instead, needing to shift focus to something that doesn't involve my broken brain. "Tyler treating you right?"

Grace's face transforms the way it always does when someone mentions her husband. "He's wonderful, Sheila. Really wonderful. Patient and funny, and he makes me feel like I can be completely myself." She pauses, a soft smile playing at her lips. "Remember how I used to overthink everything? Plan out every conversation before I had it?"

I nod. Grace has always been the careful one, the sister who made pros and cons lists for everything.

"With Tyler, I don't have to do that. I can just... be. And somehow that's enough."

There's something in her voice—a contentment I've never heard from her before. It should make me happy, and part of me is. But mostly it makes me aware of how empty I feel, how disconnected from the possibility of that kind of peace.

"I'm glad," I say, and I mean it even if I can't quite feel it. "You deserve that."

Grace studies my face for a moment, and I can practically see her trying to figure out how to help me without overwhelming me. It's such a Grace thing to do—always looking for ways to fix things, to make people comfortable.

"The friend Maggie mentioned," she says carefully. "He's... well, he's having a rough time too. Different reasons but, sometimes it helps to be around people who understand that not everything has to be okay all the time."

Something about the way she says it makes me look at her more closely. "What kind of rough time?"

"Accident in his workshop. Hurt his hands pretty badly. He's been..." She searches for words. "Isolated. Stubborn about accepting help."

I feel a flicker of something—not quite interest, but maybe recognition. Someone else who's used to being capable and suddenly isn't. Someone else who doesn't know how to ask for things from other people.

"What's his name?"

"Jasper. Jasper Finch." Grace stands and brushes imaginary wrinkles from Tyler's sweatshirt. "You don't have to meet him if you don't want to. No pressure. But Maggie's worried about him, and I thought maybe..."

She doesn't finish the sentence, but I can fill in the blanks. She thought maybe two broken people could help each other somehow. It's the kind of gentle matchmaking that would normally make me roll my eyes, but right now it just makes me tired.

"We'll see," I say.

After Grace leaves to check on whatever's burning in the kitchen, I sit in the quiet of the guest room and try to imagine tomorrow. Sitting around a table with people I barely know, making small talk about their lives and their jobs, and their plans for the future. Pretending to be someone who has opinions on stuffing recipes and football games.

And maybe meeting someone else who's hiding from the world.

I open my duffel bag and start pulling things out, not because I'm ready to settle in but because I need something to do with my hands. The routine of folding clothes and organizing toiletries is familiar, even if everything else feels foreign.

At the bottom of the bag, my fingers find the small leather journal I've been carrying for months but never writing in. I bought it thinking I might want to process some of what I was seeing and doing. But every time I opened it, the blank pages felt like they were asking questions I didn't know how to answer.

Now I set it on the nightstand and stare at it for a moment before turning away.

Outside the window, the little girl and her father have moved on, leaving behind neat piles of colorful leaves. The yard looks peaceful, tidy. Like someone cares enough to maintain it.

Maybe Grace is right. Maybe I just need time to remember how to exist in a world where not everything is life or death. And maybe meeting someone else who's struggling with his own version of that will help somehow.

Or maybe it'll just be another person I don't know how to connect with, another conversation I have to fake my way through.

But sitting here in this comfortable room with its soft bed and peaceful quiet, I can't shake the feeling that I want to feel useful again. Not in the life-or-death way, but in some smaller, gentler way that doesn't require me to be perfect or brave or unbreakable.

Maybe that's what I'm really looking for. Not rest, exactly, but a way to matter that doesn't cost me everything I have to give.

Tomorrow I'll meet Tyler's friends and try to be the kind of person who can enjoy Thanksgiving dinner conversation. I'll smile and ask appropriate questions, and maybe, if I'm lucky, I'll find someone who understands what it's like to be lost in your own life.

But tonight, I'm going to lie in this too-soft bed and listen to the silence and try not to count all the ways I don't fit anywhere anymore.

Thanksgiving Plans

JASPER

The doorbell rings at exactly eleven-thirty, which means it's either Maggie Foster or the universe playing a joke I'm not in the mood for. I consider not answering, but she's persistent enough to stand there ringing until my neighbors start complaining, and I've already caused enough talk in this town.

I push back from my workbench—carefully, because everything takes twice as long when your hands are wrapped like a mummy's—and make my way to the front door. The gauze catches on the doorknob as I try to turn it, and I have to bite back a curse that would make my mother roll over in her grave.

"Jasper Finch, I know you're in there." Maggie's voice carries through the door, warm but determined. "I brought soup."

Of course she did. In the week since my workshop decided to explode on me, half the town has shown up with casseroles and well-meaning advice about how I should be taking better care of myself. What they don't understand is that I was taking perfectly good care of myself before some faulty wiring decided to turn my latest invention into a small bomb.

I manage to get the door open, and Maggie's standing there with a thermos in one hand and that look on her face—the one that says she's already made decisions about my life that I'm not going to like.

"You look terrible," she says, pushing past me into the living room.

"Good morning to you too, Maggie."

She sets the thermos on my coffee table and turns to survey the disaster that is my house. Newspapers scattered everywhere because I can't hold them properly to read. Empty takeout containers stacked on every surface because cooking requires fine motor skills I don't currently possess. A pile of mail I can't open sitting by the door like a monument to my incompetence.

"When's the last time you showered?" she asks.

"I shower." It's technically true. I stand under hot water and let it run over me, though shampooing is pretty much impossible and shaving is completely out of the question. The scraggly beard I'm sporting makes me look like a hermit, which maybe isn't inaccurate.

"Jasper." Maggie sits down on my couch and looks at me with the kind of patient expression that usually precedes someone trying to manage my life. "You can't keep living like this."

"It's temporary." I hold up my bandaged hands. "Dr. Martinez says another two weeks and I should have most of my dexterity back."

"Two weeks of eating nothing but Chinese takeout and avoiding human contact?"

"I'm not avoiding human contact. You're here, aren't you?"

She gives me a look that suggests this interaction doesn't count as meaningful socialization, which is probably fair. I haven't exactly been charming company lately.

"Grace and Tyler are having Thanksgiving dinner tomorrow," she says, and I already don't like where this is going. "Small group. Just family and a few friends."

"Have fun with that."

"You're invited."

"No."

"Jasper—"

"No, Maggie." I move away from her, pacing to the window that looks out over my backyard. The workshop is still there, looking innocuous now that I've cleaned up the burnt wreckage of what was supposed to be a self-warming lantern for elderly residents. Three months of work, gone in thirty seconds of spectacular failure. "I'm not showing up to someone's Thanksgiving dinner looking like a vagrant and needing help cutting my turkey."

"So you're planning to spend the holiday alone, eating lo mein with chopsticks you can barely hold?"

The accuracy of that assessment is uncomfortable. "My plans are my business."

"Your plans are terrible." She stands up and joins me at the window, her voice gentling slightly. "Look, I get it. You're proud, you're independent, you don't like asking for help. But this isn't about pride anymore, Jasper. This is about being human."

I want to argue with her, but the truth is I haven't felt particularly human lately. More like a broken machine that someone forgot to repair. Before the accident, my days had structure, purpose. I'd wake up, work on whatever project was currently consuming my attention, maybe walk into town for supplies or groceries. Simple routines that made sense.

Now I wake up and stare at my hands until the pain medication kicks in. Then I sit in my living room and try to remember what I used to care about.

"There's someone I'd like you to meet," Maggie continues, and there's something in her tone that puts me on alert.

"No."

"Her name is Sheila. She's Grace's sister, just back from overseas. Military nurse."

"Absolutely not."

"She's been through some things. Could probably use a friend who understands what it's like to feel disconnected from everything."

I turn to stare at her. "Are you seriously trying to set me up right now? While I'm temporarily disabled and living like a hermit?"

"I'm not setting you up." But there's a flush in her cheeks that suggests otherwise. "I'm just thinking that sometimes when we're struggling, it helps to be around other people who get it."

"Maggie." I keep my voice very calm, very patient. "I appreciate your concern. I do. But I am not going to be your charity case Thanksgiving guest, and I'm certainly not going to be anyone's rehabilitation project."

"That's not what this is about."

"Isn't it?" I gesture around the disaster of my living room with one bandaged hand. "Look at me. Look at this place. What exactly am I supposed to contribute to someone's nice family dinner? Colorful stories about electrical fires? Tips on how to eat soup when you can't grip the spoon properly?"

Maggie is quiet for a long moment, studying my face with the kind of attention that makes me uncomfortable. She's always been good at seeing through people's bullshit, which is probably why she's managed to talk half the town into participating in her various community projects over the years.

"You know what I think?" she says finally.

"I'm sure you're going to tell me."

"I think you're afraid of being seen as less than perfect."

The words hit differently than I expected. Not harder, exactly, but more precisely. Because she's not wrong—I've spent the last ten years being the go-to guy for everything from furnace repairs to custom shelving and garage door opener troubleshooting. Being useful has become who I am.

"And what's wrong with wanting to be capable?"

"Nothing, when it comes from the right place. But when it comes from thinking you don't have value unless you're fixing everyone else's problems..." She shrugs. "That's not capability. That's hiding."

"I don't need—"

"Everyone needs, Jasper. That's what makes us human."

I turn away from her and walk back toward my workbench, where the remnants of my latest failed project sit like an accusation. Twisted metal and scorched wiring that were once something useful, something that might have helped people. Now it's just expensive garbage.

"The nurse," I say without looking at her. "What's wrong with her?"

"Nothing's wrong with her. She's just... tired. Really tired, in the way that happens when you've given everything you have to give and there's nothing left."

I know that feeling. Not from military service, but from the two years I spent trying to keep my father's electronics repair business running while watching him die by inches. He'd built that shop with his own hands, taught half the town how to fix their radios and televisions, and later their computers. When the Alzheimer's started taking him, I thought I could honor that by keeping it going.

Turns out there's a difference between fixing things because you love the work and fixing things because someone else's legacy depends on it. The exhaustion that comes from carrying someone else's dreams—it goes bone-deep, makes everything feel impossible even when it shouldn't be.

"She doesn't want to be set up either, does she?"

"Probably not." Maggie's voice carries a smile. "But maybe two people who don't want to be set up can just enjoy a nice dinner and some decent conversation. No expectations, no pressure. Just... company."

I pick up a piece of the ruined lantern, turning it over in my bandaged fingers. Before the accident, I could have had this rebuilt in a week. Now I can barely hold it without dropping it.

"I look like hell, Maggie. And I smell like antiseptic and failure."

"So take a shower. I'll help you wash your hair if you need it."

The offer is made so matter-of-factly that it doesn't even register as embarrassing until a few seconds later. That's Maggie—practical to the point of being utterly unsentimental about things that would make other people squeamish.

"You don't have to do that."

"I know I don't have to. I'm offering because you're my friend and you need help, and there's no shame in either of those things."

I set the piece of metal back on the workbench and really look at her for the first time since she arrived. Maggie's gotten happier since she and Sam got back together—there's a lightness in her eyes that wasn't there before, a sense of settledness that makes her seem more like herself somehow.

"You're not going to let this go, are you?"

"Not a chance."

I sigh, feeling the fight go out of me. Maybe it would be nice to spend a few hours with people. Maybe it would be good to remember what normal conversation sounds like, what it feels like to sit at a table with food I didn't order from a menu.

And maybe this Sheila person will be as uninterested in socializing as I am, and we can just sit quietly and avoid each other while everyone else enjoys their holiday.

"Fine," I say. "But I'm not staying long. And if anyone tries to make a big deal about me being there, I'm leaving."

"Deal." Maggie grins like she's won something important. "Dinner's at four. I'll pick you up at three-thirty."

"I can drive myself."

"With those hands? I don't think so."

She's probably right, though I hate admitting it. Simple things like gripping a steering wheel and working the turn signals are still beyond me.

"What should I bring?" I ask, because my mother raised me with manners, even if I've been ignoring them lately.

"Just yourself. Cleaned up, preferably."

After she leaves, I stand in my living room and try to remember the last time I looked forward to anything. It's been months, maybe longer. Even before the accident, my life had fallen into a routine that was more about maintaining than actually living.

Work on projects. Eat when I remember to. Sleep when exhaustion finally wins.

Rinse and repeat.

Not exactly what anyone would call a full life. But it was *my* life, built around work that felt meaningful because I chose it. After I finally closed Dad's shop—after I admitted I wasn't him and never would be—I thought I'd found my way to something that was mine. Turns out losing the use of your hands puts a real damper on being an inventor.

I look around at the mess I've been living in—the newspapers, the takeout containers, the general air of neglect—and feel something that might be shame. This isn't who I used to be. Before my father got sick, before I inherited a business I didn't want and responsibilities I couldn't escape, I used to care about things like keeping my house clean and wearing shirts that weren't wrinkled.

Maybe Maggie's right. Maybe it's time to remember how to be human.

I walk to the bathroom and stare at myself in the mirror. The man looking back at me is a stranger—hollow-eyed, scruffy, wearing the same flannel shirt I've had on for three days. My hair is sticking up at odd angles, and there are dark circles under my eyes that make me look like I haven't slept in weeks.

Which isn't far from the truth.

Tomorrow I'll sit at Grace and Tyler's table and try to make conversation with people I barely know. I'll probably spill something on myself, struggle to cut my food, and generally make everyone uncomfortable with my helplessness.

But maybe that's okay. Maybe being helpless for a while is part of learning how to be helped.

And maybe this tired nurse who understands about giving everything you have until there's nothing left—maybe she'll understand that too.

First Meeting

SHEILA

I sit in Grace's car in their driveway for a full minute after returning from picking up last minute groceries, trying to work up the nerves to go inside where the dinner party is already underway. The windows are golden with warm light, and I can hear laughter drifting from inside—the kind of easy, comfortable sound that happens when people genuinely enjoy each other's company.

It should make me happy. Instead, it makes me feel like an imposter preparing to crash a party I don't belong at.

A knock on the driver's seat window startles me. "You coming in?" Maggie asks. She's bundled up in a jacket patiently waiting for me to get out of the car.

"Yeah." I unbuckle my seatbelt and grab the bottle of wine I picked up—something to contribute, something to do with my hands. "Just... preparing myself."

"For what?"

I look at the house again, at the warm light and the sounds of people being normal together. "For pretending I know how to be around people anymore."

Maggie opens the car door for me. She's pretty in that under-stated small-town way, with kind eyes and an air of quiet competence that reminds me a little of the nurses I worked with who'd been doing it long enough to stay calm in any crisis.

"Sheila," she says, and there's something in her voice that makes me actually listen instead of just waiting for her to finish talking. "Nobody in there is expecting you to perform. Grace just wants you fed and comfortable. Tyler wants to meet the sister that Grace talks about constantly. Sam and I are happy to have new people to talk to who aren't involved in festival politics."

"And Jasper?"

A small smile tugs at her lips. "Jasper doesn't want to be there any more than you do. Which means you're probably the two people in that room who'll understand each other best."

Before I can ask what she means by that, she's heading for the house. I follow her up the walkway, my boots crunching on the fallen leaves that Tyler apparently hasn't had time to rake yet. The house is a small craftsman-style with a wide front porch and window boxes that still hold the remnants of fall flowers.

Grace appears from the kitchen as we come through the front door, and the warmth that hits me isn't just from the temperature difference. It's the smell of roasted turkey and sage, the sound of a football game playing quietly in the background, the sight of my sister in an apron that says "Thankful" in elaborate script.

Grace must see the panic in my eyes, because she pulls me into a side hug and whispers "Don't be overwhelmed, it's just friends and family." Before I can react, she's grabbing bags from Maggie and asking her to taste the gravy.

The living room flows into the dining area, which opens to the kitchen—one of those layouts that's supposed to make everything feel connected and communal. Right now, with five people already there, it feels like a lot of humanity in a small space.

Tyler appears from the kitchen, wiping his hands on a dish towel.

He's taller than I expected, with dark hair and the kind of smile that reaches his eyes. The kind of man who clearly adores my sister and doesn't mind showing it.

"Ready to meet everyone?" he asks, wiping his hands on a dish towel. He's been nothing but welcoming since I arrived last week, giving me space when I need it and including me in conversations when I seem ready for company. "As ready as I'll ever be," I say, adjusting the wine bottle in my hands.

He gently takes the bottle from me. "You're going to be great. Besides, Grace has been planning this menu for weeks. She's been looking for an excuse to make your grandmother's cornbread stuffing."

A man, I assume, is Sam emerges from what looks like the den, beer in hand, and the relaxed posture of someone completely at home. He's got sandy hair and laugh lines around his eyes, and when Maggie introduces us, his handshake is warm and uncomplicated.

"Sam Walker," he says. "Maggie's told me you're just back from overseas. Army?"

"Army Nurse Corps," I confirm, bracing for the usual follow-up questions about where I was stationed and what I saw and whether I'm glad to be back.

Instead, he just nods. "My cousin did two tours in Iraq. Says the best part of coming home was sleeping through the night again."

It's such a simple, understanding comment that I feel some of the tension in my shoulders ease. Not everyone needs the whole story.

And then I see Jasper.

He's sitting in an armchair near the fireplace, slightly apart from the main conversation area. Dark hair that's a little too long, scruff that suggests he hasn't been shaving regularly, and hands wrapped in gauze bandages that he's trying to keep inconspicuous. He's wearing a flannel shirt that's clean but wrinkled, and jeans that have seen better days.

He looks like a man who's been having a rough time of it.

When our eyes meet across the room, there's a moment of mutual assessment. I see someone who's here under duress, who'd rather be anywhere else, who's probably counting the minutes until he can politely escape. Someone who understands what it's like to be managing something difficult while everyone around you tries to help in ways that don't actually help.

He gives me the smallest nod—not unfriendly, just acknowledgment that we're both enduring this together.

"Jasper," Maggie says, drawing him into the introductions, "this is Sheila, Grace's sister. Sheila, meet Jasper Finch. He's our local inventor and the reason half the town has the most creative holiday decorations you've ever seen."

Jasper shifts in his chair, as if he's uncomfortable with the praise. "Nice to meet you," he says, and his voice is quieter than I expected. Rough around the edges but not unkind.

"You too."

Tyler claps his hands together. "Alright, everyone, dinner's ready. Sheila, can I get you something to drink? Wine, beer, cider?"

"Wine would be great."

The dining table is set for six, with mismatched chairs that somehow work together and candles that cast a warm glow over everything. Grace has gone all out—there's the turkey, obviously, but also mashed potatoes, green bean casserole, cranberry sauce, and rolls that smell like they came straight from heaven.

I end up seated across from Jasper, which gives me a clear view of how carefully he's managing his bandaged hands. He's trying to be subtle about it, but I notice the way he positions his water glass closer to his right hand, the way he waits a beat longer than everyone else before reaching for the serving dishes.

"So Sheila," Tyler says as we start passing food around, "Grace mentioned you're thinking about what comes next. Any ideas yet?"

It's a kind question, the sort of thing people ask when they're genuinely interested but not prying. Unfortunately, it's also the question I've been avoiding thinking about for weeks.

"Not really," I say, accepting the bowl of mashed potatoes from Sam. "I'm still in the figuring-it-out phase."

"That's fair," Maggie says. "Sometimes you need time to just be before you can decide what you want to do."

Across from me, I catch Jasper trying to grip the serving spoon for the green beans. His bandaged fingers can't quite manage it, and I watch him pause, jaw tightening slightly with frustration.

Without thinking, I reach across and take the spoon from him, serving myself a portion before setting it down closer to his plate. "Those look great," I say casually, like I haven't just helped him. "Grace, did you make them from scratch?"

"Tyler did, actually," Grace says, beaming at her husband. "He's got this whole system with almonds and bacon that's completely addictive."

Jasper glances at me, and there's something in his expression that might be gratitude, though it's carefully controlled. He doesn't say anything, but when I pass him the rolls a few minutes later, he murmurs a quiet "thanks" that feels like it means more than just the bread.

The conversation flows around us—stories about Tyler's work, updates on festival planning, gentle teasing between Sam and Maggie that suggests they're still in the honeymoon phase of whatever they have going on. It's comfortable in the way that comes from people who genuinely like each other, and I find myself relaxing despite my earlier anxiety.

Until Grace starts clearing plates and insists that everyone stay seated while she and Tyler handle dessert.

"Absolutely not," Maggie protests, standing up. "You cooked, we clean."

"I'll help," I say, already reaching for empty serving dishes.

"You're guests," Grace argues, but Sam is already stacking plates, and Tyler is waving us all toward the kitchen.

"Too many cooks," Tyler says cheerfully, "but we'll make it work."

In the shuffle of clearing the table, I end up in the kitchen at the same time as Jasper, who's trying to rinse his water glass one-handed at the sink. It's not going well—the glass keeps slipping, and he's gripping it so tightly with his functioning fingers that I'm genuinely worried he's going to break it.

"Here," I say quietly, moving to stand beside him. "Let me."

He tenses, and for a second, I think he's going to refuse. But then he steps back and lets me take the glass, watching as I rinse it quickly and set it in the drying rack.

"I used to be able to do simple things," he says, so quietly I almost don't hear him over the sound of conversation from the dining room.

"You still can," I tell him, drying my hands on the dish towel. "You're just temporarily inconvenienced."

He looks at me as if trying to determine whether I'm being condescending or genuinely matter-of-fact.

"I'm a nurse," I add. "I've seen a lot of people struggle with temporary limitations. The keyword is temporary."

"How temporary?"

I glance at his bandages, taking in the way they're wrapped and the slight stiffness in his movement. "What degree burns?"

"Second. Both hands. Some fingers are worse than others."

"How long ago?"

"About ten days."

I nod, mental calculations running automatically. "Another week, maybe two, and you'll have most of your dexterity back. Full healing in a month if you don't push it too hard."

For the first time since I met him, Jasper's expression softens slightly. Not into a smile, but into something less guarded.

"Dr. Martinez said six weeks."

"Dr. Martinez is being conservative, which is smart. But I've treated a lot of burn patients." I lean against the counter, keeping my voice low so the others won't overhear. "The hardest part is the waiting. Feeling useless while your body does what it needs to do."

He studies my face for a moment, and I have the strangest feeling that he's seeing something in me that I haven't said out loud.

"Is that what you're doing?" he asks. "Waiting for your body to do what it needs to do?"

The question catches me off guard. Not because it's inappropriate, but because it's unexpectedly perceptive.

"Something like that," I admit.

We stand there for a moment in oddly comfortable silence, the sound of the others cleaning up around us fading into background noise. There's something about Jasper that doesn't require performance—no need to smile when I don't feel like it or make conversation to fill the space.

"Sheila," Grace calls from the dining room, "do you want coffee or tea with dessert?"

"Coffee," I call back, but I don't immediately move to rejoin the group.

"I should probably go," Jasper says, glancing toward the door.

"Probably," I agree. "But you don't have to."

He looks at me questioningly.

"I mean, if you want to leave, leave. But if you're just leaving because you think you should, or because you don't want to be a bother..." I shrug. "You're not bothering anyone. And from what I can tell, we're both pretty good at enduring things we don't particularly want to do."

The corner of his mouth twitches—not quite a smile, but close.

"Besides," I add, lowering my voice to a conspiratorial whisper, "I heard Grace mention pie, and I'm pretty sure if we both disappear now, we'll never hear the end of it."

This time, he does smile, just a little. "Apple or pumpkin?"

"Both, apparently. Tyler's been bragging about his crust technique all week."

"Well," Jasper says, and there's something almost playful in his voice, "I suppose I can suffer through some pie."

"Very noble of you."

When we rejoin the others, the conversation has moved on to holiday plans and the upcoming Christmas festival. I settle back into my seat and notice that Jasper seems slightly less tense than he did before. When Tyler brings out two perfect pies and starts cutting generous slices, Jasper doesn't protest when I quietly switch our plates so he gets the piece that'll be easier to manage.

He doesn't thank me, but when our eyes meet across the table, there's an understanding there that feels like the beginning of something I can't quite name yet.

Later, after helping with dishes and saying goodnight to everyone, I sit in the guest room and realize that for the first time since coming home, I made it through an entire evening without thinking about Jeremy Martinez or counting the ways I don't fit anywhere.

Maybe that's progress. Or maybe it's just what happens when you meet someone who understands what it's like to feel temporarily broken without needing to fix it right away.

Either way, it was better than I expected.

And tomorrow, if Grace has her way, I'll probably see Jasper again.

I'm not sure yet how I feel about that. But for tonight, it's enough that I'm curious to find out.

Routine and Resistance

JASPER

I'VE BEEN DREADING this for two days.

Ever since Grace called on Friday morning with her carefully casual suggestion—"Sheila's between things right now, and you're supposed to be changing your dressings every day. You need someone who knows what they're doing,"—and by the time I could object, they'd apparently already coordinated a time, I've been bracing for this moment like it's a dental procedure.

It's not that I don't appreciate the offer. My attempts at changing my own bandages have been exercises in frustration and medical futility. The gauze ends up too loose or too tight, the antiseptic gets everywhere except where it's supposed to go, and I can't properly assess whether anything looks like it's healing or getting infected.

But there's something uniquely humbling about having a stranger come to your house to perform basic care tasks you should be able to manage yourself.

Especially when that stranger is someone who looked at you across a dinner table and seemed to understand exactly how much you hate needing help.

I've spent the morning cleaning. Well, attempting to clean. The living room is marginally less disastrous than it was yesterday, though I had to give up on vacuuming when I couldn't grip the handle properly. The kitchen counter is clear of takeout containers, and I managed to wash the dishes by sheer stubborn determination and a lot of careful maneuvering.

Now I'm sitting in my kitchen, staring at the medical supplies Dr. Martinez sent home with me—sterile gauze, antiseptic solution, medical tape—and trying not to think about how pathetic it is that I need someone else to use them on me.

At exactly ten o'clock, there's a knock on my door.

No, not a knock. Two quick raps, followed by the sound of the door opening.

"It's Sheila," her voice calls from the entryway. "Hope you don't mind. I figured knocking and waiting would just give you time to pretend you weren't home."

Despite myself, I almost smile. She's not wrong.

"Kitchen," I call back, because there's no point in pretending this isn't happening.

She appears in the doorway carrying a small canvas bag, wearing jeans and a gray sweater that makes her dark hair look almost black. No makeup that I can tell, no effort to dress up for a medical house call. Practical boots, sleeves already pushed up to her elbows like she's ready to get to work.

"How are the hands feeling today?" she asks, setting her bag on the counter and washing her hands at the sink without being asked.

"Stiff. Tender around the worst spots."

"That's normal." She dries her hands on the clean dish towel I left out and turns to look at me properly. "Any increased pain, unusual discharge, fever?"

"No."

"Good." She gestures to the kitchen table. "Sit down and let me see what we're working with."

I sit, trying not to feel like a child being managed, and extend my hands. She takes the chair across from me and begins unwrapping the gauze, her movements quick and sure. Her touch is gentle but impersonal—the kind of careful handling that comes from years of practice, not from any particular concern for my comfort.

Which is exactly what I need, though I hadn't realized it until now.

"These are healing well," she says, examining the burns on my palms and fingers. The skin is still angry red in places, with patches of new pink tissue growing in around the edges. It looks better than it did a week ago, but it still looks like something that shouldn't belong to me. "No signs of infection. You've been keeping them clean?"

"As best I can."

"That's good enough." She reaches for the antiseptic solution. "This might sting a little."

It does sting, but not as much as I expected. She works efficiently, cleaning each area with careful attention before applying fresh gauze. Her hands are steady, competent, and she doesn't wince or make sympathetic noises when she gets to the worst spots.

"You're good at this," I say, more to fill the silence than because it needs saying.

"I should be. I did it for two years straight under considerably less ideal conditions."

There's something in her voice—not bitterness, exactly, but a kind of matter-of-fact acknowledgment that she's seen things I haven't. It makes me curious about what those conditions were, but I don't ask. If she wanted to tell me, she would.

"There," she says, securing the last piece of medical tape. "That should hold for about twenty-four hours. I can come back tomorrow, or you can try managing it yourself if you're feeling ambitious."

The smart thing would be to say I can handle it myself. To thank her politely and send her on her way so I can go back to managing my temporary disability in private.

Instead, I hear myself saying, "Tomorrow works."

She nods like this was the expected answer. "Same time?"

"Sure."

I expect her to pack up her supplies and leave, but instead she glances around the kitchen and frowns slightly.

"When's the last time you had a proper meal?"

"I've been eating."

"Takeout doesn't count as proper." She moves to the refrigerator and opens it, taking inventory of the sad collection of condiments and expired leftovers inside. "Do you have anything that resembles actual food?"

"I have... cereal."

She looks at me like I've just confessed to living on sawdust.

"Okay," she says, closing the refrigerator door. "I'm making you eggs and toast. Don't argue with me about it."

"I don't need—"

"You don't need charity, I know. But you do need protein, and I need something to do with my hands for ten minutes. So we're both getting what we need."

There's something about the way she says it—practical, unromantic, like she's solving a problem rather than doing me a favor—that makes it impossible to object. I sit at the table and watch her move around my kitchen with surprising familiarity, finding the eggs and bread, locating a pan and a spatula.

"How do you like your eggs?"

"Scrambled is fine."

She cracks four eggs into the pan and starts them cooking, adding a pinch of salt and pepper from the shakers I didn't even know I had. The toast goes into the toaster, and she puts the kettle on for tea without asking if I want any.

It's been so long since someone moved around my kitchen like this—with purpose, making decisions, creating something from nothing—that I find myself just watching her work. There's something soothing about the routine domesticity of it, the simple competence of someone who knows how to take care of things.

"You don't have to do this," I say.

"I know." She plates the eggs and butters the toast, setting everything in front of me before making herself a cup of tea. "But you need to eat real food, and I'm between jobs and bored out of my mind. So this is as much for me as it is for you."

She sits across from me with her tea, not eating herself but not hovering either. Just present, keeping me company while I eat the first home-cooked food I've had in over a week.

"It's good," I tell her, because it is.

"It's eggs and toast. Hard to mess up."

"Still."

We sit in comfortable silence for a few minutes, her hands wrapped around her mug, steam rising between us. There's something peaceful about it—no pressure to make conversation, no need to fill the quiet with pleasantries.

I didn't expect to want her to stay. And I definitely didn't expect her making eggs in my kitchen to feel like the first quiet moment I've had in weeks.

"Can I ask you something?" she says eventually.

I tense slightly. "Sure."

"What were you working on when the accident happened?"

It's not the question I expected, and it takes me a moment to decide how to answer.

"A heating device," I say finally. "For elderly residents. Something they could use on their porches or in their garages when the weather gets cold. Self-contained, energy efficient. Safe."

"What went wrong?"

"Faulty wiring in the heating coil. Created a feedback loop that turned the whole thing into a small bomb." I set down my fork, my appetite suddenly gone. "Three months of work, and it nearly burned my house down."

She doesn't offer sympathy or reassurance, nor does she tell me that these things happen or that I'll figure it out next time. She just nods, like this is useful information she's filing away for later.

"Can I see it?"

I stare at her. "What?"

"The workshop. Where it happened, I'm curious about what you were building."

Every instinct I have tells me to say no. The workshop is my private disaster zone, the place where my competence failed spectacularly. It smells like burnt wiring and disappointment, and it's full of half-finished projects that remind me of everything I can't do right now.

But there's something about the way she asks—not like she's looking for evidence of my failure, but like she's genuinely interested in understanding what I was trying to accomplish.

"Okay," I say. "But it's a mess."

"I've seen worse."

I lead her through the back door to the converted garage that serves as my workshop. She follows me inside, taking in the organized chaos of workbenches and tool racks, half-built inventions and salvaged electronics. The air still carries a faint smell of smoke, and there's a scorched area on the main workbench where the lantern exploded.

But she doesn't focus on the damage. Instead, she moves to examine some of my finished pieces—a self-watering planter system, a motion-activated bird feeder, a series of LED lanterns powered by small solar panels.

"These are beautiful," she says, picking up one of the lanterns and turning it over in her hands. "Did you make all of this?"

"Most of it."

"It's like functional art."

There's something in her voice—not just politeness, but genuine appreciation. Like she understands what I was trying to create here, even if the latest attempt went catastrophically wrong.

"The heating device," I say, gesturing toward the scorched workbench, "it was supposed to be simple. Just a small, portable unit that seniors could use when they needed a little extra warmth. Nothing fancy, nothing complicated. But I couldn't get the temperature regulation right, and when I tried to fix it..."

"It fought back."

"Something like that."

She sets the lantern down carefully and looks around the workshop again, taking inventory of the tools and materials, the works in progress.

"You'll figure it out," she says, and it doesn't sound like empty encouragement. "When your hands heal, you'll be able to work with the fine wiring again. And you'll have learned something from this failure that you can apply next time."

"How do you know?"

"Because you're not the kind of person who gives up on something important to you. And helping people stay warm in the winter —that's important."

She says it with such quiet certainty that I almost believe her.

We walk back to the house in silence, and she packs up her medical supplies while I finish my tea. When she's ready to leave, she pauses at the door.

"Same time tomorrow?"

"Yeah."

"Jasper?" She looks at me directly, brown eyes serious but not pitying. "Try to eat something that isn't delivered in a cardboard container before I get here."

After she leaves, I sit in my kitchen and try to process what just happened. She came here to change my bandages—a simple medical procedure that took less than fifteen minutes. But somehow she also made me breakfast, looked at my workshop without judgment, and managed to make me feel less like an invalid and more like a person who's temporarily inconvenienced.

She walked through the wreckage of my worst failure and didn't flinch. Just saw what I was trying to do, and told me I'd figure it out.

I can't remember the last time someone treated me like that. Like I'm still fundamentally capable, even when I can't manage basic tasks. Like the man I am isn't defined by what I can't do right now.

Tomorrow she'll come back, and we'll probably follow the same routine—medical care, maybe some food if she thinks I need it, quiet conversation that doesn't require me to perform or pretend to be better than I am.

For the first time since the accident, I find myself looking forward to something.

It's a dangerous feeling. But sitting here in my clean kitchen, looking at my properly bandaged hands, I can't quite bring myself to regret it.

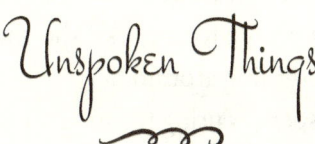

Unspoken Things

SHEILA

By the fourth day, visiting Jasper has become the most normal part of my routine.

Wake up in Grace's guest room, drink coffee while she and Tyler get ready for work, then walk the six blocks to Jasper's house at ten o'clock. Change his bandages, assess the healing, and maybe make him eat something that doesn't come from a delivery bag. Back to Grace's by eleven-thirty, where I spend the rest of the day reading or helping with small household tasks or staring out the window, wondering what I'm supposed to do with the rest of my life.

It should feel like a chore. Medical care for a stranger who barely talks, who accepts my help with the kind of resigned politeness that suggests he'd rather be managing alone.

Instead, it's become the hour of my day when I feel most like myself.

Not the self I was in Afghanistan—that version of me who could run on three hours of sleep and pure adrenaline, who could make life-or-death decisions without flinching, who thrived on the constant urgency of keeping people alive under impossible circumstances. And not the self I'm supposed to be now—the veteran who's successfully transitioned back to civilian life, who has plans and goals and a clear sense of what comes next.

Just me. Sheila. Someone who knows how to clean a wound and wrap gauze and make decent scrambled eggs. Someone who can sit in comfortable silence without feeling like she should be doing more, being more, fixing everything around her.

This morning, Jasper's waiting for me at the kitchen table when I arrive, hands already unwrapped and a cup of tea steaming beside him. He's wearing a clean flannel shirt—blue this time, instead of his usual gray—and his hair looks like he actually combed it.

"You're prepared today," I say, setting my supplies on the counter.

"Seemed easier than making you watch me struggle with the gauze."

I wash my hands and sit across from him, taking his left hand first. The burns are healing well—new pink skin growing in around the edges, less redness and swelling than there was even two days ago. His fingers are regaining flexibility, though I can tell he's still favoring his right hand for anything that requires fine motor control.

"How's the pain level?"

"Better. Still stiff in the mornings, but the sharp pain is mostly gone."

"That's good progress." I start cleaning the worst spot on his palm, a patch where the burns went deepest. "Another week and you should have most of your dexterity back."

"What you said before. About it being temporary."

"Yes."

He's quiet while I work, but I can feel him watching my hands as I clean and dress each area. There's something different about him today—not more talkative, exactly, but less guarded. Like he's stopped bracing for this interaction and started accepting it.

"Can I ask you something?" he says as I'm securing the last piece of tape.

"Sure."

"What made you want to be a nurse?"

I pause, not because it's a difficult question, but because it's been so long since anyone asked me about the before. The reasons I had for choosing this work, back when it felt like a calling instead of something I'd burned out on.

"My grandmother," I say finally. "She had a stroke when I was sixteen. Spent three months in the hospital and then another six months in rehab. I saw how much difference the good nurses made—not just in her medical care, but in how she felt about herself, whether she had hope, whether she kept fighting to get better."

I finish with his bandages and start packing up my supplies, but I don't move to leave yet.

"The nurses who really helped her weren't necessarily the smartest or the most technically skilled," I continue. "They were the ones who saw her as a person instead of just a patient. Who remembered that she used to teach fourth grade and loved crossword puzzles, and worried about her garden. Who treated her like she still mattered, even when she couldn't do basic things for herself."

Jasper nods slowly. "And you wanted to be that for other people."

"I thought I could be."

"You can't anymore?"

The question is asked gently, without judgment, but it still hits something tender in my chest. I look at my hands—still steady, still competent, still capable of providing the technical care people need. But the other part, the emotional generosity that made me good at this work, feels depleted in a way I don't know how to fix.

"I gave everything I had for two years," I say. "Every shift, every patient, every emergency. And it was good work, important work. I saved lives, helped people heal, made a difference."

"But?"

"But there was always another emergency. Always someone else who needed everything I had to give. And eventually I realized I'd been running on empty for months without noticing. The compassion, the emotional connection that made me good at this job—it was just gone."

I expect him to offer some kind of reassurance, to tell me it'll come back or that everyone goes through periods like this. Instead, he just nods like he understands exactly what I'm talking about.

"Is that why you came here? To figure out how to get it back?"

"I don't know if I want it back," I admit. "That version of myself who could give everything to everyone—she was useful, but she wasn't sustainable. Maybe I need to figure out how to be useful without emptying myself completely."

We sit in silence for a moment, morning light filtering through his kitchen window and casting long shadows across the table. There's something about the way he listens—without trying to solve my problems or minimize what I'm struggling with—that makes it easier to be honest than it's been in months.

"What about you?" I ask. "What made you want to invent things?"

He considers the question for a long moment, flexing his fingers experimentally.

"My father," he says finally. "He ran an electronics repair shop here in town for forty years. People would bring him their broken radios, televisions, computers—things other people would throw away—and he'd figure out how to make them work again."

"Sounds like he was good at it."

"He was brilliant at it. Could diagnose problems just by listening to the sounds something made, or feeling how the circuits responded. But what I remember most was how happy he was when he got something working again. Like he'd rescued something that mattered."

There's a wistfulness in his voice that makes me think there's more to this story.

"When he started getting sick—Alzheimer's—I tried to keep the shop running. Thought I could honor what he'd built by carrying it on. But I wasn't him, and I wasn't happy doing repair work. I was good enough at it, but it felt like I was wearing someone else's clothes."

"So you started inventing instead."

"Eventually. After I finally admitted I couldn't be him and closed the shop." He looks toward the back door, in the direction of his workshop. "Building new things instead of fixing old ones. Trying to solve problems that don't have obvious solutions yet."

"Like heating devices for seniors."

"Like that. Or solar-powered holiday displays so people don't have to worry about their electric bills spiking in December. Or automatic watering systems for people who want gardens but can't maintain them consistently."

There's something in the way he talks about his work—quiet pride mixed with genuine care for the people who might use what he creates—that reminds me of why I became a nurse in the first place. The desire to solve problems that matter, to make life a little easier for people who are struggling with something difficult.

"You'll get back to it," I say. "When your hands heal."

"Maybe. If I can figure out what went wrong with the heating coil."

"You will."

He looks at me questioningly, and I realize I've spoken with more certainty than the situation probably warrants.

"You're not the kind of person who gives up on something important," I explain. "And helping people—that's important to you."

"How do you know?"

"Because you let a burned-out army nurse come to your house every day to change your bandages, even though you hate needing help. Because you've been polite and patient with me, even though I'm probably not the most cheerful company these days."

"You're better company than you think."

The comment catches me off guard. Not because it's particularly profound, but because he says it like he means it. Like spending an hour a day with me isn't just something he's enduring until he can manage on his own again.

"I should let you get on with your day," I say, standing up and shouldering my bag.

"Actually," he says, and there's something almost hesitant in his voice. "If you don't have anywhere you need to be... I was thinking about making soup for lunch. Nothing fancy, just something from a can, but you could stay. If you want."

The offer surprises me. Not because it's inappropriate—we've moved well past the boundaries of a strictly medical relationship—but because it suggests he's been thinking about our interactions as more than just necessary care.

"I don't want to impose on your day."

"You wouldn't be imposing. I'd... like the company."

There's something vulnerable about the way he says it, like he's admitting to something he wasn't planning to reveal. And there's something about the idea of staying, of having lunch in his quiet kitchen and maybe talking about things that aren't related to wound care or our respective struggles, that appeals to me more than I expected.

"Okay," I say, setting my bag back down. "But I'm making the soup. You're still technically under medical orders to avoid unnecessary strain on those hands."

He smiles—the first real smile I've seen from him since we met.

"Deal."

While I heat up tomato soup and make grilled cheese sandwiches, Jasper sits at the table and tells me about the other projects in his workshop. A wind chime that doubles as a bird feeder. A motion-sensor light that only activates for larger animals, so it won't go off every time a squirrel runs past. Small inventions that show a mind that pays attention to everyday problems and thinks about creative solutions.

"You really see things differently," I say, setting a bowl in front of him.

"What do you mean?"

"Most people would just buy a regular bird feeder and a regular light. You see ways to make them better, more thoughtful. More useful."

"I guess I just notice when things could work better than they do."

"That's a gift."

He looks skeptical. "Even when my attempts to make things work better result in small explosions?"

"Especially then. Because you're not letting one failure stop you from trying."

We eat in comfortable quiet, the afternoon sun warming the kitchen and making everything feel peaceful and unhurried. It occurs to me that this is the longest I've sat still in one place since coming home without feeling restless or hollow or like I should be somewhere else doing something more important.

Maybe this is what healing looks like—not a dramatic recovery, but quiet moments where I remember how to exist without measuring my worth by how useful I am to others.

When we finish eating, I help him clean up—or rather, I clean up while he protests that he can manage it himself.

"I know you can manage," I tell him, rinsing our bowls. "But I'm here, and it's easier with two people, and there's no reason for you to struggle with dishes when I have two perfectly functional hands."

"When you put it like that."

"I'm very logical."

"You are."

There's something in his voice that makes me look at him more closely. He's watching me with an expression I can't quite read—not grateful, exactly, but something warmer than that. Something that suggests this afternoon has been as nice for him as it has been for me.

"Same time tomorrow?" I ask, drying my hands on his dish towel.

"Yeah. And Sheila?"

"Yes?"

"Thank you. Not just for the medical stuff. For... this."

He gestures vaguely around the kitchen, but I know he means the conversation, the meal, the hour we spent together, without it being about his injuries or my burnout or any of the things that brought us together in the first place.

"Thank you for the soup invitation."

"Anytime."

Walking back to Grace's house, I find myself thinking about the way Jasper looked at his workshop yesterday. Not with shame or frustration, but with the kind of longing you have for something you love and miss and know you'll return to eventually. And I think about the way he talked about his inventions today—with quiet pride and genuine care for the people who might benefit from them.

I didn't think about Jeremy Martinez once while stirring soup or listening to Jasper talk about solar lanterns. That has to mean something.

Maybe that's what I've been missing. Not the ability to give everything I have to everyone who needs it, but the ability to care about my work without letting it consume me completely. To find meaning in helping people without requiring that work to be everything I am.

Tomorrow I'll go back to his house and change his bandages and maybe stay for lunch again if he offers. And slowly, carefully, I'm starting to think that maybe we're both healing in ways that have nothing to do with burned hands or combat fatigue.

Maybe we're learning how to be useful to each other without giving more than we have to give.

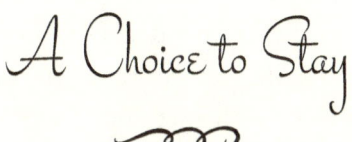

A Choice to Stay

JASPER

The bandages come off for good on a Tuesday.

Sheila examines my hands with the same careful attention she's shown every morning for the past two weeks, turning my palms over to check the new pink skin, testing the flexibility of my fingers. The burns have healed into pale patches that will probably always be visible, but the pain is gone, and my dexterity has returned to something close to normal.

"How do they feel?" she asks, releasing my hands.

I flex my fingers, make a fist, pick up a pencil, and test my grip. Everything works the way it's supposed to. "Good. Normal."

"Any stiffness or sensitivity?"

"Some. Nothing I can't manage."

She nods and starts packing up her supplies—gauze and antiseptic solution, and medical tape I won't need anymore. She doesn't ask if I want tea. Doesn't set the kettle to boil like usual. Just zips her bag like she's already somewhere else.

The routine we've built over the past two weeks is ending, and we both know it.

"You should keep them moisturized for another week or so," she says without looking at me. "And wear gloves if you're doing anything that might irritate the new skin."

"Okay."

"Other than that, you're cleared for normal activity."

She zips up her medical bag and stands, shouldering it like she's done dozens of times before. But this time, she doesn't sit back down for tea or ask if I need help with anything. This time, she's leaving.

"Thank you," I say. "For everything. The medical care, the company, the meals. All of it."

"You're welcome."

There's something different in her voice—more formal, like she's putting distance between us now that our arrangement is officially over. Like she's already halfway out the door.

"What will you do now?" I ask, because I can't let her leave yet. Not when I don't know if I'll see her again.

"I'm not sure. Grace has been patient about me staying with her, but I can't impose indefinitely." She glances around my kitchen like she's memorizing it. "I've been thinking about heading back to Virginia after Christmas. Find an apartment, maybe look into hospital positions."

The words hit me like cold water. She's leaving. Of course she's leaving—she has a life somewhere else, a career, reasons to be places that aren't here. But somehow in the past two weeks, I'd started thinking of her as a permanent fixture. Someone who belonged in this kitchen, at this table, in this space I've shared with no one else.

"Virginia," I repeat.

"That's where my things are. I was supposed to return to Fort Belvoir after my deployment, but when it got extended, they had to reassign my housing. The Army packed up my stuff and put them in storage there. I need to figure out what to do with all of it."

"Do you want to go back?"

She pauses, considering the question. "I don't know what I want. That's part of the problem."

I should say something supportive. Something about how she'll figure it out, how she's young and capable and can build a life anywhere she chooses. But the thought of her packing up and leaving, of going back to my solitary routine without her daily visits to anchor my mornings, makes me selfish.

"You could stay," I say.

"Here?"

"In Maplewood Grove. There's a clinic in town, and the regional hospital's always looking for experienced nurses. It's not exciting, but—"

"Jasper." She stops me gently. "I can't base major life decisions on changing someone's bandages for two weeks."

"That's not what this was."

The words come out more intensely than I intended, and she looks at me sharply.

"Wasn't it?"

"No." I stand up, suddenly unable to sit still. "Maybe it started that way, but it hasn't been just medical care for days. You know that."

"I know we've become friends."

"Friends."

"Yes."

There's something careful in the way she says it, like she's testing whether that's the right word. Like maybe she's been thinking about this as something more than friendship too, but isn't sure if she should admit it.

"Is that what you want?" I ask. "To be friends?"

"I want..." She stops, runs a hand through her hair. "I don't know what I want, Jasper. That's the problem. For the first time in years, I don't have a mission or an assignment or a clear sense of what I'm supposed to be doing. And sitting in your kitchen making soup and listening to you talk about solar lanterns has been the most peaceful I've felt since I left the Army. But that doesn't mean I should upend my entire life to stay here."

"Why not?"

"Because it's not realistic. Because we barely know each other. Because I'm emotionally exhausted and you're recovering from an accident and neither of us is in a position to make smart decisions about the future."

She's being logical, practical, all the things she's always been. But there's something underneath the logic—a kind of fear that suggests she's talking herself out of something she actually wants.

"What if I don't care about smart decisions?" I say.

"Then you're not thinking clearly."

"Maybe I'm thinking clearly for the first time in months."

We stare at each other across the kitchen, and I can see her internal struggle playing out on her face. She wants to stay—I can see it in the way she keeps glancing around like she's trying to memorize everything, the way she hasn't actually moved toward the door despite saying she needs to leave.

"Sheila—"

"I should go." She adjusts her bag strap and takes a step backward. "Grace is making lunch, and I promised I'd help."

"Will I see you again? Before you leave for Virginia?"

"I don't know."

It's an honest answer, but it's not the one I wanted to hear.

After she leaves, I sit in my kitchen and try to process what just happened. For two weeks, she's been the bright spot in my days—competent and calm and quietly funny, someone who made even the frustration of being temporarily disabled feel manageable. Someone who looked at my failed inventions and saw what I was trying to accomplish instead of what had gone wrong.

Someone who made me remember what it felt like to have something to look forward to.

And now she's gone, and I'm back to the silence and the empty hours and the workshop full of half-finished projects I don't have the motivation to complete.

I walk out to the garage and look around at the scattered remnants of my pre-accident productivity. The heating device that exploded remains on the main workbench, a stark reminder of my most recent failure. But for the first time since it happened, I find myself studying it analytically instead of just seeing it as evidence of my incompetence.

The wiring that caused the problem is clear now that I can examine it properly. A simple oversight in the connection between the temperature sensor and the heating coil—the kind of mistake that happens when you're tired and rushing and not paying close enough attention to details.

Fixable. Definitely fixable.

I pick up a pair of wire strippers, test my grip on the handles. My hands are stiff but functional, good enough for basic work. Not perfect, but good enough to start again.

Three hours later, I have the heating device partially rebuilt and a much clearer sense of what went wrong the first time. The work feels good—familiar and purposeful in a way I'd forgotten was possible. But every few minutes, I catch myself listening for the sound of Sheila's knock on the door, expecting her to appear with tea and questions about what I'm building.

She's not coming back. She made that clear.

But maybe I can give her a reason to reconsider.

The next morning, I wake up early and drive to the hardware store for supplies. Betty Morrison, who's worked there for thirty years, raises her eyebrows when she sees me.

"Jasper Finch, as I live and breathe. Haven't seen you in weeks. Heard you had some trouble with one of your inventions."

"Nothing I can't fix," I tell her, loading screws and electrical wire onto the counter.

239

"Course not. You're too stubborn to let a little setback stop you."
She rings up my purchases, then leans forward conspiratorially. "Also
heard you've been getting some help from Grace Thompson's sister.
The army nurse."

Word travels fast in small towns. I shouldn't be surprised that
people have noticed Sheila's daily visits to my house.

"She was helping with medical care," I say carefully.

"Sure she was." Betty's grin suggests she thinks there was more to
it than that. "Pretty girl. Seems nice. Shame she's not planning to
stick around."

"What do you mean?"

"Agnes Carlton saw her at the post office yesterday, asking about
shipping boxes to Virginia. Looks like she's getting ready to head out
after the holidays."

The information sits heavy in my stomach. Sheila's not just
thinking about leaving—she's actively making plans for it.

"Shame," Betty repeats. "This town could use more good nurses.
And you could use someone to keep you fed and make sure you're
taking care of yourself."

I pay for my supplies and leave before Betty can offer any more
unsolicited observations about my personal life. But her words follow
me home, and before I left the hardware store, I'd asked her if she
thought people in town might actually use something like this. The
way her eyes lit up told me more than a dozen surveys ever could.

I spend the rest of the day working on the heating device with
unusual focus and determination.

If Sheila's planning to leave, I need to finish this before she goes.

By Thursday evening, the device is complete and functional. I've
tested it extensively, checked every connection twice, and built in
multiple safety features to prevent the kind of failure that caused the
original accident. It works exactly the way it's supposed to—clean,
efficient heat that can be controlled precisely and shut off automatically if anything goes wrong.

More importantly, it works the way I intended it to work before everything went sideways.

I should be satisfied. I've solved the problem that's been haunting me for weeks, proven to myself that I can still build things that matter. But sitting in my workshop holding the finished device, all I can think about is how much I want to show it to Sheila. How much I want to see her face when she realizes I figured out what went wrong and fixed it.

How much I want her to understand that this isn't just about the heating device—it's about remembering who I am when I'm not defined by what I can't do.

Friday morning, I walk to Grace and Tyler's house carrying the heating device and a thermos of coffee, and no clear plan for what I'm going to say when Sheila answers the door.

She doesn't answer the door. Grace does, wearing an apron and a surprised expression.

"Jasper! What brings you by?"

"I was hoping to see Sheila."

"She's not here. She went into town to run some errands." Grace glances at the device in my hands. "Is that what I think it is?"

"The heating unit that exploded. I fixed it."

"That's wonderful! Come in, come in. Tyler's at work, but I'd love to hear about it."

She ushers me into the kitchen and pours coffee while I explain what went wrong originally and how I solved it. Grace listens with genuine interest, asking thoughtful questions about the safety features and the efficiency ratings.

"This is really impressive, Jasper. You should be proud of yourself."

"Thanks."

"But you didn't come here to show it to me, did you?"

Grace has always been perceptive. It's one of the things that makes her both kind and occasionally uncomfortable to be around.

"I wanted Sheila to see it," I admit.

"Because she was there when you were struggling with it."

"Because she told me I'd figure it out. When I couldn't see past the failure, she saw what I was trying to accomplish." I pause, looking down at the device. "She saw me."

Grace nods slowly. "She's good at that. Seeing the person someone is instead of just the crisis they're dealing with."

"She is."

"Jasper," Grace says gently, "what's going on between you and my sister?"

It's a fair question, and one I should have an answer for. But the truth is complicated and probably doesn't make sense to anyone who hasn't lived it.

"I don't know," I say finally. "We became friends. Good friends. And now she's leaving, and I'm trying to figure out if there's anything I can say or do that might convince her to stay."

"Do you want her to stay because you'd miss her friendship? Or because it's something more than that?"

I look down at the heating device, at the hours of careful work and problem-solving it represents. The proof that I can still build things that matter and solve problems that help people.

"Both," I say.

Grace is quiet for a moment, refilling our coffee cups.

"She's been through a lot, Jasper. The military, the burnout, trying to figure out what comes next. I think she's scared of making decisions based on emotions instead of logic."

"And I'm not logical?"

"You're a man who spent three hours walking around town yesterday asking people if they'd be interested in buying portable heating devices for their elderly relatives. That's not logic—that's hope."

She's right. I've been thinking about production and distribution, about turning this single device into something that could actually help multiple people. About building a business around solving problems that matter.

About creating a life here that Sheila might want to be part of.

"What should I do?"

"Show her what you built. Tell her what it means to you. And then let her make her own choice about what she wants her life to look like."

"What if she chooses to leave?"

"Then you'll have to respect that choice."

When I get home, there's a note tucked under my front door. Sheila's handwriting, quick and practical.

Jasper—heard from Grace that you've been working on something. Would love to see it if you're willing to share. I'll be at the coffee shop on Main Street around 2 if you want to meet. —S

I look at my watch. It's 1:30.

I grab the heating device and head into town.

Sweet Return

SHEILA

The coffee shop on Main Street is busier than I expected for a Friday afternoon three days before Christmas. Holiday shoppers warming up between errands, teenagers on winter break claiming the corner table with their laptops, and the usual collection of retirees who treat Maggie's Café like their unofficial social club.

I choose a table by the window where I can watch for Jasper, ordering a latte I don't really want just to have something to do with my hands. Outside, Maplewood Grove looks like a postcard—fresh snow dusting the sidewalks, shop windows glowing with warm light, people bundled up in coats and scarves moving at the unhurried pace of a small town that knows Christmas will arrive whether you rush or not.

It's beautiful. Peaceful in a way that makes me understand why people choose to build their entire lives in places like this.

Which doesn't mean I should be one of them.

I've spent the last two days making lists—practical considerations about moving back to Virginia, job applications I should submit, contacts I should reach out to. The kind of logical planning that usually makes me feel more in control of uncertain situations.

Instead, every item I write down feels like I'm talking myself out of something I actually want. I've been practical. Cautious. But none of that planning gave me back the steadiness I felt in Jasper's kitchen.

The bell over the door chimes, and Jasper walks in carrying something wrapped in a canvas tool bag. He spots me immediately, raises one hand in greeting, and makes his way over after stopping at the counter to order coffee.

He looks different than he did Tuesday morning in his kitchen. More settled, less guarded. His hands move normally as he stirs sugar into his coffee, no hesitation or careful positioning to accommodate healing burns.

"How are they feeling?" I ask when he sits down across from me.

"Good. A little stiff in the morning, but otherwise back to normal." He flexes his fingers demonstratively. "I've been working on something."

"Grace mentioned you'd been busy."

"Did she tell you what I was working on?"

"She said you'd rebuilt the heating device. The one that exploded."

He nods and reaches for the canvas bag. "I figured out what went wrong originally. Simple oversight in the wiring connection—the kind of mistake that happens when you're rushing and not paying attention to details."

He unwraps the device and sets it on the table between us. It's smaller than I expected, about the size of a large book, with a sleek metal housing and simple controls. It looks professional, purposeful, like something you might actually see in a store rather than a garage workshop.

"It works?"

"Perfectly. Clean, efficient heat that can be controlled precisely. Built-in safety features to prevent the kind of failure that caused the original accident." He runs his hand over the smooth metal surface. "I tested it extensively."

"That's wonderful, Jasper. You should be proud of yourself."

"I am. But that's not why I wanted to show it to you."

I look at him questioningly.

"You were right," he says. "When you told me I'd figure it out, when you said I wasn't the kind of person who gives up on something important. I didn't believe you then, but you were right."

"Of course you figured it out. You're brilliant at this kind of work."

"Maybe. But I never would have gotten back to it without you."

The intensity in his voice catches me off guard. This isn't just pride in completing a difficult project—there's something more personal in the way he's looking at me.

"All I did was change your bandages."

"No." He leans forward slightly. "You made me feel like I was still fundamentally capable, even when I couldn't manage basic tasks. You looked at my workshop full of failed projects and saw what I was trying to accomplish instead of what had gone wrong. You treated me like I was temporarily inconvenienced instead of broken."

I think about the first time I saw him struggle with simple tasks, the frustration and shame he tried to hide. The way he gradually relaxed into accepting help, stopped bracing for pity that never came.

"You weren't broken," I say quietly. "Just hurt."

"Same thing you are."

The observation is gentle but direct, and it lands with more accuracy than I'm comfortable with. Because he's not wrong—I am hurt, in ways that have nothing to do with physical injury and everything to do with giving too much of myself for too long.

"Jasper—"

"I know you're planning to leave." He keeps his voice low, but there's something urgent underneath the calm tone. "I know you've been looking into jobs back in Virginia."

"I have to be practical about my future."

"Do you want to go back?"

It's the same question he asked in his kitchen Tuesday morning, and I still don't have a clear answer.

"I don't know what I want," I admit. "For two years, every decision was made for me. Where to go, what to do, who to save, how to prioritize my time and energy. Now I have complete freedom to choose, and I have no idea how to do it."

"So choose based on what feels right instead of what makes sense on paper."

"That's not how I make decisions."

"Maybe it should be."

A burst of laughter from the teenagers in the corner breaks the tension, reminding me that we're having this conversation in a public place where anyone might overhear. Where people are already starting to glance our way with the kind of curious attention that comes from recognizing the local inventor and the army nurse who's been visiting him every day.

"People are staring," I murmur.

"Let them stare."

"Jasper—"

"I'm in love with you."

The words are spoken quietly, matter-of-factly, like he's stating an observable truth rather than making a declaration that changes everything between us.

"You barely know me."

"I know you're kind without being soft. I know you're competent without being cold. I know you notice when people are struggling and help them without making them feel helpless." He pauses, his eyes never leaving my face. "I know that sitting in my kitchen talking to you has been the best part of every day for two weeks."

I can feel heat rising in my cheeks, and I'm suddenly very aware of the other conversations happening around us, the normal life of a small-town café continuing while my world shifts on its axis.

"This is happening very fast."

"Is it? Or have we both been thinking about it for days and just not saying it out loud?"

He's right, and we both know it. The careful way we've been watching each other, the way our conversations have moved from medical necessities to genuine intimacy, the way neither of us wanted our daily routine to end—none of that was about friendship.

"Even if that's true," I say, "love isn't enough. I don't have a job here, or a place to live, or any kind of plan for what I'd do with my life."

"What if we figured that out together?"

"What does that mean?"

He reaches across the table and turns the heating device slightly, so I can see the small plate on the back that reads "Finch Innovations."

"Betty Morrison at the hardware store thinks half the senior citizens in town would buy one of these for their porches and garages. Agnes Carlton wants to know if I can make a version that's portable enough for outdoor events. Dr. Martinez asked if I could develop something similar for the clinic's waiting room."

I can hear the excitement building in his voice, the same quiet passion he had when he talked about his other inventions.

"I want to turn this into a real business," he continues. "Small-scale manufacturing, custom solutions for local problems. And I want you to be part of it."

"I'm not an inventor."

"No, but you understand people. You know what they need, how to take care of them, how to solve problems in practical ways." He leans forward. "You could handle the business side, work with potential customers, and help me understand what problems are worth solving."

It's a generous offer, and I can tell he means it. But there's something about the way he's presenting it that feels too neat, too much like he's trying to solve the problem of my uncertain future by giving me a role in his.

"Jasper, you can't create a job for me just to convince me to stay."

"That's not what I'm doing."

"Isn't it?"

He's quiet for a moment, considering my challenge.

"Maybe partly," he admits. "But mostly I'm offering you a partnership because I think we'd be good at it together. And because I think you want something to care about that doesn't require you to give everything you have."

The accuracy of that assessment takes my breath away. Because that is exactly what I want—meaningful work that doesn't empty me completely, a way to be useful that's sustainable instead of consuming.

"What if it doesn't work? The business, I mean."

"Then we'll figure something else out."

"What if we don't work? As partners, or... whatever this is between us."

"Then we'll deal with that too." He reaches across the table and covers my hand with his. "But Sheila, what if it does work? What if this is exactly what we both need?"

His hand is warm and steady over mine, no trace of the careful movements he had to make just days ago. Completely healed, ready to build new things.

"I'm scared," I say quietly.

"Of what?"

"Of making a decision based on how I feel instead of what makes logical sense. Of getting attached to a life here and then having it not work out. Of disappointing you when you realize I'm not as put-together as I seem."

"You think I don't know you're not put-together?" His mouth

quirks up in a small smile. "Sheila, you've been staying in your sister's guest room for three weeks because you couldn't face going back to Virginia. You create lists of practical considerations, only to ignore them because none of them actually matter to you. You're one of the most capable people I've ever met, and you have no idea what you want to do with your life."

The description should sting, but it doesn't. Maybe because it's completely accurate, or maybe because he says it with the kind of affection that suggests he finds my uncertainty endearing rather than frustrating.

"You're not exactly the poster child for having everything figured out either," I point out.

"No, I'm not. But for the first time in months, I'm excited about something. About this business, about the possibility of building something meaningful. About the idea of doing it with you."

I look down at our joined hands, at the heating device sitting between us like a symbol of second chances and new beginnings. Outside the window, snow is starting to fall again, dusting the sidewalks and making everything look clean and possible.

"I'd want to take it slow," I say. "The personal stuff, I mean. I'm not ready for anything too intense too fast."

"Neither am I."

"And I'd want my own place. I can't keep staying with Grace indefinitely, and if we're going to try working together, I should probably have some independence."

"There's an apartment above the bakery that's been empty for months. Dot Simmons has been looking for the right tenant."

He's thought this through. Not in a controlling way, but in the practical way of someone who's been hoping for a specific outcome and considering how to make it possible.

"You really think we could make this work?"

"I think we understand each other in a way that doesn't happen very often. I think we're both looking for the same thing—work that matters, a life that feels sustainable, someone to share it with who doesn't need us to be perfect."

He's right about that. The past two weeks, I haven't had to perform for him or prove my competence or be anything other than exactly who I am in this moment. Tired, uncertain, healing at my own pace.

"Okay," I say.

"Okay?"

"Let's try it. The business partnership, I mean. And... something more. Whatever this is between us."

His smile is brighter than I've seen from him since we met. Not relief, exactly, but satisfaction. Like he knew I'd eventually come around to seeing what he could see.

"There's one more thing," he says, reaching into his jacket pocket and pulling out a small wrapped package. "An early Christmas gift."

I unwrap it carefully, revealing a small solar lantern similar to the ones I saw in his workshop. But this one is different—more delicate, with intricate metalwork that creates patterns of light when it's illuminated.

"It's beautiful."

"For your new apartment. Whenever you find one."

I turn the lantern over in my hands, studying the careful craftsmanship. It's clearly been made specifically for me, designed with attention to details I mentioned in passing—my love of intricate patterns, my preference for warm light over harsh brightness.

"When did you make this?"

"I started it the day after Thanksgiving. Just in case."

"Just in case what?"

"Just in case I got the chance to convince you to stay."

I look at him across the table—this quiet, thoughtful man who sees problems and creates solutions, who makes beautiful things with his hands and wants to share them with people who will appreciate them. Who looked at my uncertainty and offered me a way to build something new instead of trying to fix what was broken.

"Thank you," I say. "For the lantern, for the offer, for... seeing something in me that I couldn't see in myself."

"Thank you for helping me remember who I am when I'm not defined by what I can't do."

We sit in comfortable silence for a moment, both of us holding pieces of what he's built—the heating device that represents his recovery, the lantern that represents his hope for our future. Outside, the snow is falling steadier now, and the afternoon light is starting to fade into the early twilight of late December.

"So," I say eventually. "Partners?"

"Partners."

He extends his hand for a formal handshake, and I take it, laughing at the seriousness of the gesture. But when our hands meet, neither of us lets go right away. Instead, we sit there connected across the small table in the warm café, surrounded by the gentle hum of other people's conversations and the promise of something new beginning.

When we finally release our handshake, Jasper glances toward the window where the snow is still falling steadily.

"It's getting pretty heavy out there," he says. "Can I give you a ride back to Grace's? I drove today."

I look outside at the thickening snowfall, then back at him. "Thanks, but I like walking in the snow. Helps me think."

"You sure? It's supposed to get worse."

"I'm sure. But I appreciate the offer."

He nods, understanding. "Walk carefully then."

Later, walking back through the snow to Grace's house with the lantern tucked carefully in my coat pocket, I realize I haven't thought about Jeremy Martinez or my empty apartment in Virginia or any of the reasons I should be making different choices.

Instead, I'm thinking about apartment hunting with Dot

Simmons, learning the business side of small-scale manufacturing, and what it might feel like to wake up every morning with something meaningful to look forward to.

Maybe this is what coming home really means. Not returning to the place you left, but finding the place where you want to build what comes next.

And maybe love doesn't have to be loud or dramatic or perfectly timed to be exactly what you need.

Sometimes it just has to be true.

The End

Sweet Solstice

❦

A CLEAN SMALL TOWN HOLIDAY ROMANCE

The Spark

LENA

The Carlton house smells like rosemary, peppermint tea, and the faintest tinge of something burning. Probably one of Aunt Agnes's "seasonal incenses," which she insists on lighting whenever there's a change in weather, mood, or cosmic alignment. Which, apparently, happens a lot.

The house creaked under my feet, the way it always had. Like it was welcoming me back... or warning me to be sure. Because this time, leaving again wouldn't be so easy.

I stand in the entryway with my arms full of labeled crates—"Dried Flowers," "Crystals + Stones," "Tincture Tools"—and take a slow breath. This house hasn't changed since I was a kid: same creaky floors, same ivy-covered porch, same questionable wiring that flickers when too many lights are on at once. Chaotic, cozy, eccentric. Like my aunts. Like me.

Mabel's voice drifts in from the kitchen. "Lena! Did you bring your moon calendar? We need to know when to start the solstice cider!"

"I literally just got here," I call back, nudging the front door closed with my hip. "Give me five minutes to find a clear surface to breathe on!"

I drop the crates onto the floral-patterned rug and let out a long sigh. The house smelled like beginnings. And like endings too, if you breathed deep enough. Moving back to Maplewood Grove was never part of the plan. I've spent years bouncing between spiritual retreats, healing workshops, apothecary apprenticeships—following the rhythm of the seasons and my own restless heart. But something shifted this fall. I wanted more than the next new thing. I wanted roots. A genuine community. A place where people remember your name and ask about your aunt's cats and come to your herbal shop for more than just a social media photo.

But deep down, it wasn't just about wanting. It was about needing. I couldn't outrun the hollow spaces anymore—the ones you only notice when the noise stops. Maplewood Grove wasn't just home. It was my last good idea.

Maplewood Grove tugged at me like a tide I hadn't even realised I was swimming against—one morning I woke up and knew I was already halfway back. Maybe I'd been drifting too long. Maybe I needed something older and sturdier than ambition to hold on to. Something that wouldn't change when the next shiny thing caught my eye.

Past the Carlton house, Main Street shimmered with tiny white lights strung between the maple trees—an old Maplewood Grove tradition to "guide the returning sun."

The thump of boots on the porch makes me turn just as the front door creaks open again.

"I knocked," a low voice says. "No answer."

My stomach flips before I even see him. When I do, I wish I had a better poker face. Because the man standing in the doorway—tool belt, black knit beanie, rain jacket speckled with sleet—carries a quietness that feels almost defensive, like someone used to expecting the worst.

There was something about the way he stood—shoulders slightly hunched, like he wasn't sure if he was welcome here or anywhere. I recognized it. It was the posture of someone who knew how quickly things could disappear.

"I'm Ben Brooks," he says, holding out a calloused hand. "Electrician. Here to fix the disaster your aunts are calling a breaker box."

Oh. Of course. The Brooks brothers. Patty mentioned them in one of her emails. Liam's the contractor who's been renovating half the town. This must be the younger one. The quiet one. The one who's building a house out near Stony Hill with his own two hands.

I clear my throat and shake his hand. Firm grip. Warm. Ugh.

"I'm Lena Sullivan. Their niece." I gesture vaguely toward the back of the house. "They're... somewhere between the root cellar and Jupiter, depending on who you ask."

His eyebrows lift, just slightly. "Good to know."

He steps inside, taking in the leaning coat rack, the bundles of drying herbs hanging from the ceiling beams, and the vintage lamp flickering ominously by the stairs.

"You're the one opening the... shop, right?"

"Yes." I nod toward the storefront space off the side of the house. "*Solstice Remedies.* Grand opening in three weeks, on the winter solstice."

He glances toward the doorway but doesn't comment. I get the feeling he has *thoughts*. Probably along the lines of "what is this crystal-loving nonsense?" But he doesn't say it. Which, for a small-town man wielding wire cutters, is something.

I tilt my head. "You're Liam's brother?"

"Unfortunately," he deadpans. "He sends me to handle the messier jobs. And this wiring system is... something."

I smirk. "It's got personality."

"It's got exposed wires next to a spice rack."

"Also personality."

Maybe he didn't hate the chaos as much as he thought. Maybe he just needed someone who spoke its language.

He shakes his head, but I catch the tiniest twitch of amusement. He crouches near the fuse box like a man preparing for battle and mutters, "This may take a while."

Two hours later, I've unpacked four boxes, burned sage in every corner of the shop, and started labeling glass bottles with hand-lettered tags. Ben is still in the back hallway, tracing wires like he's hunting ghosts.

I peek around the corner just as a spark flies from an outlet, and he jumps back, swearing under his breath.

"Protection charm," I say innocently, leaning against the doorframe.

He blinks at me. "Excuse me?"

"There was an old sachet of rosemary and iron filings tucked behind that outlet. My aunts like to hide them in places where energy tangles."

He stares at me for a beat. "You're telling me the wiring exploded because the house didn't like my vibe?"

I grin. "Technically, it might have just been overloaded. But the charm didn't help."

Ben sighs and wipes his hands on a rag. "This is going to be a long week."

I tilt my head. "Planning to stick around that long?"

"I'll be here off and on until I finish the work," he says, then adds, "I'm moving back full time as soon as my house is done."

Something tilts inside me—not panic, nor fear, just the soft, unsteady pull of something I didn't realise I'd been reaching for.

"Well," I say, lifting my mug of tea, "in that case, you might want to prepare. The Carlton house tests people."

He meets my gaze, and his mouth twitches again. "So do I."

Challenge accepted, I think. I just smile and disappear back into the shop.

———

Later that night, after the tools are packed, and the house is quiet, I light a single candle in the front window of my shop. A simple ritual. One flame to bless the new beginning.

From across the street, I glimpse Ben tossing his gear into Liam's truck. He turns and sees me standing there, silhouetted by the light.

He doesn't wave. But he doesn't look away either.

And just like that, the spark catches.

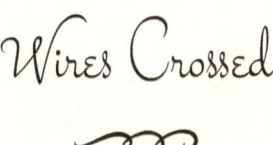

Wires Crossed

BEN

The Carlton house hums like it's alive. Not in the way most houses hum—the way of quietly buzzing appliances or wind rustling through gutters—but in a way that makes the hair on the back of my neck stand up.

Every time I flip a switch or open an access panel, I swear I hear something creak back at me, like the house is thinking it over before it decides if it'll let me work today. It's ridiculous, but then again, so is the place.

The wiring is a mess—circuits branching where they shouldn't, bundles of outdated cables wrapped in cloth insulation. It's a miracle this place hasn't spontaneously combusted.

Or maybe it's been protected by the small army of charms I keep uncovering in the walls.

Today alone, I've found two bundles of dried sage and what I'm fairly certain was a pinecone stuffed with salt and lavender. When I pulled it out and set it on the kitchen table, Agnes gasped like I'd unearthed an ancient relic.

"Careful with that!" she said, snatching it up like a toddler with a toy. "That's our winter protection cone. Mabel made it during the lunar eclipse of 2002."

"... Of course she did," I muttered.

I head to the shop entrance to grab my wire strippers and find Lena standing barefoot on a woven mat, adjusting a dried floral wreath over the doorway. She's in an oversized sweater and leggings, her hair pulled back loosely, with strands falling in her face. The scene feels like it belongs in one of those seasonal catalog photoshoots: *Rustic Apothecary Aesthetic: Limited Solstice Edition.*

"You're barefoot," I say without thinking.

She glances down. "Yup."

"In November."

"Helps me ground."

"To frostbite?"

She laughs. "You're always this cheerful, or is this a special mood just for me?"

"Just you." I grab my gear and straighten up. "Though it's not personal. I've got a short fuse with old wiring and houses that fight back."

Her mouth twitches. "Well, the house is eccentric, not malicious. You just need to work with her."

"Her."

"Her," she confirms. "She responds best to people who pay attention."

Grounded, she said. Maybe that's what had been missing all this time—something solid enough to stand on, someone stubborn enough to stay.

I raise an eyebrow but don't argue. Logic sputters and dies when you're talking to someone who tucks bowls of water into dusty corners and nods solemnly at their reflections, as if listening for a reply.

But even I have to admit—she's not just floating around throwing herbs in the air. She's focused. Hands steady. Movements intentional. She's setting up shelves with a coherent plan. She's been sanding old crates for display stands and labeling tiny vials of something that smells like clove and orange.

Everything about her shop feels...warm. Inviting. Like she wants people to feel something when they walk in.

"Is that rosemary?" I ask, surprising myself.

She looks over her shoulder. "It is. Good for memory, clarity, and energetic cleansing."

"It's what Mom used to put in stew," I whisper.

Lena turns, her face softening. I almost say more—about the days when things felt whole—but the words stick like burrs in my throat.

"I like that. It's both comforting and cleansing. Food and feeling."

I nod, not sure what to do with that kind of response. Most people either ignore what I say or turn it into a joke. Lena just listens —and then layers on something thoughtful, like it's the most natural thing in the world.

A few hours later, I'm under the house, swearing at a junction box and crawling over cobwebs, when Liam calls.

"You good over there?" he asks.

"Define good," I grumble. "I think I just got hexed by a jar of cinnamon sticks and rose petals."

"That sounds about right." He laughs. "The Carltons always did have their own brand of logic."

"I don't get it," I say, shrugging. "It's like the whole place is built on wishes and duct tape."

"You're just not used to things being soft," Liam says casually. "You've been in survival mode for years. Maybe it's time to shift gears."

I go quiet. Liam doesn't bring up my past often. It's nice. Because most of the time, I don't want to think about it.

"I'm not saying you should start burning sage and reading moon charts," he adds, "but Lena? She might be good for you."

I snort. "She's infuriating."

"So are you."

By the time I finish the day's work and wipe my hands clean, Lena is sitting cross-legged on the floor of her shop, surrounded by candles and mason jars.

"Want to stay for tea?" she asks, glancing up at me.

I start to say no. To make some excuse. But, I hear myself say, "Sure."

It wasn't the tea I wanted. It was the quiet she carried. The way she made stillness feel like a choice, not a punishment.

She rises smoothly and disappears into the kitchen. I follow, because... I don't know. I just do.

The Carltons are out at book club—or, more accurately, their "Divine Women's Circle," which I'm ninety percent sure is just them drinking mulled wine and pulling tarot cards—so the house is unusually quiet.

Lena sets a steaming mug in front of me and sits across the table. "Chamomile and honey. Nothing too mystical."

"Appreciate it," I say, wrapping my hands around the mug. It smells like calm.

We sit in silence for a minute before she speaks.

"You ever celebrate the solstice?" she asks.

"Nope."

She doesn't look surprised. "It's my favorite night of the year. The longest night, but the turning point. After that, the light returns. Even if you can't see it yet, it's already shifting."

I nod slowly. "That's kind of... beautiful."

She smiles softly. "It is."

And for the first time in a long time, I feel like maybe things are changing for me, too. Just a little.

Unraveling

~~~

LENA

I've always believed in thresholds—moments when everything feels like it's holding its breath. The last golden light before dusk. The final few minutes before a year turns over. Or now, when the shop is still quiet, the floors freshly swept, the windows fogged with morning mist.

Solstice Remedies isn't open yet, but this space already hums. The shelves are full—jars of dried herbs, beeswax candles, a small wall of teas with hand-written labels: *Nurture, Focus, Ease.* The room smells like cedar and orange peel and soft resolve.

Tonight, I'm hosting a small candle-making circle. Nothing huge —just a few people from the community who signed up via the little flyer I pinned on the library board. I'm not sure who will show. Probably Patty, bless her soul, and at least one of the Carltons, if I can convince them to stay in one spot for over fifteen minutes.

What I *don't* expect is for Ben Brooks to walk in.

He stands awkwardly near the doorway, one hand still gripping his car keys. "Uh... Agnes told me this thing was open to anyone?"

I blink, surprised. "It is. But you... came?"

"I brought you that fixed outlet plate," he says quickly, like it's a reasonable excuse for crashing a candle-making workshop. "And I was already here."

I arch a brow. "Sure. Come in."

He walks in slowly, taking in the setup—low tables, cushions, little bowls of herbs and oils arranged neatly in a circle. He stands out here, all flannel and restraint, like a lumberjack who wandered into a spa by mistake.

"You're going to have to take your shoes off," I add with a smirk.

He glances down at his boots, sighs once, then toes them off. "You enjoy testing me, don't you?"

"Constantly."

The others trickle in: Emily from the post office, Patty—of course—with a reusable shopping bag full of cinnamon scones, and Livy, the young assistant from the library. It's not a full house, but it's enough.

I guide everyone through the process of melting the wax, choosing their intention—calm, courage, clarity—and blending their oils. Each person pours their wax into a glass jar and adds a sprinkle of herbs over the top. Lavender for peace. Rose for love. Peppermint for truth.

When I glance at Ben, his candle's labelled "Renew," and something in my chest pulls tight. Not because it's sweet, but because it's raw. It's a word you choose when you know what it feels like to be worn down.

Simple. Clean. Intentional. Interesting.

Maybe he's not the one who needs saving. Maybe he's the one who knows what saving feels like.

After the final jar is poured, we sit in a soft circle, the candles still warm and unlit in front of us.

"This is my favorite part," I say, keeping my voice low. "This time of year, we're surrounded by holiday chaos—noise, glitter, expectations. But the solstice asks something simpler: just light a candle. Just mark the moment. Choose to bring warmth into the dark."

Everyone sits still, heads slightly bowed as the light flickers across their faces. The room is so quiet I can hear the hum of the heater in the corner and the faint crackle of wax cooling.

Ben leans forward just a little, hands loose in his lap, candlelight playing in the lines of his face.

He's not smiling, exactly—but he's present. Grounded. And when he meets my eyes across the circle, something tips. The air, maybe. Or me.

After everyone leaves, I clean up, stacking the extra jars and gathering wax-stained rags.

"You meant all that, didn't you?" Ben asks from behind me.

I turn, finding him still barefoot, leaning against the doorway between the shop and the house. He looks a little dazed. Or maybe just disarmed.

"Of course I did," I say. "It's not a performance."

"I didn't think it was," he replies. "Just... it's rare to see someone mean something so much without trying to sell it."

I pause, a little taken aback. "That might be the kindest thing anyone's said to me all month."

He rubs the back of his neck. "I'm not great at compliments. That came out weird."

"It didn't," I say softly.

We stand in the half-light, surrounded by the fading scent of herbs and melted wax. My hands are still sticky from beeswax. His shirt smells like cedar and the faint metallic tang of electrical work. We're a strange pair—earth and wire.

He takes a step closer, then stops. "What do people usually do after one of these workshops?"

I shrug. "Depends. Some people go home and journal. Others take baths. Some just... sleep better than they have in months."

"And you?"

I smile faintly. "I usually clean. And then sit in the dark with one candle and let the quiet settle."

Ben looks down, then back at me. "That doesn't sound so bad."

I reach for the broom, grounding myself before I do something foolish—like lean into him, or tell him he's welcome to stay.

"Thanks for coming," I say instead. "Seriously. I didn't think you'd... show up."

"I didn't think I would either," he replies.

And then, after a pause that buzzes just under my skin, he adds, "But I'm glad I did."

That night, I light a single candle in my bedroom and write *renew* on a slip of paper. I'm not sure if it's for me or for him. Maybe it's both.

And for the first time in months, I fall asleep with the door ajar.

Just in case he walks back through it.

Static

***

BEN

The Carlton attic smells like cedar, dust, and regret. Mostly mine.

I'm up here running new lines through exposed rafters, trying not to fall through the boards while replaying last night in my head like some teenager who got his first genuine smile from the girl next door.

Lena's candle workshop wasn't anything like I expected. I thought I'd show up, roll my eyes, maybe get a laugh out of it. Instead,I walked out with a jar of melted wax that smelled like rosemary and bay leaf, and a strange feeling I couldn't name—something tight but not painful, like the first breath after a long swim.

Renew. That was the word I picked.

I didn't say it out loud. Just read it to myself and thought, *Yeah, okay. Sure. Try again.*

But sitting in that warm circle, hearing Lena speak with this soft steadiness, it hit harder than I was ready for. She doesn't pretend the world's perfect. She just makes space for it to be okay anyway.

And then there's the way she looked at me when everyone else had gone. Like I wasn't the most skeptical person in the room. Like I belonged there.

That look is what's still messing with me.

I'm halfway through routing a junction box when I hear the soft sound of footsteps on the attic stairs.

"I brought tea," Lena calls up.

Because of course she did.

I look down through the opening in the floor, and there she is—barefoot again, balancing two mismatched mugs with a dish towel tucked into the crook of her arm. Her hair's piled on her head in a messy twist, and she's wearing a knit sweater so big it swallows her. She looks like comfort incarnate.

I crouch down and take the mugs so she can climb the last few steps. "Thanks," I say, suddenly very aware of the dust on my shirt and the cobwebs stuck to my sleeve.

She settles on an old wooden trunk near the edge of the attic. "You've been quiet today."

"Just thinking."

"Dangerous," she teases, sipping her tea.

I smile but don't answer. I'm still trying to work out what to say.

She glances around. "You know, I always thought this attic would make a great reading nook. Or meditation space."

I raise an eyebrow. "More candles?"

She shrugs. "Always."

A beat of silence settles between us.

Then she says, "You really don't believe in any of this, do you?"

I hesitate. "It's not that I don't believe. I just... don't get it."

"That's fair."

She's not offended. If anything, she looks thoughtful.

"It's not about magic spells," she says softly. "It's about making time to mark things. Little rituals. You'd be amazed at what five minutes of intention can do."

"I don't think I've ever done anything with intention in my life," I admit.

She looks at me then, really looks, and my throat tightens.

"Then maybe it's time," she says gently.

We go back to work. I wire a new switch. She sets out a collection of small vials to photograph for her website. We work in silence, but it's not the hollow kind. It's a weight in the air, like dust motes hanging in a sunbeam—bright, tangible, alive.

Until the phone rings.

She picks it up on the second ring, her voice light and pleasant—until I hear the tone shift.

"No, it's okay," she says, her back to me. "You don't have to apologize. I understand... Yes, I know. Of course."

She hangs up slowly and sets the phone down like it weighs a hundred pounds.

"You good?" I ask.

She doesn't answer right away. Then: "That was my dad. Canceling our winter solstice lunch. Again."

"Ah." I move uncomfortably. "He's not... around much?"

She shakes her head. "Hasn't been, not since Mom died. I think I remind him too much of her. Which is ironic, since she's the reason I do what I do."

"I'm sorry."

She brushes a curl behind her ear, smiling like it doesn't hurt, but I can see the effort it takes. "It's okay. I don't need him to show up to validate my life choices. It just would've been nice."

I set down my tools and cross the attic, sitting beside her on the old trunk. "You make people feel seen, Lena. That matters. What you're building here? It matters."

Her eyes meet mine, wide and surprised. "Thank you."

"Don't thank me for telling the truth."

She's still holding her mug, but her fingers are trembling just slightly. I reach out, covering her hand with mine. Her skin is warm, and I swear I feel her pulse skip.

She doesn't pull away.

"I should go check that panel downstairs," I say eventually, standing before I do something I can't undo.

She nods, but her eyes linger on me as I descend the attic stairs.

And for the first time since I came back to Maplewood Grove, I wonder if this house—this town, this *woman*—might be more than just a job.

It might be the beginning of something I didn't know I was still allowed to want.

Rooted

～

LENA

The wind picks up the day before the solstice.

It slips through the cracks in the old shop windows, whistles around the eaves, and dances through the branches of the cedar tree outside my bedroom like it's rehearsing something ancient. It feels right. Wild, but right.

I light a candle, just one, and press my palms together.

Tomorrow's the opening. The culmination of months of slow preparation and decades of dreaming. *Solstice Remedies* will finally open its doors. People will come. Some curious. Some skeptical. Some maybe even needing something they can't name.

And I'll be there, ready—with jars and candles and kind words. With room for quiet and space for belief.

My stomach churns like a storm in a teacup. I scrub my palms down my jeans for the third time. Right now? I'm a mess.

"Stop fussing," Aunt Mabel says from the kitchen as I pace the hallway for the third time. "You've saged this space so many times even the mice are enlightened."

Agnes doesn't look up from her crossword. "You're making it

worse, dear. Try steeping some lemon balm. Or better yet—go outside."

"You want me to go outside in *this* wind?" I ask, tugging my sweater tighter.

They look at me in unison. "Yes."

I mutter something about witchy aunts and boots and grab my coat.

The air bites as soon as I step onto the porch. It smells like cold bark, chimney smoke, and snow that hasn't fallen yet.

The storefront is dark except for the string of lanterns along the awning. I walk to the door, keys in hand, but I don't unlock it. Not yet.

I just stand there, staring at the painted sign above the window: *Solstice Remedies — Light, Root, Restore.*

It felt poetic when I chose it. Now it feels... terrifying.

"What if no one comes?" I murmur.

"Then I'll come twice."

I turn at the sound of Ben's voice. He's standing a few feet away, hands in the pockets of his coat, hair windswept. There's a dusting of sawdust on his jacket and a calm steadiness in his eyes that wraps around me like flannel.

I smile, surprised and stupidly relieved. "You're out late."

"Liam sent me to drop off a box of hooks your aunts ordered. For hanging herbs or... dreams or whatever."

"Hooks for bundles," I correct, teasing. "Very sacred hardware."

He holds up the box. "Your sacred tools, milady."

I take it from him with a grin. "Want to come in?"

Inside, the shop is dim and soft, lit only by candlelight. I haven't turned on the main lights yet—don't want to ruin the mood.

Ben glances around as I set the box on the counter. "This place is... cozy."

"Go on," I murmur. "Say it: weird."

He shrugs. "It's kind of peaceful. Like you expect something good to happen when you walk in."

My chest tightens. "That's exactly what I want people to feel."

We stand in the center of the space, surrounded by jars and herbs and shadows. The wind howls outside, but in here, it's still.

He runs a hand along one of the shelves. "You did all this yourself?"

"With help from my aunts. And... well, you. Electrical stability is an underrated feature in mystical healing."

He chuckles. "So this is really it? Your dream?"

I nod slowly. "Yeah. It took me a while to admit it, even to myself. I used to think it wasn't enough. That I had to keep moving, keep chasing something 'bigger.' But now?" I exhale. "I think I just wanted a place to land. Somewhere to be real. And rooted."

Ben looks at me for a long moment. "You ever think this place was waiting for you to be ready?"

That gets me. Hits me low and warm in the belly. "Sometimes," I whisper.

We're quiet again, only the flickering of a candle between us. Then Ben steps closer, slowly, cautiously.

"I don't usually get pulled into things like this," he says. "Feelings. Plans. People."

"You don't have to explain," I start, but he shakes his head.

"I want to," he says, voice low and steady. "Because I think this town might finally feel like something I don't want to run from. And you—you're part of that."

My breath catches. "Ben..."

His hand brushes mine on the counter. And then, so softly it feels like a question, he leans in.

And I meet him halfway.

The kiss is a little clumsy at first—noses bumping, a startled laugh—but it settles, slow and warm, like finding a heartbeat under layers of winter. When we break apart, I rest my forehead against his chest, feeling the steady thump of his heart beneath his jacket.

"Stay," I whisper. "Just a little longer."

He kisses the top of my head. "I've got nowhere else I'd rather be."

Later, we sit on the floor by the window, sipping peppermint tea and watching the lanterns sway in the wind. He tells me about his unfinished house, how he's building it by hand with too much pride and not enough planning. I promise to help him bless it, and he groans good-naturedly.

And in that quiet space between words and warmth, I realize something.

He's not a detour.

He's part of the path.

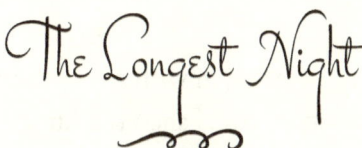

The Longest Night

LENA

I wake before dawn, before the first spill of gray-blue light touches the frost on the windows. The house is quiet in that way only old homes are—settled, creaky, half-asleep. I pad softly down the hallway, past the Carlton twins' bedrooms. Agnes snores faintly. Mabel murmurs something about cinnamon in her sleep. My heart tugs with affection.

In the kitchen, I light a small candle. One flame. One breath.

Today is the solstice. The longest night of the year.

And it's the beginning of something. I feel it humming beneath my skin, subtle but steady.

The hours blur as I prep the shop: baskets of wrapped teas, linen sachets filled with lavender and pine, candle jars lined neatly beneath twinkling garlands of dried orange slices and bay leaves. I hang the *OPEN* sign just as the sky turns a rich shade of dusk blue.

The lights glow low and warm. The tea is steeped. The doors are unlocked.

And now, I wait.

At first, it's just Patty, breezing in with a velvet scarf and a tray of tiny ginger cakes. "So proud of you," she says, hugging me fiercely. "You did it."

Then comes Livy from the library, then Emily from the post office, then two couples I don't recognize who smile and take their time browsing the shelves. The air fills with soft conversation and the scent of cinnamon and clove.

It's exactly what I hoped for.

But I keep glancing toward the door.

Then it opens—and he's there.

Ben, standing in the golden spill of lantern light, cheeks pink from the cold, hair wind-tousled and a little damp. In his hand, he cradles a small wooden lantern, the candlelight inside catching the tiny carved moons and pine trees—and the silhouette of a woman holding a flame. He shifts his weight, almost sheepish, like the offering might burn him if he holds it too long.

"Made you something," he says gruffly, stepping inside. "Kind of a 'happy solstice' gift."

My heart rises into my throat as I take it. It's beautiful. Detailed. Thoughtful. The light flickering inside dances across his face as he watches me.

"It's perfect," I whisper. "Thank you."

We stand there for a moment, just looking at each other while the room buzzes gently behind us.

"Want to help with the candle ritual?" I ask.

He raises a brow. "Do I have to chant anything?"

"Just breathe," I say with a smile. "And hold a flame."

We gather the guests around as I pass out small beeswax candles, each tied with a sprig of rosemary. The lights are lowered, and I speak softly.

"The winter solstice is the longest night," I begin. "But it's also the turning point. After this, the days grow lighter. Slowly, but surely. Tonight, we hold our own light in the dark—and we offer it forward. For healing. For hope. For love."

I light my candle from the central lantern—the one Ben made—and pass the flame to the person beside me. One by one, the room fills with flickering light, and I swear the air itself changes. Softer. Stronger.

Ben watches the flame travel, his expression unreadable but so deeply *present*.

When it reaches him, he cups the light carefully and glances at me.

"You really believe this matters, don't you?"

"I know it does," I say, my voice quiet but steady.

He nods once, and then—he smiles. It's the kind of smile that's not for show. The kind that says, *I see it now.*

After the ritual, as people drift out into the cold night, Ben lingers. We walk out into the backyard of the Carlton house, quiet now, the trees still and glistening with frost. The stars are sharp and clear above us.

He takes my hand in his.

"I've been building something out at my place," he says. "A house, yeah, but... something else too. I didn't realize what it was until I came here. Until I met you."

I turn to face him, my breath visible between us. "What have you been building?"

He exhales slowly. "A reason to stay."

My heart squeezes.

"I don't have all the answers," he adds. "I still don't understand half of what you do in that shop. But I want to. I want to understand you."

I step closer, the soft crunch of frost underfoot. "I don't need you to understand it all. I just want you to *believe* in it. In me."

He brushes his knuckles along my cheek, his voice rough. "I do."

And then he kisses me. Not rushed. Not hesitant. Just real. Grounded. Rooted.

The lantern light glows in the window behind us, and the longest night wraps around us like a blanket—not empty, but full of promise.

Sweet Solstice

LENA

The morning after the solstice always feels like an exhale.

The shop is quiet, bathed in soft gray light from the overcast sky outside. The garlands are still up, the candles still resting in their bowls of melted wax. Last night's tea kettle is washed and drying, and the smell of cinnamon still lingers in the air.

I'm sitting cross-legged on the shop floor, sipping coffee, wrapped in one of Aunt Agnes's knit shawls that smells like cedar chest and peppermint. A mug of tea steams beside me—one for Ben, who said he'd stop by "when it's decent out."

It's barely 8 a.m., and I already miss him.

I think about last night—his lantern, his kiss, the way he looked at me like he was ready to stop running from himself. The way he didn't flinch when I said I wanted him to believe in me.

I've never felt so seen.

The shop bell chimes, and I glance up to find him standing in the doorway, snowflakes in his hair, cheeks pink, a lopsided smile on his face.

"You're early," I say.

"Didn't sleep," he admits, stepping inside and closing the door behind him. "Been thinking."

I tilt my head. "Dangerous."

"Yeah," he says, crossing to me and crouching on the floor beside me. "But this time I think I got it right."

He reaches into his coat pocket and pulls out a set of keys.

"I'm finishing the house in a few weeks," he says. "And it's got this room—the front room, right off the entry. It's got south-facing windows and a ton of light. I wasn't sure what to do with it." He pauses. "Now I think I do."

My heart skips. "What are you saying?"

He shrugs, eyes steady. "I'm saying I want that room to be something we choose together. A space we fill with whatever we want—plants, books, candle jars, probably too many mugs. I want to build something with you, Lena. Not just a house. A life."

My hands tremble slightly as I set down my mug. "Ben—"

"I don't need a ritual. Or a charm. Or the right moon phase. Just... tell me you want that, too."

I reach for him, fingers curling around his jacket collar as I press my forehead to his. "I want that too," I whisper. "So much it scares me."

"Yeah," he breathes. "Me too."

Later that afternoon, we visit the construction site together. His house is quiet, bare, the windows fogged from the heat of our breath. We walk through it hand in hand—he points out where the kitchen will go, the fireplace, the wall where he wants to hang some kind of art piece I'll no doubt find at a local maker's market.

We end up in that front room, sunlight pouring through the windows. It really is the brightest space in the house.

"You were right," I say, twirling slowly in the middle of it. "It feels like it's waiting."

He leans in the doorway, watching me. "So, what should we do with it?"

I smile. "Let's keep it simple."

He raises an eyebrow.

"A big rug," I say. "A low table. Floor pillows. A candle shelf. Maybe an herb drying rack."

"So... basically your shop, but in my house."

"Our house," I whisper.

Ben crosses the room and pulls me into his arms. "I like the sound of that."

Back in town that evening, I light a single candle in the shop window again. Not because it's the solstice this time. But because it's still dark early, and some part of me wants to keep the ritual going—not for the meaning, but for the *feeling*. For the warmth that lingers.

The Carlton twins pass by the front of the store, arms linked and laughing at some private joke. Mabel gives me a thumbs-up through the window. I laugh and press a hand to the glass in return.

Ben joins me a few minutes later, his hand brushing mine as we stand there in the golden light.

"It's funny," I say. "I used to think finding peace meant going far away. Climbing mountains. Sleeping under stars. Always searching."

"And now?"

I smile at him. "Now I think maybe peace is something you build. Brick by brick. Jar by jar. Kiss by kiss."

He wraps his arm around my shoulders. "Let's build it slowly. The good way."

"Rooted," I whisper.

And as snow begins to fall outside, soft and steady, I lean into him, my hand resting over his heart.

This winter, I didn't just open a shop.

I didn't just light candles.

I found the place I belong.

And this solstice?

It's just the beginning.

The End

Did you enjoy Small Time Miracles?

Consider reviewing it on Goodreads, Bookbub or your favorite bookstore. Reviews help me reach new readers.

Have you read *Small Town Moments* and *Small Town Memories*?

Get this FREE Maplewood Story when you join my newsletter.

Subscriber Exclusive!

About the Author

Daisy Landish is a clean romance and cozy mystery author whose clean and sweet novellas have tugged at readers' heartstrings around the world. When she's not writing love stories, Daisy spends her time reading, hiking at dawn, and riding into the sunset on her horse, Rosebud.

Join Daisy's Newsletter for updates and giveaways!
www.daisylandishromance.com

facebook.com/daisylandishromance

x.com/daisy_landish

instagram.com/daisylandishbooks

amazon.com/author/daisylandish

bookbub.com/authors/daisy-landish

goodreads.com/Daisy_Landish

Also by Daisy Landish

Clean Regency Romance

Christmas with the Earl

The Lady Series - The Allington Collection

The Lady Series - The Gillingham Collection

The Lady Series - The Blackmore Collection

The Lady Series - The Norrington Collection

Clean Contemporary Romance

Timeline Retreats

Maplewood Grove Series

Love on Spruce Island

Second Chance

Cherry Tree Island

The Wedding Trio

Extra Credit

Counting on the Cowboy

Focusing on the Cowboy

Mistletoe Magic

Grounded at Christmas

Cozy Mysteries

Lady Ashcoombe Mysteries

Sophie Brooks Mysteries

Jane and Kennedy Daniels Mysteries

Pine Grove Mysteries

Annie Archer Paranormal Mysteries

Wilma Wade Holiday Mysteries

Mike and Maddie Mysteries

Mystic Moonhaven Mysteries

Cozy Mystery Samplers

Sweater Weather: Cozy Mysteries for Fall

Summer Vibes: Cozy Mysteries for Summer

Let it Snow: Cozy Mysteries for Winter

Spring Break: Cozy Mysteries for Spring

www.ingramcontent.com/pod-product-compliance
Lightning Source LLC
Chambersburg PA
CBHW020647030726
47498CB00002B/405